Dark World
The Surface Girl

Kell Frillman

For Lily, my most faithful listening ear.

My name is Ruby, like the gem. I was born on May 5, 2062. I have never smelled fresh roses. My eyes have never seen the earth's sky and the soles of my feet have never felt the tickle of grass underneath them. I have hair as red as fire, eyes as green as ivy, and freckles that dance across my face like the solar system. My grandfather used to say that I was as beautiful as a candle flame. We were very close when he was still alive. Even though he wasn't supposed to, he encouraged me to dream of a better life. He called me his princess and when Mom and Dad weren't listening, he used to whisper to me that he knew someday, somehow, I would change the world.

I've always been fascinated with stories about what life was like before the invasion. When I was young I used to sit on my grandfather's lap for hours as he spoke about what it felt like when the sun shined down on his face, or when water from the ocean washed over the tops of his feet and wrapped around his ankles like a soft blanket. He claimed back then everyone took their freedom for granted. Kids always wanted to stay inside and watch "Netflix" instead of enjoying nature when it was still habitable. Modern technology such as "cell phones" and "iPads" were so much more important to them than life's so-called simple pleasures. I have never been able to wrap my head around that concept; how did people not care about freedom? How did anyone not relish every second they could in the outdoors, doing things like swimming in the ocean, running barefoot in the sand or climbing a tree? I learned about oceans in the classroom when I was younger but the stories that touched my heart came directly from my grandfather's lips because he actually experienced them. He once swam with a dolphin when he was a young boy. I know it's impossible now because we no longer have oceans or dolphins, but I wish I could have experienced that more than anything else in this broken world.

I miss Grandpa Logan. I felt cheated out of more time with him when they came to take him away. He wasn't senile or incapable of taking care of himself, but Doctrine is absolute. Sixty years is all we get. "All men and woman on the eve of their sixtieth birthday shall be escorted to the *transitional containers* to be put to sleep." I can't even recite that in my head without both rolling my eyes and wrapping my arms around myself as a cold shudder skitters its way across the surface of my skin. Sarcasm first, fear second. That's how I always felt about Doctrine and all that it entailed.

I was naïve at ten years old and I thought my parents would appeal to the government and try to make a case for Grandpa's life, but they sat on their chairs quietly, numb and defeated as he was escorted out of our barracks. Why weren't they telling the flatfoots that he was still healthy and working? Why weren't they prepared to prove how much Grandpa could still lift, or that working on his feet did not cause his joints to ache yet? I knew of the demands of Doctrine, but I was still a child. I wanted to believe that exceptions could be made when Doctrine was unfair. I made the mistake of relying on my parents to ask for these exceptions, but in the moments that mattered, they did nothing. They were statues.

I on the other hand was not made of stone. I lunged for the door only moments after Grandpa was dragged through it. Only then did the statues come back to life. Immediately my dad lurched forward and reached for me. His arms wrapped firmly around my chest and practically lifted me off of the ground as I clawed my fingers desperately forward to grasp only air. "NO! Grandpa, come back! COME BACK!" I screamed until my dad covered my mouth with his palm. A shift of my panicked gaze in my mothers direction cause my protests to die in my throat. Her skin had paled even whiter than usual and her green eyes just like mine were so wide that I was afraid they would pop out of her head. She leapt to her feet and embraced me from the front so tightly that my small body was practically squished between the two of them.

"Don't you ever, EVER do that again," she scolded, but while her voice was angry, her arms trembled with the same fear I had just seen on her face. "NEVER show defiance to a flatfoot. Do you hear me, they could *put you to sleep!* If they had seen and heard you.." she shook her head. Her arms trembled with even more instability as they pulled me with desperate force against her chest. "I can't lose you, Ruby. Do you understand? I can't *ever* lose you. Obey. Be a good girl." My vision blurred and large, salty tears that signified my first true moments of heartache slid down my cheeks. Her words swam around in my mind among a tumultuous sea of confusion. I felt betrayed, broken inside, hit in the chest by a hammer the size of a human head. For the first time in my young life I understood the true sorrow of helplessness.

I tossed and turned with sleeplessness that night. The fear I had seen and felt from my mother frightened me like a monster in my closet. My parents told me monsters weren't real but I knew now they were wrong. Monsters were all around us. They wore navy blue uniforms with big white buttons and they dragged healthy people away from those who loved them. I kept thinking of Grandpa and I was so afraid of what he was going through. Was he in pain? Was he trembling as he was put to sleep the way my mom had trembled when she embraced me? Why couldn't we at least be there to hold his hand as he took his last breath? It wasn't fair. Mom wanted me to behave, obey, and be a good girl because she didn't want me to die. She didn't understand my thirst for knowledge the way Grandpa had. That's why he only encouraged my curious nature when Mom wasn't around.

Grandpa's last words to me earlier that day were, "You have a strong spirit, Ruby. One day you're going to find out that things aren't as they seem and you're going to have to be strong. Do you understand?" I remembered his words every single day but it would be six long years before I actually understood them.

When Grandpa was a little boy, the magnetic force the aliens had used to suck entire oceans up into their space ships messed up our planets rotation on its axis. I remember a teacher explaining to me when I was younger that Earth now moves much, much slower. It once took our planet only 24 hours to do a full days rotation, but now that same rotation took approximately 100 years. Because of this, the world above our heads has been suffering the unbearably cold temperatures of perpetual night. The other side of Earth, the side now that now faced the sun burned with constant fires of searing heat. Nothing could survive in such a hostile atmosphere so here we were – living out entire, meaningless lives underground until someday a new planet with compatible living conditions for humanity was found.

Gratitude for the "protection and comfort" of The Complex and the scroll of laws that governed it was demanded from us unconditionally. We were not allowed

4

to even acknowledge our own autonomy, much less celebrate it. *Doctrine was for our own benefit.* But it was the government and their silly Doctrine that dragged Grandpa away from me when I was ten years old and not ready to lose him so how did that benefit anyone? I would never forgive them for that day. I would never appreciate life in The Complex. I would never view Doctrine as something held in place for my protection.

Mom and Dad refused to discuss Grandpa's last words with me or shed any light on what he might have meant. To be fair, death was the punishment for noncompliance. We were taught about Earth in the classroom but we were strongly discouraged from asking questions that weren't already answered in the curriculum. As a child I couldn't help but wonder, how exactly did an axis work in the first place and how did the aliens manage to mess with ours? Why had they done so in the first place when all they wanted was our oceans? My elementary teacher, Rita, grew irritated by my questions very quickly and soon began answering them with nothing more than the narrow side of a ruler smacking down on the back of my hand. I suspected part of the reason I was disciplined so much for simple curiosity was because Rita didn't know the answers either and she didn't want to admit it. After all, she had been born right here underground just like I was. Every year as the elderly were put to sleep at age sixty, fewer and fewer people that had seen or lived in the outside world existed. Grandpa's tales about what life was like Before-Invasion, or "B-I" were the only stories I knew for certain to be true because they were first-hand accounts and he never would have lied to me.

Grandpa Logan was ten years old in 2022 when the invasion happened. His story was terrifying, but enthralling. There he was, leisurely fishing late in the evening on Lake Superior at twilight with his father when the world around him suddenly felt like it was spinning like the teacup ride at a place called *Disney World*. Grandpa said he could literally feel the earth rushing and tilting as it was forced on an accelerated turn, as if natural gravity couldn't quite keep up with the magnetic pressure from the alien ships. The water churned and the boat tipped over. Grandpa's father yelled at his son, "SWIM! SWIM! GET TO THE CELLAR!" Grandpa swam like a shark was after him. He made it to the shore but when he looked back, his father was nowhere to be seen. Believing his father would be okay because he was a strong swimmer, Grandpa crawled into the storm cellar under the cabin just before the invasion officially began.

The aliens came to pillage natural resources from our oceans and seemingly had no interest in humanity itself whatsoever. That isn't to say they had any concept of mercy, all of the people that got in their way were quickly annihilated. The attack happened so quickly that not many people had the chance to get out of their way. The invaders simply had an agenda and whether we lived or died was less than trivial to them.

The not so stealthy attack and pillage supposedly lasted close to a full day. Once the aliens got what they came for they were gone as suddenly as they arrived, only nothing about our world was ever the same.

This side of the earth at the time of the attack was in the tale end of daytime and now struggled in darkness, and the even less fortunate people on the other side that were at first thrust into darkness were now left to burn in the unrelenting heat. The ecosystem went on a quick downward spiral of destruction, and our planet became a dud that could no longer sustain life on the surface.

Grandpa was a wee child of four back in 2016 when the government officially, publicly announced the first genuine alien transmission caught by satellites. Everyone was afraid because no one knew what to expect next. It wasn't until after the invasion that the government admitted they suspected some type of attack was going to happen, but they swore up and down they had no idea what the aliens were planning ahead of time or when. Still, after that first transmission they began construction on top-secret massive underground living quarters that could essentially serve as an enormous fall-out shelter, just in case.

I have a particularly noticeable scar on the back of my right hand from the ruler slap I received for asking Rita, "If the government knew aliens might attack so they built this whole place, why didn't anyone get any warning?" My question was viewed as insolence and a notice was sent home to my mother later that day. She forced me to bed without an evening meal that night but Grandpa Logan snuck into my room after lights-out and whispered, "I've wondered that my whole life, too."

Approximately half of the people that lived in what was once the United States, parts of a country once called Canada and even some parts of what was once Mexico died during the invasion. Once the aliens were gone, the US government sent massive rescue teams to search for survivors. They found approximately 10% of the initial survivors before thirst and starvation killed them off and brought down into The Complex. By the time they found Grandpa, still hiding in the cellar under his cabin, he was nearly dead.

As for how anyone could have survived in other

countries – we don't know. Staying hidden from anything or anyone that could have otherwise survived in the outside world was supposedly critical to our safety. That seemed like such a silly excuse to me. If the other side of the world was lost in eternal flame either they were living like we were in their own shelters – or everyone on that side of the planet was dead. The government had an explanation for every question they tolerated though, and when their explanations and tolerance ran out, the punishments began. If they singled you out as a troublemaker they would find an excuse to put you to sleep. That's why my mom was always so afraid for me.

The Complex has been our home for the last 56 years. It only exists to sustain humanity; to keep us locked down in a holding pattern until some unforeseeable day in the distant future when we find another planet with suitable conditions for human life. Every five years we send out a select group of people in a small space shuttle built in the heart of The Complex in Core City, where all the high-up government officials lived. The chosen group's mission is to find and explore nearby planets in the hope that they will discover one that is habitable. It seems so silly to me that we live with limited, controlled resources and the government sees fit to build space ships instead of trying to find a way to salvage our own planet, but that's just one more thought I am not allowed to voice.

No one has ever returned from a shuttle mission and my generation is taught not to hope for a new home within our lifetime. I'm not important as an individual. I only exist to breed and sustain my species. Here in The Complex when we reach fifteen years of age we are required to undergo genetic screening in order to be matched with a mate. With so few of us left compared to the numbers humans used to have, it's important to the government that we breed only with those with whom we have compatible genes. No room for misfits or freaks.

When females achieve pregnancy the fetus is regularly monitored and if any test reveals significant problems, termination is mandatory. Yet another decree put in place *for our benefit.* The government claims they are doing my gender a service by forcing termination if the fetus is problematic rather than making us suffer the emotional consequences of having to put a defective baby to sleep after its born. No one is allowed to live unless we have the potential to be a useful, functioning member of The Complex. The good of the many outweighs the importance of the one.

My name is Ruby but my ID number identifies me as Complex Resident R-1046. I'm almost sixteen years old. Last year after genetic testing, I was assigned C-2246, otherwise known as Connor, as a future mate. I don't know anything about him and I am expected to spend my life with him. This "sense of security" does not comfort me like it does so many others. I already resent Connor just for existing. I know that isn't fair but neither is the fact that I have no say in the matter. The government uses Doctrine to control and dictate our lives. They can put us to sleep, smack us with rulers and force us into visible compliance, but they cannot go into my head and take my dreams and feelings away from me. I won't let them.

My mind still asks questions. I still want something more for myself than the life that is being forced upon me. Maybe I got my unwavering desire for adventure by holding on to Grandpa Logan's last words, or maybe that longing has been in my heart since the day I was born. Lately, I feel endlessly torn between wanting to sooth my mothers constant fear for my life by outwardly cooperating with "simple expectations" like accepting without questioning, marrying Connor and having my own child with him, and wanting to know more, be more, see more, and do more. Grandpa Logan was the one that told me one day I would change the world and I wanted that more than anything – I just didn't know how. Even though I had learned to keep my mouth shut, my eyes were always open. The only question now before me was if an opportunity to change the world ever presented itself during my lifetime, would I have the courage to take it?

Chapter 1

When I was twelve I asked my mother if she thought I would have a chance at someday being chosen for a shuttle mission. Her eyes immediately narrowed and her lips pressed tightly together like she was trying to hold back an explosion. Anxiety displayed itself as lines tightening across the corners of her mouth and it frightened, and guilted me.

Another question I shouldn't ask. Noted.

Sigh.

It wasn't that my mother's paralyzing fears about my discontented spirit finally broke my naturally adventurous curiosity, but I learned that the more complacent I appeared to be, the less likely people were to keep a watchful eye on me. If everyone assumed I finally accepted my virtually meaningless life they wouldn't feel the need to pay me any special attention. As I got older my questions and dreams, although still very prominent in my mind, had to settle for resting behind a false smile and an obedient nod.

I knew the geological facts about what happened to our planet after the invasion. Nothing currently remained on the surface above us but darkness and the possible terrifying living mutation, and on the other side of the planet, fires that spread far across the land. My only real chance to escape from the confines of The Complex would have been landing a spot on one of the five-year shuttles, but last year my genetics were found to be compatible with someone in another division. My inevitable destiny to marry and mate with Connor C-2246 made me want to throw up in my mouth. Being mated meant that any chance I had to be chosen for a shuttle mission was officially extinguished. I hated him for that. His very existence was a snake wrapping itself snugly around my lungs and squeezing until I could no longer breathe. Those who were chosen for missions were often found to have minor but not life-threatening physical imperfections that make them ineligible for breeding. Besides, none of the shuttles had ever returned from a mission, so for all we knew, getting chosen for a one might be the prolonged equivalent of getting put to sleep.

I barely got any rest last night. Tiny buzzing flies circulated within the bile in my stomach and no amount of tossing and turning was succeeding in calming them. Sixteen. *Sweet sixteen, yeah right.* There was nothing sweet about it. Tonight would be my first mandatory "date" with Connor and I couldn't even fathom the idea of having to be in the same room with him. I didn't want him to look at me and think that I was *his*, because I would never be his. Not where it counted.. not in my heart.

The flashing wakelight in my chambers refused to allow me to stay in bed with my eyes closed so I gave in and rose. The vulturous flies in my stomach beat themselves against its walls even harder. I rubbed bathing powder over my skin and through my hair, but I still didn't feel clean. It was only when I began raking my fingernails down my right forearm that I realized I might never feel clean again, especially after Connor laid eyes on me. My body was not my own to keep to myself or give away to a person of my own choosing. I didn't want to admit that it never was in the first place. How lucky people were B-I when they got to choose their own mates freely, and in their own time. I knew the moment I walked out of my chambers my mother would invasively cling to me as desperately as she had on the day Grandpa

Logan was taken to the transitional containers. She would go on and on about how fast I have grown up and how she can hardly believe that it was already the day I would meet my mate for the first time. I would have to hold my breath and count to five before I would be able to put on a fake smile, nod a few times and choke back all of my own weepy tears and cries of protest. For her sake I would have to at least half-heartedly pretend that I was looking forward to tonight. If she knew how I really felt, she would be terrified for me again and her fear would be my fault.

I slipped on my regulation uniform; an aqua shirt with a single pocket over my left breast and a pair of slightly loose-fitting slacks of the same color with an elastic waistband. I ran a comb through my freshly cleaned hair and watched how it floated around my shoulders as if gravity barely existed. My shining auburn hair was thin when it came to the individual strand, but there was a lot of it so it had a certain flow when I moved, almost like water. Anything that moved like water was considered beautiful.

I briefly considered cutting all of my hair off down to my scalp before meeting Connor tonight. Maybe if I was ugly he would refuse to mate with me. I knew that was wishful thinking, refusal wasn't allowed (if it was, I would be the one refusing before he even had the chance) but maybe he would at least find it hard to look at me and that would make this better, easier. I continued to stare at my haunted reflection and the longer I stared, the less I could imagine myself nearly bald. What frightened me was that it wouldn't just be Connor who might look away from me if I were ugly – but someone else might, too. Someone who mattered to me more than Connor ever would.

I tore my eyes away from my own reflection and tightly squeezed them shut. I tried to push away thoughts of the person I would lose forever after tonight but consciously trying to reject those intrusions inevitably drew them closer. I wouldn't feel so dirty if it were his eyes on me instead of Connor's. His doe-brown, glistening orbs were endless and profound. When they gazed at me they became heat lamps. Electricity would birth itself at the base of my spine and work its way upwards, causing my body to shudder but in a good way. When the backs of his fingers brushed against mine I would bite down on my lower lip to contain a gasp. Dimples appeared on his cheeks when he smiled, and when he moved his hand to his forehead and absentmindedly brushed back thick strands of longish chocolate brown hair, it was like watching an artist stroke a paintbrush across a canvas. Reese was a work of art, the embodiment of everything that was perfect in this world. Watching even the tiniest of his movements was like watching a ballet. Everything about him was graceful and mesmerizing.

I would never be gifted the opportunity to dance with Reese. I would never know the all-consuming internal fire of his fingertips grazing across my skin nor the explosion of his warm, moist lips pressing against my own. I would spend my whole life with nothing but daydreams that faded and an imagination that was constantly betraying me. Would the only way I could force myself to tolerate Connor's touch be to close my eyes and imagine he was Reese instead?

The back of my hand rose to the slightly darkened circle under my eye and wiped away a few tears.

Stop it. You can't cry today. You have to hold it together.

Commanding myself to accept my fate was as useful as boobs on a man. All I could do was wipe my eyes one more time, straighten my shoulders and force myself to begin this dreadful day.

Sure enough, the moment I stepped out of my chambers I was crushed against my mothers chest. "Happy Birthday, Ruby!" She squealed happily into my ear. We were polar opposites right now. I knew why she was happy. I knew my resistance to accept my duties in life made her fear that I would be sent to the transitional containers, but once I met Connor tonight my marriage two years down the road would seem officially underway and that would help calm her uneasiness. I was obviously not a mother myself but I could still understand her basic point of view. I would never forget how I felt when I watched the flatfoots drag Grandpa Logan away. I would never forgive them. I was the only person my parents had and I knew that losing me would break them beyond repair and make them feel like failures.

Crap.

I had to figure out some way to get through this. If not for myself, then for my parents.

"Thanks Mom," I finally replied as she loosened her grip. She raised her hands and brushed back a few straying strands of my hair, catching my gaze with her own.

"You look beautiful, Ruby. You really do. You've grown up so much." I shifted my eyes. My mother's barely audible sigh had not been lost on me. "Someone special is here to see you."

It was actually amazing to me how one single, simple sentence could manage to send me through three different extreme emotional moments in about two seconds flat.

WHAT IF ITS CONNOR OH MY GOD NO I'M NOT READY I'M NOT READY FOR THIS I DONT WANT THIS

No, it couldn't be Connor. Our "date" was not scheduled until six o'clock in the evening. I would be formally escorted to our meeting room because the "date" was to take place in Connor's home division Connecticut, which I would then be forced to transfer to after our wedding. I didn't even have the option to pick which division I wanted to live in. I would be forcibly wed to Connor and then I would only be allowed to see my own parents on designated visiting days once every six months. Unauthorized, unescorted and/or frequent traveling between divisions was not permitted. Connor could not be here this morning because that would not be in accordance with Doctrine. This was the first moment in my life that I was thankful for something dictated in that stupid law scroll.

WAIT, WHAT IF ITS REESE? I CAN'T FACE HIM RIGHT NOW! IF I LOOK AT HIM I WILL CRY AND MY PARENTS WILL KNOW AND THEY WILL BE AS TERRIFIED FOR ME AS THEY WERE WHEN GRANDPA LOGAN WAS TAKEN.

Reese wouldn't have come in the morning, though. He was not an early riser and he avoided my parents whenever he could. He never said why, but there was always a small part of me that hoped he was carrying the same secret I was. Maybe he was worried that if they saw his lingering gaze or the way he would step just a bit closer to me than he needed to, they would know and they would be afraid. But that was all in my imagination, maybe. I don't think his gaze lingered, I think time just slowed down in my head whenever he looked at me. I don't think he deliberately stepped closer to me, I think I just read too much into his habit of shifting his weight from foot to foot while standing.

Honestly, it wouldn't be comforting if he felt for me the way I felt for him. It would make me hate Connor even more. It would make spending my last two years in my own division being able to see Reese almost every day that much more difficult.

I BET IT'S WILLOW!!

That possibility cheered me up a bit and because it was a realistic guess. It eased my panic. Willow was my best friend and she often stopped by our barracks unannounced. She was my better half in so many ways. She covered for me when I opened my mouth too often. She provided encouraging words to help me through my struggles. She kept me in line but she never judged me for being different even though my differences sometimes put me in danger.

My mother loved Willow so much that she considered her to be a second daughter. Sometimes I secretly thought she would have preferred Willow to have been her real daughter instead of me but I never let it bother me. Sometimes I wished that were true, too. I loved my mother very much but I knew raising me wasn't easy for her. Mom was delicate, like a butterfly. Fear controlled every choice she made and with me being naturally inquisitive, she was scared all the time. Grandpa Logan said it was because her own mom, my grandmother, died when Mom was only fourteen. Realizing Grandpa forgot his lunch, my grandmother decided to bring it to his work site for him despite knowing that her presence there was forbidden by Doctrine. The ceiling of the older passageway that Grandpa was helping seal off caved in. My grandmother was not wearing a helmet and a large rock crushed her skull.

Mom doesn't know I know this, but Grandpa told

me she had been convinced that the rock story was a ruse. She thought the government had secretly sent my grandmother to the transitional containers for breaking Doctrine. Even though Grandpa never actually admitted it out loud to me, I got the impression he suspected it too. After all, he didn't actually *see* the accident. A flatfoot approached him and delivered the news. If he thought the story of her death was a ruse, maybe thats what he meant when he told me "one day you're gonna find out things aren't always as they seem." Thinking about it now sent a cold chill up my spine so I tried to force my attention back on the present. My mom's expression had relaxed and that made the worry-lines across her cheeks disappear. I assumed I was probably right. I shifted my weight excitedly to the balls of my feet and walked past her only to see Willow sitting on our couch. Willow was also my better half in a physical way. My skin was ridiculously fair but hers was almost olive, like what I would imagine a "tan" would look like on someone. What a strange concept, that being out in the sunlight used to actually change the shade of our skin! Her jet black hair was so long that it went down to the small of her back, and so thick that it literally shined. When she moved, it moved with her like the millions of strands were one cohesive entity. I considered my hair to be my best feature, but Willow's was still far superior to my own. Her lips were full and pouty, her intense eyes were dark brown and uniquely shaped like almonds and her lashes were naturally long and elegantly defined. Her figure was full and curvy, causing all of the boys to become puddles at her feet. Compared to her, I looked and felt like a mouse. My physique was a whisper while hers was a roar.

Willow immediately rose and faced me. Her arms

18

curled around me in a tight hug but this one was much less suffocating than my mother's. Willow's hug was one of pure excitement. I did not share her enthusiasm but it felt reassuring nonetheless.

Willow dropped her arms but she curled three of her fingers around my elbow and tugged on it as her gaze shifted toward my chambers. We had been best friends since we were small children so I understood her hint right away. I raced behind her and before I closed my door I shot my mom a slightly apologetic, but anticipatory thankful expression and explained, "girl talk!"

Once the door was closed, Willow and I assumed our usual chatty positions with me sitting by my pillow and her curling up her legs indian-style at the foot of my bed. I rested my hands over my knees.

"Are you scared?" Willow asked carefully. She knew I wasn't looking forward to this day at all. I shrugged a shoulder trying to put on airs of being nonchalant, but immediately dropped the act because I knew Willow would immediately see through it.

"I just wish we could do this in our own time."

Or not at all.

I gazed at Willow with profound sadness in my eyes. I was helpless to stop the path my life was about to lead me down. I could dream of other things up until now but reality was about to hit me like a freight train.

I'm not ready! I don't want this.

Willow shifted her weight on my bed. "What do you think of your dad?" Her question caught me off guard and I tilted my head.

"What?"

"Do you love him?" That was a silly question.

"Of course I do, he's my dad."

19

"Does your mom love him?" I paused and briefly closed my eyes. Did my mom love my dad? That wasn't something I had ever thought to ask myself or anyone else before. My parents were mated. That was Doctrine. But beyond that, I rarely ever saw them fight or argue. My mother was a butterfly and my father was a tree. His roots were firmly planted and nothing made him sway. He comforted her when she was afraid. He steadied her when she stumbled. If I really thought about it I would have to admit they complemented each other almost perfectly.

"Yeah, I think she does." Willow shifted her weight again and ran her tongue over her lips as if trying to choose her next words very carefully.

"Maybe this genetic matching system is really a good thing, you know? Have you ever heard of the word *divorce*?" I bit down softly on my lower lip and crinkled my eyebrows. Something about that word seemed vaguely familiar but I just couldn't place it. Because I didn't respond right away, Willow explained. "B-I, there wasn't any genetic matching system and half of the couples that mated voluntarily split up. Their marriages were basically cancelled. It was called *divorce*. People were getting married randomly without knowing if they were a good match and they ended up getting in too many disagreements." That sounded like such a crazy concept, didn't it defeat the entire purpose of marriage? Marriage to the government meant to be mated and to be mated meant optimal to breed, but the added benefit was supposed to be for us to have a companion there for us always. Supposedly it kept us content, which kept us obedient. I sighed in partial defeat.

Crap.

Willow was doing this on purpose. She was trying

to get me to look forward to being mated to Connor and to see it as a positive thing. I knew she was just trying to be my friend and help me accept my path but it was still frustrating. I frowned and rested my hands behind me so I could stretch my back.

"*Divorce* sounds terrible," I admitted, "but I wish I had more time. I know I don't have to get married for two years but I don't even feel like that matters. I have to meet Connor tonight and then I belong to him whether I want to or not." Willow pressed her lips together and I assumed she was going to try and bring up another positive thing about being mated, but instead she reached forward and tapped my arm. She drew her hand back to herself, reached into the pocket on her shirt and pulled out a piece of folded paper. Before I could ask any questions she held her index finger on her other hand up to her lips. What was she doing?! Willow wasn't secretive! She hadn't passed a note to me since we were thirteen years old, and when our teacher Rita caught Willow she made her bend over and receive her ruler slaps right on her butt cheeks in front of everyone. I cautiously reached forward and grabbed the note. I carefully unfolded it and perused its contents.

There's something important I have to show you. Meet me at the place where we found the butterfly.

That was it. That was all. There was no signature but there didn't need to be.

A few months ago Reese and I had been walking down a hallway that lead from classes toward my barracks. We heard a strange chirp-like sound and we paused. The sound continued. I looked left, he looked right and soon we found the culprit; a single, undersized butterfly who couldn't quite fly. We were amazed because although our labs had various larvae, it was extremely rare to see an insect free from laboratory confines. Anything and everything that happened in our labs was carefully monitored. The only other insects I had ever seen roaming free were ants who occasionally got in through very minor, overlooked cracks in the foundation of The Complex. I was six the first time I saw one. I was fascinated and I brought it into our barracks to show Grandpa. He picked me up, plopped me onto his lap and told me stories about how he used to watch entire ant colonies marching through the grass when he was my age.

Mom screamed when she had seen the ant crawling over my hand and immediately killed it. She made me tell her where I found it and promptly reported the incident to a flatfoot.

Reese and I were fascinated by the butterfly we ran across. I bent down and watched it struggling, scraping its tiny little feet against the wall and trying to spread its wings but something was wrong; one of its wings stuck out at an odd angle. Reese bent down next to me and when I shifted my eyes toward him, I saw that being partially in the way of one of the lights on the ceiling was casting a shadow over his cheek. The shadow was reminiscent of his sadness. It touched me to witness how much compassion he felt for this poor little creature who couldn't fly like it was supposed to. It was as if Reese was actually experiencing its struggle right along with it.

The butterfly, although still small, was considerably larger than any of the three ants I had seen before so I doubted it had found its way into the complex through a crack exposing us to the earth's deep soil. This little guy had to have escaped from a lab, but how, if it couldn't even fly? How could it have gotten all the way out here near our barracks?

I didn't ask Reese any of these questions because the soft, saddened expression that made his cheeks sink downward told me that knowing how this happened was not going to help this little guy now. Reese cupped one of his palms and carefully laid it next to the insect. It paused in its frenzied but fruitless attempt to scamper up the wall and seemed to consider Reese's offer of assistance. My lips parted in actual amazement as it carefully climbed into his hand. He was magical like that.

Carefully, Reese stood up straight. "I'm going to take him home," he said very quietly. "I'll try to make him comfortable." His words caused me to shiver and I curled my arms around my chest. I understood what he was saying. A butterfly who could not fly could not survive. I imagined Reese would probably put the little guy into some kind of container and offer him food (what did butterflies eat? I had no idea and I doubted we had access to what they probably needed) but it would probably spend all of its moments trying to climb out of the container, its little legs sliding helplessly against the sides until it was so exhausted and disheartened that it finally gave up and gave in to inevitable death.

A butterfly, an insect, knew that to be alive meant to be free and if there was no such thing as freedom there was no reason to live. Why didn't humans understand that, too? Why did we continue to breed if there was no real possibility of life outside of the confines of The Complex? *Always have hope*, the government tells us, but they've also told us there was no hope for my generation. I would never see anything but walls to my sides and a ceiling above my head.

Reese took the butterfly back to his barracks and never spoke of it again. I knew why. I knew it didn't survive. Maybe he even put it to sleep himself just to save it from its misery but he wanted to spare me knowing about it. It touched my heart to know that although Reese was incredibly vulnerable and sensitive himself, he still wanted to protect me from the worst things.

I tore my eyes away from the note and jumped off of my bed like it was on fire. My fingers, resting on either side of the paper as my fingers gripped it, yanked in opposite directions tearing it right down the middle. Before I could stop myself I stuffed the paper into my mouth. The compressed tree root seemed to dissolve on my tongue and an unpleasant sourness invaded my tastebuds. I involuntarily gagged and covered my lips but I forced myself to swallow the paper-turned-chalk. I shifted my guilty eyes back over to Willow, a bit terrified that my extreme response gave something away. It relieved me to witness the way her styled black brows furrowed in pure confusion. Still, I detected worry.

"I don't know if you should go," she said openly, "but I promised I'd get the note to you." I knew that tone. It was akin to my mother's tone when she was afraid for me. I looked away. "Do you remember when people used to call us *the three amigos*?" I couldn't help but crack a small smile. Willow, Reese and I had known each other practically all our lives. It felt strange to think about that because although nothing ever changes within the constricting walls of The Complex, in another way – everything constantly changes. I could glance upon Willow right now and so easily recall what she looked like as a child. When we first met, she resembled a tiny, tanned cherub. Her cheeks had that cute puff to them while her arms and legs still carried residual baby-fat. She was picturesque innocence, a perfect little angel.

It was different to think back on Reese's younger days. Myself, Reese and Willow truly were *the three amigos* back when we were kids. We were equal. I was the one with my head in the clouds (clouds I had never actually seen), Willow was the one with her feet firmly planted on the floor and Reese was the scientific one that balanced us out. Back then, we were three sides of one person and we were only complete when we were together. As we grew older the friendship between Willow and Reese became more strained, but in a subtle way and without any substantial cause. I was the one Reese always tackled, until we turned eleven and my mom sat me down and told me it was time to act more ladylike. Reese and I developed our own silent language and maybe Willow felt left out. It was something I noticed, but I noticed it alongside my far-fetched dreams of wanting more than friendship with Reese so it was never something I spoke out loud. "Yeah, I remember," I responded carefully. A lump began to form in my throat. It would make absentmindedly swallowing access saliva a slightly difficult feat.

"I know things haven't been the same lately." Willow's voice was barely above a whisper. Her eyes darted around the room as her pupils dilated. I couldn't help but follow suit. I knew the government claimed they did not monitor conversations in private barracks but I never quite trusted that they were telling the truth. I supposed that was what they wanted though; to always keep us afraid and on edge so we never stepped out of line. My parents, to my knowledge had never been informed that I was officially on a Watch List (which would be the only legal instance in which the government would have surveillance inside barracks to monitor in-home conversations) but with my incessant childhood questions I wouldn't refer to that possibility as a paranoia. "You're still my best friend, though. I still want you to be safe." I got it. Message received. Yet another person who cared about and loved me was telling me I had to go through with meeting Connor tonight and accept him as my mate in order to preserve my life. What I wish they understood was that Connor did not feel like an assurance of my life, but instead, he symbolized the inevitability of my eventual death that could only follow and unsatisfactory life. Still, Willow had given me Reese's message and that meant that some part of her, even if it was forever silent and buried deep, didn't want Reese and I to have unfinished business.

I reached one of my hands forward and gave Willow's a squeeze. I would do it – I would meet Connor tonight like I was supposed to, but first I had to see Reese. I had to look at him one last time and let go of my secret feelings on my own terms. Willow's relief was temporary because although I knew I had assured her that I would go through with tonight, I was almost positive she knew what I was going to do first. "I need your help," I said softly. Willow apprehensively twitched.

"With what?"

"I know it's Saturday, but I'm going to tell my parents that I forgot something in the lab that I need for homework due on Monday. Tell them you'll walk there with me?" Willow bit her plump lower lip. She was just as bad at lying as I was. "All I really need you to do is stand there and look agreeable. Can you do that?" Willow shifted her weight and her eyes before lowering them toward her lap with a defeated sigh that sank her shoulders.

"Only if you absolutely promise me that you'll be

back well before your escort arrives." I nodded firmly.

"You know I will. I honestly think my mother would have a heart attack if I were late." Willow managed to crack a small smile, but I was being utterly serious and I knew she knew that.

I swung my legs over the side of my bed and hopped to my feet. I winced when I saw the 'flower' on my dresser; a hairpiece designed to look like a rose that was made out of tissues and some dye that my mom made for me to wear tonight when I met Connor. I pressed my arms to the side of my body to resist picking it up because I wanted to wear it now instead. I wanted Reese to see me wearing it. I would much rather his eyes gaze upon me looking my best than Connor's.

I turned away from my dresser, and my mirror. There was no longer any reason to look at myself. "Lets go," I said calmly but firmly as I turned to Willow. She rose and we headed toward my barrack door. I paused and glanced at my parents in the living room. They were both on our couch, sitting as still as statues just like the day the flatfoots took Grandpa Logan away. But why? "Mom? Dad?" I addressed them apprehensively. "I left something in the school lab and I need it for homework due on Monday. Can I walk there with Willow to pick it up?" My tone was fearful. I knew I didn't sound convincing. Mom slowly turned her head toward me and blinked a few times, forcing her chin downward in a curt nod. She hadn't been paying attention to my tone, thankfully. Her mind was definitely somewhere else.

"Sure honey, but come right back. Your father and I have a present for you and then I want to help you get ready for your big night." Because obviously I needed yet another reminder of the dread I felt about tonight. I tried not to let my annoyance show.

"Mom, are you okay?" Mom rested her hand over Dad's. I shifted my eyes toward my father and noticed his work shirt was torn. "Dad, what happened?" Immediately my dad came back to life, turning toward me and moving his hand away from my mom's to rub at his fire-red beard.

"What? Oh – yes, I'm fine Ruby. Just coming down with a slight cold. If I'm still achey in the morning I'll see the GP." He covered his mouth and nose as he sneezed. He didn't seem to realize I had been asking about his shirt.

Still, Dad's oncoming cold explained my mother's distant attitude. Mom always got especially frightened if Dad or I got sick. Getting sick didn't happen often for anyone. The Complex was pretty sterile and very few viruses circulated, but nasopharyngitis was highly contagious even though not lethal and sometimes even careful procedures couldn't stop its occasional spread inside of a division. When a case was confirmed, everyone in the division in which it was diagnosed was given mandatory medication as a preemptive strike and the virus usually waned within one to two weeks. The first person to be diagnosed was usually interrogated because the government always wanted to know exactly where and how a virus originated. Honestly, I suspected that more often than not the government probably released the occasional virus on purpose to study how it spread but that wasn't something I ever dared voice out loud. The government did much worse things to focus on in my opinion, such as putting people like Grandpa Logan to sleep and forcing us to accept a mate and to breed whether we wanted to or not.

"Okay, feel better Dad, I'll be back soon!" I grabbed Willow's arm and dragged her to our door, hustling out of it and shutting it firmly behind us. I exhaled with relief. "Okay, free and clear." Willow's face was etched with apprehension lines, vastly different than my happy grin. "Will, I promise I'll be back soon. I'm just gonna go see what Reese wants. I'm not gonna stay long and worry my mom and I promise I'll be ready to go when my escort gets here. Okay?" I was not the kind of person who broke promises and I knew Willow was aware of that. She seemed to relax a bit.

"Okay." She threw her arms around me in a desperate hug as if this was the last time she would be able to hug me, and then abruptly let go, turned around, and walked away. I sighed. She was being silly. This was definitely not goodbye.

I began walking down the hallway, ignoring the squeaky sound my sneakers made on the polished floor. I walked past a mother and child, Tina and her daughter Zion, and kept going until I reached the end of the hall. I turned to the right as if I were headed toward the labs and there he was; Reese, standing tall but still, like the way Grandpa Logan used to describe a giant tree that shaded a meadow he liked to play in as a young boy. I paused in my forward motion and tried to force the blush that threatened to spread across my cheeks to retreat back the way it came, but unsurprisingly it refused to dissolve. I would just have to hope that it wasn't very noticeable.

As I got closer to Reese, he shifted his weight from foot to foot. His jaw muscles clenched.

Something's wrong.

My heart skipped a beat and began an erratic, rapid climb up the speed ladder. Reese grabbed my arm and pulled me close to the wall as if leaning against it would make whatever he was going through easier to bear. He leaned to the side to look behind me, then twisted his neck to glance over his shoulder before resting his eyes on my face. I usually loved his eyes, warm like chocolate, deep like a canyon. Today though, they were piercing and I had never seen him look at me that way before. His glare was...accusing.

"Ruby," Reese began at almost a whisper. "I need you to come with me." He slipped his hand under my elbow and lead me further down the hall. I assumed we were going to turn left but he paused at an old, sealed off door. "Are we alone?" I blinked a few times, even more intimidated by the tone than the accusing nature of his eyes.

"Willow didn't follow us, if thats what you're asking.." the blush was nearly gone from my cheeks now. I stiffened, feeling defensive without even knowing what I was being accused of. Reese rose to the balls of his feet to look over my shoulder again, then glanced behind himself. He was acting *paranoid.* My comfort level declined by the second. I rubbed my throat and couldn't help but glance around at nothing, too. Then Reese did something that I have never done – never even *thought* of doing – he reached for the handle on the sealed off door. My breath caught in my throat. The yellow ribbon across it signified the entry to an old passageway that has since been closed down. When The Complex was first built, it contained passageways so that people could travel freely between divisions. When the government decided to limit our freedom even more, those original passageways were sealed off and a tram system was created in their place. Only authorized personnel could use the tram and only for pre-approved travel reasons, like distributing and transporting basic supplies or personal, pre-authorized individual travel such as my "date" with Connor in his division tonight. An officially assigned government escort would take me from my barracks to the tram, travel with me to my date, and then escort me back again when it was over.

"Reese, NO!" I squealed on impulse, subconsciously channeling my mom's inability to control her fear. Reese yanked on the handle and threw his shoulder against the door. Miraculously, it submitted to his weight and budged. He yanked my arm and forced me behind the door. He let go of my arm and immediately brought a finger to his lips telling me to hush. Overwhelmed with Reese's unexpected behavior, I became the statue I had seen my parents embody and I obeyed. He pushed on the door to close it again and its rusty hinges groaned in protest. I bit down on my lower lip, hard.

The passageway smelled and I wrinkled my nose. I recognized the scent but only vaguely. It was reminiscent of when we got to hold dirt and soil in science class. Only, the scent in here was moist, like dirt and clay combined. "I have a confession to make," Reese spoke. Before this, I would have been terrified, hopeful, and all over the place anticipating the slight possibility he had feelings for me but now my mind was somewhere else entirely. "I've been exploring these passageways for a while now. I do it when I get bored, or when I feel claustrophobic and cooped up." Half of me was terrified for him and what he was doing but the other half was furious. My palms shot forward and pressed against his chest, literally shoving him up against the wall. I hadn't done this in years since we quit wrestling each other, but this was not a playful gesture. It was a shove of fury.

"We've known each other almost our whole lives, and you've been doing this *without* me? You KNOW how much I wish I could escape this place!" Reese threw up his hands in a cease-fire motion but I wasn't finished. "How could you be so *selfish*? Don't you care about me AT ALL?" I stopped and suddenly froze. "...They'll know we're here! They're probably listening to this right now and we're gonna get caught and put to sleep-"

"Ruby, no," Reese was shaking his head. "They're not monitoring us." My heart was racing, threatening to jump right out of my chest and run away from me on invisible, panicked little legs.

"How – how do you know?" My voice was shaking. It was as if my mom was secretly inside of my body taking over my reactions. This wasn't me...

"These passages were built in the beginning, *before* everything was monitored. They were abandoned only ten years A-I and I don't think they started bugging The Complex until at least five years after that. I've been walking these passageways for a while now and no one has come for me." Well, he *did* have a point. I let my hands fall from his chest but my body still trembled. I took a deep breath and pulled my shoulders back.

"So... you thought a good birthday gift for me would be to show me these tunnels only hours before I have to meet my future husband? Do you know badly I want to just – just run away -" I curled my arms under my chest and tried to force my betraying eyes from blurring with salty liquid but the dreaded tears began running down my cheeks anyway. This was too much. This was overwhelming. I didn't know what to do. And then I felt them; strong, muscular arms curling around my shoulders and drawing me closer. My chin bumped against Reese's shoulder and my chest rested against his. His body was warm. My heart pounded against his shirt. I fit perfectly against him like a shoe or a glove. My heart responded immediately to the comfort and its rapid beating began to slow. But - this was wrong. I was letting Reese comfort me when I shouldn't be comforted. I squeezed my eyes shut.

"I'm sorry Ruby, but that isn't why I brought you here."

Oh.

Of course not.

I immediately felt like an absolute fool. Reese didn't bring me down here to touch me, comfort me or confess that he wanted me for himself. This was real life; a trapped, pointless life and not a story or a fable. I squirmed out of his embrace and turned around to wipe the tears from my face. Maybe I needed this. Maybe this was a good thing. Maybe I had to be angry at Reese in order to get through tonight. "No, thats not what I meant -" I could literally hear him running his fingers through his hair with frustration even though I could barely see him in the dark. I knew him well enough to know his movements. I wished I didn't. "I brought you down here because theres something – someone – you need to meet."

...Huh?

I wiped my remaining tears and turned toward Reese in pure confusion. What the heck was he talking about? I could hear him fumbling in his shirt and suddenly a pocket-light illuminated the darkness. I stepped away from the tiny beam. I didn't want Reese to see my face right now. "Come with me," he requested and reached for my hand again. I almost impulsively pulled it away but I managed to stop myself and not visibly react. I followed him in silence, choosing instead to focus on the unfamiliar feeling the dirt floor had on the soles of my shoes. I had never walked on uneven ground before and I felt a bit wobbly. It was a strange and foreign sensation to have solid ground under parts of my feet and uneven ground under other parts. I walked slower. After a few minutes Reese abruptly stopped. A sudden scratching noise made me jump a bit and I moved closer to his side. "It's okay," he spoke assuringly and crouched down. My eyes followed where he was aiming the light beam and I gasped. *There was something there!* It shifted. I covered my mouth with my hand to prevent myself from screaming. Reese moved the beam again.

The moving thing was a person. A child. "It's okay," Reese spoke again and I realized he was not speaking to me. He was speaking to the child. "The friend I was going to bring, this is her. This is Ruby." The child's eyes widened and she clutched her knees with her little fingers. Her impossibly blonde hair was extremely long, endlessly matted together in tangles and extra dirty as if she hadn't used bathing powder in weeks. A strange, unpleasant smell waifed off of her. I tried not to be incredibly rude and wrinkle my nose in distaste. She was wearing, well, I couldn't tell what it was. It was some kind of suit that covered her entire body, but it was very puffy, as if filled with stuffing. It definitely didn't resemble any kind of division uniform I had ever seen. The odd, unrecognizable one-piece garment seemed just as filthy as the rest of her. Reese reached into his pocket again and pulled out something wrapped in a napkin. He held it toward the girl. For about five seconds she didn't move, but then her dirty hands shot forward, grabbed the napkin out of Reese's grasp and pulled it back possessively toward her chest. I bit my lip and carefully crouched down next to Reese so she could see me a bit better in what little light there was.

"Are you lost?" This was not good. This was not good at all. How did a little girl get in here in the first place? These passageways were sealed off and forbidden. She could be put to sleep if she were to get caught. We couldn't bring her out to a flatfoot and say she was lost because *we* could get put to sleep, too. We had no excuse for being in here. "What division are you from?" The little girl raised her head fearfully. I could see in her eyes that she understood my questions – my language – but she wasn't answering me. Was she simply afraid? I would be, too, if I had somehow gotten lost at such a young age. "Can you tell me where you're from?" I tried one more time.

Then, the little girl did something I will never forget. She did something that would change the direction of my life forever. No pun intended. She pointed *Up.*

I leapt backwards as if flames ignited in front of me.

OMIGOD, SHE WAS FROM THE SURFACE! SHE WAS A MUTANT, A MONSTER! SHE WOULD EAT US! HOW COULD REESE BRING ME HERE, DID HE REALLY THINK BEING EATEN ALIVE WAS A BETTER FATE FOR ME THAN MARRYING CONNOR?

Was it, though?!?

Reese scampered to his feet and rested a hand over my shoulder. I couldn't tell if he was forcing me, or requesting from me that I didn't immediately run. I happened to notice that the little girl wasn't jumping up to attack me. "It's okay, she won't hurt you!" I don't know why, but suddenly, I believed him. That did not however bring me any relief nor did it do anything to aid in lessening my utter confusion. "There's something else you need to see, though." He kept his one hand on my shoulder and shined the little pocket light downward toward the girl's hand. In it, she clutched a piece of torn aqua fabric about the size of the chunk missing from my father's shirt. Both of my hands rose to cover my mouth once more.

"Oh...my...god." Her fingers clutched the fabric even tighter and then, she sneezed.

Chapter 2

When we're young we think of our parents as one-dimensional beings that take care of us. As we grow older we learn that they are actually individuals, complicated people just like us that have feelings; dreams, hopes, fears, and pasts all their own before we ever existed. We struggle to figure out how and where we fit in to their complicated lives.

I learned bits and pieces about my mom's autonomy as the years went on, but my dad – he was always just my dad. He was quiet, strong, and thoughtful. He was my mom's rock and my protector. When I was a little girl he would get down on the ground and pretend to be a *horse*, a huge animal that used to exist on the surface B-I that people would actually ride. I would get on his back and he would crawl around our barracks. Sometimes he would rub his prickly red beard on my cheek and it would tickle so I would giggle. When I got older we stopped playing "horsey" and he no longer tickled me with his beard. Our conversations became a little bit more awkward. My mother explained my period to me and helped me understand my changing body. It made sense that my dad wasn't around for those conversations. Mom said it was hard on fathers to see their little girls growing up, and that when she was my age, she wasn't very close with Grandpa Logan, either.

As I crouched in the dark in a passageway I was not supposed to be in while staring at a little girl who seemed to be trying to tell us that she was from the surface while clutching a piece of fabric from my dad's work shirt, I suddenly realized that maybe I didn't know my father at all. My mind started listing off facts about him as if it wanted to prove the rest of me wrong. I knew his name was Robert R-1045. I knew he worked in the artificial gardens growing and cultivating food for our division. I knew he was quiet and he always chose his words carefully so he never had to put his foot in his mouth. He kept his head down, he worked hard, and he took care of us. He never raised his voice in anger. He never faltered. I always accepted these things at face value without pausing to wonder if that was really my dad or just a mask he wore because he loved us. I had to wear a mask, I had to pretend that I was satisfied with my life and purpose when that couldn't be further from the truth. I presented my outer self in a certain way in order to ease my mother's fear but I was an entirely different person underneath. Maybe my dad was, too. How else could I hope to explain the piece of fabric that this little girl was clutching? Had my dad also been wandering these passageways? If so, why? If he had been in the passageway and stumbled across her and she had grabbed at him and he had run, he wouldn't have been able to tell anyone. I understood that. My mom would absolutely lose her sanity if she knew he had been breaking Doctrine like that and putting his life at risk, especially with the way her mother supposedly died. I knew she always worried about me breaking Doctrine but it never occurred to me to consider that my dad might be the one to worry about, instead.

What were my dad's hopes and dreams? When he was younger, did he ever ask questions that got him smacked by rulers or did he challenge ideals that went against Doctrine? Why hadn't I thought to want to know my own father better as a person? Was I an awful, selfish daughter? Was I so wrapped up in the fear of losing my own autonomy that I never allowed myself to wonder if my dad had any to begin with?

I barely felt the cold, damp wall against my back as I slid down it. My bottom hit the floor and I ignored the momentary sting on my tailbone. I bit my lower lip, hard. "Ruby?" I heard Reese's voice but my mind was spinning far too fast to coordinate a response. My eyes fixated on the little girl; the dirty, smelly little freak who was probably a liar too. If I hadn't seen my dad alive, well and pretending things were perfectly normal less than an hour ago I would probably be convinced that this monster ate him, killed him – or both. I simply didn't understand. "Ruby?" Reese crouched down and I felt his palm on my forehead. I still couldn't respond. "Ruby, talk to me." The worry in Reese's voice finally registered in my brain and even though I was shaking, I manage to open my mouth.

"I – I – I don't understand," was all I could mutter. I couldn't take my eyes off of the girl. She still clutched the torn piece of fabric possessively like it was the last bit of food at the week's end. She appeared as afraid and confused as I was but how was I supposed to know if she was just putting on an act to get me to lower my guard? Okay, so she obviously ran into my dad somehow and didn't hurt him, and she ran into Reese before and didn't hurt him but that didn't mean she didn't have some sinister plan to lure us into a false sense of security before feeding us to her tribe of surface dwelling cannibalistic mutants. How many times had I been told that the only way anything that was once human could have survived on the surface was to mutate into a savage, animalistic beasts? What if the girl's plan was first to gain our trust, and then to lead her fellow cannibals down whatever entrance point she infiltrated The Complex through to invade and kill us all? I wouldn't let myself trust her, I *couldn't*, but there were still things I absolutely had to know. I narrowed my eyes and tried to focus on seeing her as a potential enemy. Oddly, simplifying things in my head helped me regain some of my composure. "Where did you get that?" I asked quietly but I couldn't hide the accusing tone in my voice. My eyes darted toward the piece of fabric between her small fingers and then back up to the shadows on her dirty face. She curled into herself even tighter. "Where?" I demanded a bit more forcefully. I felt Reese's hand curl gently over my shoulder. *No.* He couldn't ask me to back down right now. This was about my dad and I had a right to demand answers.

The girl's eyes, although wide with terror – unless she was faking it – still seemed to gleam with some sort of familiarity.

She understands my words!

At least, I was pretty sure she did. I had been taught that any possible mutants that were once human who currently roamed the surface were feral by now, completely uncivilized and no longer able to mimic or understand human speech. What use did they have for language when all they had to sustain them was the immediate gratification of second-by-second survival?

Then again, by that logic, why would we be any different down here?

Surface mutants were supposed to be savages. This little girl had to be some kind of trick, a well-planned ruse formulated by the government to punish us for wandering forbidden passageways. Commander SueLee might as well terrorize us before sending us to the transitional containers so we could become a cautionary tale for others who might dare to disobey, right? Reese and I would become an example to the rest

40

of The Complex; "This is what happens when you break Doctrine." I should have known this is how my life would end. And yet... the possibility of that being true did not fill me with dread. It actually calmed me.

"Can I please see your wrist? I won't hurt you," I found myself adding. I suppose in that moment I realized she seemed as genuinely frightened of us as we were of her.

Down here in The Complex, all citizens had small chips implanted on the sides of our hands when we were toddlers. The chips held all vital information about us; our ID numbers, division membership, medical statuses, etc and if you pressed down on the skin in just the right spot you could always feel them. If this was a trick, if this little girl was part of a ruse and she was a government mole who also happened to be a very good pretender, I would be able to feel her chip.

The little girl continued to eye me with fright and uncertainty. Her hesitation could be genuine confusion and possible distrust, or it could be because she knew she was about to be outed. I gently held my hand out, palm facing upward, and tried not to let my fingers tremble.

"It's okay," Reese gently tried to assure her. He probably understood my plan. "She won't hurt you, I promise. I've known Ruby almost all my life." Slowly, *very* slowly, the little girl un-clutched her hand from her knees – but not the one holding the torn piece of fabric – and reached forward. I gently pressed my finger down on the loose skin and crevice behind the groove between her thumb and fingers. I felt nothing. Keeping my eyes locked on her on her in case she panicked or tried to attack me, I moved my finger around the top of her hand and still felt nothing. This *had* to be a trick! I pressed my lips together. Maybe her chip was hidden. If she was a spy from Core City, it would make sense that they would have implanted her chip somewhere we wouldn't expect to find it. That *had* to be it, but I couldn't exactly ask her to remove her strange, puffy, body-covering outfit just so I could feel around her entire body to find it, nor did I expect her to comply with such a request, even if she wasn't a spy. Defeated for now, I drew my hand back to myself and frowned with dissatisfaction. She quickly recoiled her arm around her knees.

I turned my head toward Reese helplessly but I couldn't see his face, there wasn't enough light. I heard him sigh.

"If you came from," Reese paused. I understood why. It felt wrong and risky to even let the words flow out of our mouths. "*up there*," I sucked in a sudden breath. "can you show us how you got down here?" Reese was smart, why didn't I think of that? The little girl's eyes shifted. She definitely understood Reese's request, but she simply clutched her legs even tighter and buried her nose between her knees. How had she gotten here, indeed? Even more importantly, how had my father stumbled across her?

Why had my dad been in the forbidden passageways to begin with? None of this made sense no matter how many times I pondered the same questions. Every time I thought I was catching on to the master plan I remembered another curveball and my conspiracy ideas dissolved. There was only one thing left I could think of to try and convince the little girl to talk to us.

"Can you at least tell me about the surface?" I requested. "How do you survive up there? From what I understand, there isn't any oxygen or sunlight." I paused. She stared. "What do you eat?" I shifted as my

42

bravery began to wane. "Are.. are you going to eat *us*?" I glanced briefly at Reese but at this point I didn't actually believe she would try to eat us. She seemed.. *human*. Like us. She didn't seem like a monster at all which was why I felt convinced this had to be some kind of trick.

But she was just a little girl. She could have been trained to react this way, and yet how can someone fake being so terrified, especially someone so young? Then again, if she was from Core City she had probably been trained from infancy. Who knows how many children they had working undercover? They had even more eyes and ears than I realized. That thought send a cold chill down my spine and I bit my lower lip. I pressed my palms to my knees and stood. Suddenly this tunnel was too dark and too small. The walls were closing in on me. I tried to breathe but my chest was tight as if a rubber band was acting as a tourniquet around my lungs. Reese stepped closer to me and curled his arms around my shoulders. I wanted to push him away. He was the one that brought me here! Now, we were both probably going to die. I wouldn't even mind dying so much in itself if it meant I could escape a life imprisoned by a marriage I did not want and a Doctrine I did not support, but my death becoming an example to others who questioned things the way I did would mean that the government won. Accepting my death would mean they finally found a way to break me after all. I didn't want my death to be their triumph.

Was there any possibility – even the tiniest, slimmest possibility - that this little *wasn't* a government spy? Was it even remotely conceivable that she was really from *up there*, and somehow found her way into The Complex? I didn't see how. This place was well sealed. It *had* to be. We created and circulated our own oxygen through generators and artificial greenhouses. If there were holes in the foundation big enough for a person to fit through, by now we would have no air and we would all suffocate.

What if the scientists were wrong about the air on the surface not being breathable? What if they were wrong about surviving humans turning into savage cannibals? What if other humans found a way to survive just like we did, and we don't know about them and they don't know about us? I couldn't deny any of these possibilities but they still sounded like desperate fantasies in my head. They seemed like daydreams I had when I was younger, like running through grass or feeling sunshine on my face. Suddenly I realized I was doubting every question I had ever asked and every daydream I had ever held on to. What if that was exactly what the government wanted? What if they didn't plan on sending me to the transitional containers but instead they wanted to break me in a way that made it seem like it was my own decision? *NO!* I couldn't let that happen either! They couldn't win!

The band around my lungs tightened. I wheezed as I inhaled. Was there enough oxygen in these passageways? They were supposed to be sealed off, what if they weren't fit for breathing? I tried to inhale again, and wheezed again. I couldn't stay here. *I was going to suffocate.* **I needed air.**

I bolted. My legs jerked forward as if they were their own entities and sailed me down the pitch black hallway. I practically slammed myself against the steel door (How did I even know where it was?) as my fingers frantically groped for the handle. The moment I felt it, I yanked. It groaned in protest but finally gave. I shoved my shoulder against the door. It opened just enough for me to squeeze through. I inhaled. STILL WHEEZED! I moved away from the door and pressed my palms to my knees.

Breathe, dammit! BREATHE!

My self-commands were minimally effective but at least I was trying. My lungs seared as I struggled to draw air into them. It was as if my esophagus had swollen, leaving only the tiniest possible passage and air had to make it through a tunnel no larger than the size of a pin in order to fill my lungs. My body simply needed more air quicker than I was able to take it in. I closed my eyes. Maybe the air in the passageway was poison. Maybe I was dying. This might be *it*. These could be my final moments. I tried to inhale again but it took forever for the air to pass through. My lungs needed it NOW. How did we take such a simple thing for granted? We breathed in and out every second of every day throughout our whole lives and never understood how precious each breath was. I barely registered arms curling around my shoulders. "Ruby, you have to breathe!" I recognized Reese's voice but I couldn't respond. The harder I tried to inhale the more fruitless my efforts seemed to be. *I was going to die.* "You're having a panic attack. You have to listen to me. Listen to my voice, okay? Breathe slower. Take a long, deep breath." Was he blind, or crazy? **I COULDN'T BREATH!** His hands trembled on my shoulders but I couldn't concern myself with the fact that he was worried about me – not when I knew I was dying. "Okay – look. Don't hate me but I have to calm you down. I have to shift your attention." I barely heard a word he said. His palm pressed against my cheek and turned my head. Instantly and out of nowhere, Reese's warm lips pressed against my own.

I daydreamed about this feeling before. I used to

kiss the back of my hand in the privacy of my chambers and imagine I was kissing Reese, something I knew could never and would never happen in real life. Even so, just the mere thought of it, the imaginary impossible kiss from the only person I had ever wanted in that way sent my body into a frenzy. It felt like I was being tickled, but all over my skin in every place at once. Sometimes I would then run my fingertips across my forearm and the feeling would increase. I would shudder and my back would arch, but all too quickly, fear would rush in and replace the tingles. It wasn't that I was afraid of what I was feeling, rather, I was afraid I would never feel it for real and the more I let my imagination wake my body up, the more disappointed I would be when my mate kissed me – and I felt nothing.

Reese's breath softly rushed past my lips and all I could compare it to were the stories Grandpa Logan used to tell me about the tide from the ocean rushing over the tops of his feet. My heartbeat definitely did not slow but it was no longer blind panic that kept it pumping madly, it was desire. My lids half-closed over my eyes and my chin tilted upward as I pressed my lips back against his own. My body responded in ways I could not possibly command it to in my own consciousness. The tiniest noise escaped between my lips and the vibration moved from my mouth to his. We were connected, my movements becoming his and his becoming mine. He pillowed my upper lip between his own and I sighed again, moving closer, wanting more – but he pulled away. As suddenly as this amazing, earth-moving feeling of escape began, it was over.

The cloud of yearning I was cushioned on for only a few mere moments disappeared and I crashed back down to the hard, cold floor. Fury replaced lust. How could Reese do that to me? How could he kiss me like that, bring me to a new height, allow me to feel what was – and should have stayed – only in my imagination and then take it away just as thoughtlessly as it was given? And then I realized –

I was breathing.

My heart still raced, my mind still flashed snippets of colors and scenes and fleeting possibilities behind my closed eyes, *but I was breathing.* My breaths were short; a quick and heavy inhale and a forcefully expelled exhale, *but I was breathing.*

I opened my eyes. Reese's face was redder than I had ever seen it before. He looked like he dove head first into a barrel of tomato juice. His eyes darted around wildly, refusing to settle or even come close to looking into my own. He pressed his palms on the ground and scooted away from me like I was poison. "You were having a panic attack – I – I had to do that," he muttered with a guilty tone. Emotions became a live army and I was the target. They rushed at me with bayonets drawn, screaming, raging, swearing to take my blood to the grave with them as they clashed into each other and battled without mercy. I closed my eyes again and concentrated on breathing – it *was* easier. My lungs were actually taking in air now, the flow wasn't being forced through a pinhole.

It hadn't been the passageway, after all. I wasn't dying. Reese was probably right. I'd never had a panic attack before so how was I supposed to know?

This was all too much. I couldn't process it. I couldn't sort it out. I couldn't figure out where the lies stopped and the truth began – so I ran. I ran from the little girl who was probably a mole for the government but might possibly be from the surface somehow. I ran from Reese, who claimed he kissed me to save me from my panic attack but I didn't believe that was true, either. He had kissed me because he wanted to and that made everything I was already feeling for him that much more devastating. It was painful enough to harbor unrequited feelings that could never be acted upon but it was twice as painful to know that he might feel that same way, and yet we could still never be together. His kiss opened a doorway to how amazing and uplifting being with him could feel but I would never be able to walk through it. How could I even look at him now that I knew he wanted from me the same thing I wanted from him?

What about my father? *Who was he?* Did I know him at all? Was he anything like the man I thought he was? How many secrets was he keeping, and why? Did Mom know that he was breaking Doctrine? My mind said no, she couldn't possibly, but what did I know? It seemed like so many things I had been pressured to accept as truth were actually lies and I didn't know who to trust anymore.

I stopped running once I reached the door to my barracks. I pressed my palm on the wall near the door and let my head sink forward. My breathing was labored again but I knew this time it was because of running, not because I was dying. I closed my eyes so I couldn't get distracted by anything in the visual world. My heartbeat thundered deep within my ear canals. Blood rushed through my veins as if it had an urgent place to be. I trembled. I couldn't walk into my barracks like this, I knew my dissevered state would terrify my parents but I couldn't just stand here forever, either. Reese might be not far behind and I couldn't speak to him or face him again. At least not right now. Preferably not ever. My sixteenth birthday was turning out to be the worst day of my life.

After a few minutes, I stood up straight and rubbed my palms over my face. I concentrated on my breathing and willed my heart to slow.

Everything's fine. You're fine. Nothing happened today. It's like any other day – at least until tonight. No – don't think about tonight. Just focus on now and remember everything is fine. You can do this.

Lying to myself was helping, at least a little bit. I was calming down. I let my chest visibly rise and fall with each breath until I was semi-confident that I could convincingly appear normal when I walked through the door. I ran my fingers through my hair in an attempt to smooth out any tangles that may have happened during my experience

NO! Don't think about that!

and pulled my shoulders back. I pressed my thumb to the print-plate. A single beep followed and the door to my barracks opened. I walked inside as casually as possible and was instantly greeted by my mother. "There you are, good!" She paused and tilted her head as her eyes grazed over me. I shifted uncomfortably. "Where's whatever you had to pick up?"

CRAP!

"Oh, I – I couldn't find it so I think my lab partner must have taken it. I'll sort it out Monday morning." Mom narrowed her eyes.

"Learning is important, Ruby. Next year you'll have to decide how you want to contribute and that will become the rest of your life." I'd heard this lecture so many times before that my mother's familiar words were now water rolling off of hard plastic. Still, I obediently nodded because that was the response I knew would put her at ease.

"I know, Mom. I'm considering my options, I promise. I'm actually leaning toward working in the artificial gardens like Dad does." Mom raised her eyebrows. I didn't blame her, I had never mentioned having that desire before – and I still didn't have it – but I had to say something to ease her worry.

"Speaking of your father, he's in the living room and he wants to talk with you. I have to pick up your cake so I'll be back shortly." Mom moved some hair away from my forehead with her finger and then kissed it softly before brushing past me and heading for the door. My throat tightened. Dad wanted to talk to me? What about? He couldn't possibly know what I discovered today, could he? And even if he did, it would be incredibly risky to say anything about it even within the confines of our own barracks. I chewed on my lower lip and picked at my cuticles. I wanted to run again but there was nowhere to go. All I wanted to do since the moment I woke up today was run. First I wanted to run from tonights inevitable "date" with Connor, then from a strange little girl whose very existence challenged everything I thought was real, then from Reese who betrayed my feelings by kissing me when I never wanted to know what that would feel like, and now from my own father because even if the little girl was mole, she still had part of his shirt and that meant he wasn't the person I assumed he was all my life. I turned my back to the living room and wiped at my face again as I tried to choke back more tears.

Sometimes I felt much older than my physical age. Maybe I thought too much of my intellect, or maybe I was simply an "old soul" like Grandpa Logan used to say but in this moment I felt like nothing more than a child.

How could I look at my father and not ask him for the truth? How could I pretend nothing had changed when *everything* had changed? Was pretending everything was "normal" the right thing to do? Should I forget about the little girl and put her out of my mind? I would have to refuse to see or speak to Reese for the next two years of my life. How would I explain that to Willow? I supposed I could tell her the partial truth; that Reese kissed me but then she would be furious with him and that wouldn't be fair.

Who was I kidding? There was no possible way I could forget about the girl and my father's torn shirt. I knew I would feel haunted every second of my life until I knew and understood the truth, whatever it may be. My shoulders slumped in defeat and I slowly turned. I trudged into the living room with a downturned chin and heavy feet as if being urged to move forward while attached to a string. I plopped down on the couch next to my father and folded my hands into my lap. I still couldn't look at him. "What's wrong?" His gentle, concerned voice asked me. My fingertips pressed into my palms. I bit my lower lip.

"Dad, how well do I know you?" I had to be careful with my wording. *So* careful. He shifted his weight.

"What do you mean?" My muscles tensed.

"Do you have secrets?" He didn't respond right away. His silence was deafening.

"I suppose everybody does." So he wasn't denying it, at least. That was something. That was a start. I sighed heavily.

"How did you tear your shirt?" More silence followed. His brows furrowed.

"Ruby, where are you taking this?" It was my turn

to sit in silence. I couldn't say it out loud. Besides having trouble finding the words, I had to worry about the possibility of our conversation being monitored.

"Today, I realized there might be things about you that I don't know. I'm sorry about that. I should know you better." Still more silence.

"Ruby, is this about tonight?" My father leaned forward. "I know you're nervous. I know you wish you had more time. When I was sixteen, I didn't think I was ready to meet your mom but I saw her and wow, my feelings were instant. I knew she was the one. I think you just need to take a leap of faith and trust that this is for the best." I half-smiled, not because I was warming up to his words of advice but because he thought he was being clever by shifting the conversation onto a topic he knew was vulnerable to me and away from having to tell me the truth. It wasn't working, though. Right now I couldn't get the girl out of my mind. Dad was a smooth talker, this is something I hadn't realized before. How many times in the past had he used this tactic of diversion on me without my knowledge? The truth had power. The more I knew, the more I noticed. I was ready to face him. I shifted my body toward him and looked at him with calm, patient but firm eyes. I had grown up some today. I wasn't quite the same girl who woke up this morning. Ruby R-1046 may have spent her first sixteen years assuming her father was nothing more than a strong, caring provider but now I knew he was a man of secrets. I wanted to know what they were. No – I *needed* to know.

"This isn't about tonight." I paused and tried to find the inner strength, and nerve, to say what needed to be said. I kept my voice low, just in case. "This is about the little girl in the passageway."

The shift in my father's demeanor was instantaneous. His expression, only a moment ago creased with gentle concern now had lines of panic. His thick red brows practically leapt to the top of his forehead and his lips parted to fully show off his rows of (mostly) white teeth, gums and all. His eyes darted left, then right, and suddenly he was my mother with uncontrollable paranoia and fear taking him over. "Oh," he finally responded in an intentionally, dramatically loud voice. "You mean that story I used to tell you when you were a kid!" That could not have sounded less natural if he had tried. He leapt up from the couch like it was on fire. The only other time I had seen my dad move that fast toward me was when I was ten years old and raging as the flatfoots dragged Grandpa Logan out of our barracks. He grabbed my wrist and practically yanked me to my feet. He dragged me into our bathroom and shut the door. Only then did he let out a relieved sigh before letting go of my wrist. I brought it back to myself and rubbed at it, taking an instinctive step backwards. He was actually frightening me a bit. I wanted to run again. Maybe confronting him wasn't such a good idea after all. He leaned toward me and narrowed his eyes.

"Tell me what you know," he whispered but still in a very demanding tone. I shied away and tried to take a step back but I was already up against the wall. My own father had cornered me. I swallowed past a lump in my throat. There was no point in trying to sugar coat anything or lie.

"I was in the passageway and I *saw* her. She clutched a torn piece of our division uniform fabric, and you have a torn shirt." His eyes narrowed even more.

"Did she say anything?" I shifted my eyes and trembled.

"No." My throat tightened. "But, she indicated something, when I asked her where she was from."

"What, Ruby?" He hissed through his teeth. This was not the man I knew. This was not the man who used to get on all fours and play "horsey" with me, or even the man who hated seeing his little girl growing up and preparing to be someones wife. This was a man with secrets and things to lose.

"She pointed *up*." He visibly twitched. His tongue ran over his lips and the lines around the corners of his mouth tightened, but my words did not seem to shock him the way I assumed they would. He must have more secrets than I thought. Who *was* this man?

"Listen to me very, very carefully. Your mother will be back any moment with your cake. You are to smile and be an obedient daughter. Let her help you get ready for tonight. Don't say or do anything to trigger her fear. When your escort arrives, go willingly. Meet Connor. Be polite and courteous. Don't give anyone any reason to suspect you for – anything. Anything at all. Do you understand?"

No! That wasn't enough! What did my dad know? How, and why? I needed answers! I needed to understand what was happening here, didn't he realize that? I shook my head and felt the long ends of my hair clinging to my shirt. Dad's large hands curled around my shoulders and he shook me. He had never laid a hand on me before in my life. "Listen to me!" He hissed desperately. "Our lives may depend on this!" *Our lives?* Did that mean we were already in danger? Was it because of whatever my dad's secrets were, or was it because of me, and what Reese and I did today? "Get yourself through the rest of the day in one piece, and I swear to you as your father, you'll have all the answers I

54

can give you. But, you *have* to get through today without acting up." So this was basically blackmail. I had to agree to cooperate when it came to accepting Connor as my future husband or my father would tell me nothing.

Maybe I was looking at this all wrong. As much as I dreaded tonight, I already had no real plans to flee or try and escape because I knew what it would do to my mom. All my dad was asking me to do was what I was already planning on doing.

Then again, everything was different than it had been this morning. This morning I was a naïve dreamer but now I was an individual who had seen enough to realize that all of my silly questions and flights of fancy might not be as imaginary as I was urged to believe. My dad was involved in – something. Reese had feelings for me. There was a little girl in the sealed off passageways of The Complex who might be from the surface, or she might be a government spy. How was I supposed to pretend everything was normal when it was anything but. "You *have* to tell me the truth," I whispered. "If I do this today you **have** to tell me!" He quickly nodded. Too quickly, I suspected, but what other choice did I have right now but to believe him?

"Okay." He agreed with a determined expression etched across his worry lines. My father and I both jerked our heads as we heard the beep of the barrack door opening. Mom was back. He quickly opened the bathroom door and stepped out. I followed a moment later and tried to look calm. I cleared my throat and ran my fingers through my hair as I walked into the living room. Mom was standing there holding a small cake with a smile on her face that crinkled from ear to ear.

"This is your most exciting Birthday yet," she squealed.

Exciting. What a fitting word.
If only she knew. If only she had one single clue.

Chapter 3

I have no idea how I managed to smile while my mom fawned over me post-cake. She was blissfully, cluelessly happy when she presented me with my present, a hand-made dress. Only on very special occasions could we wear anything but our division-issued uniforms. All different types of clothes that served all sorts of purposes existed B-I, but now there was no need for choices. We were in an enclosure with limited resources so it was far easier to produce mass-quantities of the same types of clothing than to somehow make different fabrics and patterns for us to pick and choose from. That seemed frivolous even to me. But, first dates with our future mates and our wedding day called for a small exception to the practicality of uniformed clothing, and since my mom worked in the sewing rooms, she was able to personally create my dress. Girls whose moms did not work in the sewing rooms had to trade and barter for a special dress so I was expected to consider myself lucky.

"Try it on!" Mom squeaked excitedly as she shoved the dress into my hands. The privilege of wearing something *new* was the last thing on my mind right now. The dread I had been feeling about having to meet Connor tonight was barely on my radar anymore; many other things were swimming around in my brain like worms trying to move through thick mud.

Dad was involved in something dangerous.

Reese defied Doctrine regularly by exploring the old passageways.

Reese kissed me. God... it was amazing. It felt like flying.

There is a mysterious little girl wandering our passageways.

Was she a government spy, or a mutant?

*What if she really **was** from the surface? What did that mean?*

I turned and headed to my chambers, softly closing the door behind me. I glanced down at the dress. It was bright green like my eyes. Mom knew how much I loved green. This was the exact shade I had always imagined grass to be. The material felt considerably softer than what our standard-issued uniforms were made out of. I recalled Mom explaining to me once that there was some kind of weaving machine she used for special occasion dresses, but I never had any interest in her job so I couldn't recall the details. I climbed out of my shirt and pants and held the dress over my head. It slipped down my arms effortlessly and somehow managed to cling to my body below my shoulders without falling, although it was a bit loose. I turned my head after a soft knock on my door made me jump a bit. "Can I come in?"

"Sure, Mom." My door opened. Mom walked to me and gently tugged at my dress. It tightened right below my bust line and around my waist.

"There are clasps," she explained. "When they're open you can slip in and out of the dress but closing them makes the garment hug your body. Would you like to see?" It was definitely a new, strange feeling to have a piece of clothing hugging my figure but not providing a barrier between my thighs. Our regulation uniforms were designed for warmth, movement and comfort. Practicality was the goal. This dress was clearly designed for the gazing eye of the onlooker without much thought to the awkwardness the wearer would feel. I supposed the priority of my comfort was considered a distant second when it came to an obligation to visually impress my mate. I quickly closed my eyes. I didn't want to think about that.

"Yes," I finally managed to answer in a soft voice. Mom's fingers curled around my bare shoulders as she turned me toward my mirror. I gasped. I had never seen myself so outwardly exposed before. The dress had just enough tightness under my breasts to lift them a bit and cause a crease between them – *cleavage* – if I remembered correctly. That's what Willow called it. She was quite busty. Then, my waist seemed to curve inward, and my hips swayed outward. I couldn't stop a slight warm blush from spreading across my cheeks. I had stolen a glance or two at my own naked body growing up like all girls do when their chest starts to fill and their curves start to appear, but no one else had seen me without clothing since I was a small child and clothing hid or minimized attention to all of those bodily changes. This dress did not hide them at all. I turned my shoulders slightly to the right, then to the left. I stepped to one side, then the other. Every time I shifted, my whole body moved with me (obviously) but I had never paid attention to the fluidity of my own movements before. I was – *elegant.* It was strange to be pleasantly surprised by something that I had never really thought about before nor consciously wanted. My throat tightened. Was I *beautiful?*

No.

I didn't want to be beautiful. I didn't want Connor to see me in this dress and stare at my cleavage, my waist, my hips and my slightly rounded backside. I didn't want him to want me. I turned my head away from my mom so she couldn't see my face. "Can I have a minute alone?" Her hand fell from my shoulder.

"Of course, honey. I'll be right back, your father is going to want to see how perfect you look." I held my breath until she closed my door. I tore my eyes away from the mirror. The memory of Reese's lips pressed to mine was still alive inside of me. I could still feel their warmth and moisture. I still remembered the shudder that ran up my spine like being tickled from the inside out by the tip of a feather when he breathed against my mouth. I cautiously allowed my gaze to return to the mirror. If only Reese could see me in this. Would he want to kiss me again? Would his arms curl around my surprisingly slender waist and pull me close until my chest was pressing against his? Would his lips brush across mine again, and maybe my neck, and the groove that connected my neck to my shoulder? Thinking about it was too much. It was a dream that would never be reality. He had kissed me because I was having a panic attack, not because he wanted me. It wasn't Reese that would be seeing me in this dress tonight, it was Connor. I couldn't do anything to stop it. I promised my father that I would get through tonight and he promised he would tell me the truth when I did. I *had* to go through with this.

I pulled my shoulders back and tried to fill myself with resolve. I would allow the escort to take me to Connecticut. I would meet Connor. I would be polite and respectful. I would appear to be cooperative and accepting, but I would not let him put his hands on me. Not tonight. Not in this dress. If Reese couldn't touch me while I was in this dress, no one could.

My eyes stared into their own reflection. They seemed greener today but maybe it was the color of the dress bringing out their sharpness. I would never be able to look at Connor the way I looked at Reese when his lips parted from mine. I was okay with that. Maybe Connor would see the ice in my eyes and know from the very first moment that I would never truly be his. That would be for the best. I closed my eyes again and all I saw was Reese. I saw loose strands of his thick, chocolate hair resting across his forehead. I saw the dimples that formed on the corners of his mouth when he smiled. I saw the way his upper arm muscles bulged and curved when he lifted things. I opened my eyes and I could still see him. It was as if images of Reese had shifted from my imagination and burned themselves into my retinas.

"Reese.." I whispered out loud without meaning to. I pulled my shoulders back. "Connor may have me by Doctrine... but he will *never* have my heart. I promise you that." I quickly turned my head as a soft knock interrupted my pained, fleeting promises. My door opened and my mother re-entered with my father behind her. He stood up straight; tall, like a tree, and looked at me with calm eyes. How could he be so calm? He was *involved* in something dangerous, something that went against Doctrine, and he knew that I knew. How could he bury himself under such an obedient exterior and be my mom's rock when he had secrets that should be weighing him down? I could barely look him in the eye. He brushed past my mom and curled his large arms around me in a hug. It was an outwardly sweet gesture but I also suspected that he did it to hide my awkwardness.

"You look flawless," he said to me in a prideful tone. "Connor is a lucky man."

No, he wasn't. He was about to meet a future wife who could not love him. There was nothing lucky about that at all. I offered my dad a closed-mouth smile. My mother stepped to my dresser and carefully picked up the paper flower. She brushed some of my whispy red strands backward and slipped the flower behind my ear. "NOW she looks like perfection." My parents each took a few steps backward and stared at me with pride. I curled my arms protectively around my waist. Mom sighed and brought her hands under her chin. "You grew up so fast," she muttered in a sentimental tone. "Our time with you is coming to an end." I hated seeing her like this. I hated the sadness in her voice. I sympathized with her fears, but being so obedient to Doctrine when it came to my requirement to accept Connor being matched as my mate wasn't just hurting me, it was hurting her too. Seeing her tearing up like this made me despise the government even more. "Come on, darling. It's almost time."

I followed my parents into the living room. I sat and it felt strange. The dress rode up a bit and my legs felt exposed. Mom reminded me to keep my knees together so I appeared ladylike. She gave me some last-minute instructions but my brain was firing cannonballs in every direction but hers. Fear and dread flashed aimlessly in my head about having to face Connor. I tried to pretend I was even remotely interested in getting to know him in order to prepare for a lifetime of being his wife, but as soon as my thoughts started organizing, they began moving rapidly in a triangle that began with my dad, paused on the mystery of the little girl, and ended with my confusion and longing for Reese. I glanced down at my hands as they rested on my lap. They were trembling.

Our door buzzed. Grandpa Logan used to call it a 'door bell' but it was just the warning sound that came from our print-pad when someone touched it that did not have a matching fingerprint. Mom hurried to the door and opened it. She immediately took a few steps back and bowed her head. A stern-looking flatfoot entered without being verbally invited. His gaunt face was stone; expressionless. He was, in reality, about my dad's height but something about the stiff way he stood made him seem taller. His unyielding stance was intimidating. He was older than Dad. His hair was greying and his face was riddled with jutting, defined lines that ran under his eyes and across the corners of his mouth. I involuntarily shuddered. The last time a flatfoot was in our barracks was when they dragged Grandpa Logan away. I couldn't even look at this monster, he was already evil in my eyes. "Good evening," he began with a blatant lack of sincerity. "My assignment is to escort R-1046 to begin her courtship with C-2246." My eyes darted accusingly in my parents direction. I couldn't say it out loud but I knew my gaze communicated my words like a scream. *You didn't say my escort would be a **flatfoot**. YOU DIDN'T SAY. YOU DIDN'T TELL ME THAT!*

A calm part of me understood. My parents knew that Grandpa being sent to the transitional containers had frightened me to the core and caused me to resent Doctrine. They knew that to me, every flatfoot represented the one who took him so a part of me understood why they didn't tell me, but that didn't stop me from feeling betrayed nonetheless. They both shrank away from my icy stare. I shifted my piercing eyes to the flatfoot. I no longer cared if he saw my resentment. I slowly lifted my backside off of the couch and stood tall on my feet. "Let's go." I would never, ever let one of them drag me out of my barracks against my will.

The flatfoot did not introduce himself. That was

more than fine with me. I did not want to know his name or ID number. All flatfoots were the same. They were monsters.

I followed the beast semi-willingly out of my barracks without glancing back at my parents one last time. I knew that was immature of me and even a little bit cruel, but the sting of betrayal was still prevalent in my mind.

Reese. Reese. Reese. Where are you? I wanted him to appear around the next corner. I wanted him to take my hand and pull me away from the flatfoot. We would run so far and so fast that the flatfoot would never be able to keep up or find us. We would escape back into the sealed passageway. We would run even more until we were hidden so well we would never be found again. I would bend over and press my palms into my knees as my heart went wild in my chest. I would stumble and Reese would catch me in his arms, holding my weight effortlessly as if I were made of air. I would turn to him and press my body against his. Our lips would find each others and we would know with absolute certainty that I belonged to him, and he belonged to me. We would be two halves of one person. We would be together for eternity and nothing else would matter.

Every corner we rounded was empty. Reese was not going to save me. The sting of fresh betrayal, irrational as it may be, invaded me like a cancer.

We approached the door to the tram. I had stood here before, alone a few times and a few other times with Reese, staring at it longingly as if it were a symbol of escape. If only I could leave my division and see something new, the claustrophobic pressure I always felt weighted down by might lift and make this limited life just a bit easier to bear. Now though, it was no longer a doorway to freedom, but to dread. The flatfoot pressed his thumb to the plate. The door opened. I impulsively took a few steps backwards. Only then did the flatfoot turn and semi-acknowledge my presence. He lifted his hand and pointed a single finger toward the door. "Walk." The very act of his command increased my resentment and tempted my desire to resist. I refused to lower my head in resignation or look at him. I knew I had to do this but I was not going to sacrifice my dignity in the process. I allowed my hands to remain in their fisted state but I pressed them into my sides as I forced my stiffened legs forward. One step, two steps, three steps – and I was past the threshold. The door swung shut behind us with a finalizing click. My heart rate increased again so I tried to take a few slow breaths. I couldn't allow myself to have another panic attack. Reese was not here this time to warm the chill deep down in my soul and save me.

I perused my new surroundings. This all would have enthralled me just one day ago but now it was of minimal interest. The ground and walls were cemented and a few feet in front of me there was a drop-off. I looked down at the tracks. A tram would arrive and it would carry me out of my division for the first time ever. I should be looking forward to this and viewing it as an adventure but all I wanted to do was run. My body, as if wanting to obey my wishes, tensed but I forced myself to stand my ground. If I ran I would presumably be sent to the transitional containers. I had run too many times today.

I have to face this.

Silence was soon replaced with the dull hum of the soon to arrive tram. The hum grew louder and louder until it became more of a rumble. The cement under my feet began to vibrate. Then out of seemingly nowhere, the tram burst around a corner and seemed to make no distinction between full speed and a complete stop as it came to an instant halt in front of us. The entrance slid open. I simply stood there, transfixed, as I blankly stared at the open space in front of me. The inside of the tram would remain stationary around me and yet we would be moving. That was a concept I understood perfectly well when it came to the fundamentals of physics but it still seemed a bit too distant from the limited reality I had been exposed to for me to fully accept as a reality. The flatfoot cleared his throat. I still refused to offer him that "Is it okay, I need assurance" type of glance. I did not need his permission and I was NOT being forced into this. At least, not by him. I would never give him that satisfaction.

I stepped semi-willingly onto the tram, sat down and curled my fingers around a cool-to-the-touch metal poll. I fixed my gaze directly in front of me in case the flatfoot was still attempting to provoke me into a submissive glance. The doors slid closed and the tram raced off without a hitch. It was much quieter from the inside. For about fifteen seconds.

I jerked in my seat as the sudden boom of a trumpet cut through the silence like a deliberate attempt to startle me. I immediately recognized the bracing short tune as the anthem of The Complex, a jutting, dominant burst of notes meant to be bold, finalizing and intimidating. A picture formed on the front of the tram – a projection. A pre-recorded broadcast began. The silver infinity symbol that represented The Complex appeared small at first as it spun outward within the white background, but it grew in size as the anthem concluded. Etched on both rings of the symbol were the words *'We will prevail.'* I tore my eyes away from the projection. The symbol, as explained to us when we were small children, was supposed to be about perseverance; that nothing, not even the decimation of our planet could strike humanity down. Only, I wouldn't personally refer to a meaningless life lived within the confinement of The Complex as a triumph.

A stern looking older woman with white-blond hair to her shoulders, cold, steel blue eyes and long, curved lashes that looked like two rows of tiny razors stepped into the field of the projection and turned facing front. Despite being aware that this was pre-recorded, I could swear her icicles were glaring right at me, singling me out, seeing through me, piercing my defensive walls and exposing my hesitations and resistance with sadistic pleasure. A very cold chill ran up my spine and fizzled through my fingertips because I knew exactly who this woman was. She was the supreme leader that sat on the government throne. She was the woman who ruled The Complex. As if her cold, all-seeing icicles weren't enough to make a person shrink away, she then spoke with a forceful, accusing tone. There had to be speakers all over the tram because her domineering voice seemed to come at me from all sides. I involuntarily shrunk down in my seat.

"Good day. I am Commander SueLee and I want to congratulate you on being found physically and intellectually adequate for breeding. We have spared no expense in fine-tuning our genetic matching system in order to eliminate the possibility of anything being imperfect with your future offspring, and we are equally confident that you and your new partner will compliment each other well as you step into the future of humanity - together.

"Optimum reproduction is vital to the future success of humanity. As you know, we eagerly await the day when we discover a new planet and our species is able to flourish freely once again, but until that time it is your duty and responsibility to ensure that when that day comes, the human gene pool is selected to manifest the best versions of ourselves that we can possibly be.

"In front of your seat you will find a small vial. Prior to exiting the tram, you will open the vile and dab the substance on your wrist and on your neck. You and your mate should both enjoy the subtle fresh scent, but more importantly, the mixture contains a small amount of pheromones which should help ease any anxiety either of you are feeling upon your initial introduction, and assist in a quicker bonding process.

"Welcome to your future. Welcome to your contribution. Welcome to your destiny." Commander SueLee's finalizing words rang in my ears in the same way that a particularly terrifying nightmare lingers in your mind when you are just beginning to wake up. I shuddered again and forced my eyes away from the projector as her image began to fade and was replaced once more with the spinning infinity symbol as the trumpeted anthem finished off the presentation. The forceful tune finally faded into nothing and I was left once again with only the slight rumbling sound of the tram.

Commander SueLee was *evil*. I had seen photos of her before when we learned about our government as small children, but this was the first time I had heard her voice. My reaction was the same as when the flatfoots dragged Grandpa Logan away – I instinctively *knew* she was soulless.

Today had thus far been a day of discovery. First I

discovered Reese had a rebellious side, and then I met a little girl who was lost and may be a government mole, or she may live on the surface which should be impossible. Either way, this tiny human had secrets. Then I found out that my father, Mister Joe-Dependable, had far more layers than I ever imagined. He had secrets, too.

What secrets did Commander SueLee have? If the little girl really did live on the surface, did the Commander know that Earth isn't as unlivable as the government says it is? If so, what was the real reason we were all being kept down here? Whatever the reasons were, they couldn't be good and that filled me with a hypothermic fear that chilled me from the inside out.

The tram came to a sudden stop and the immediate cease of forward momentum caused my upper body to lurch in my seat. I tossed out my hand to catch myself and my shoulders slammed backwards. Quickened footsteps approached me. I still refused to look at the insidious flatfoot.

"Put it on," his gruff voice commanded me. The very intent of his command made me want to resist and for a moment I couldn't even recall what he was talking about. My eyes noticed a small bulge in the pocket in front of my seat and then I remembered. *The pheromones.*

This had to be a joke. There was no way I was going to smear perfume on my skin that would supposedly make Connor want me even more. I didn't *want* him to want me and no chemical was going to make me want him. I bit my lower lip. "NOW," the flatfoot commanded again.

Screw you! No. No, no, and hell no. No.

My mother's face formed in my mind; her wide, worried eyes, her fingernails nervously scratching at her knuckles and her head buried against my father's chest. The internal image changed to my father's face and his promise echoed in my mind. I pressed my lips together as I reluctantly reached into the pocket to pull out the vial, like someone whose body was being controlled by a robot, willing their muscles against the forced movement but failing to out-strength the control of the machine. I hated myself but I hated the flatfoot even more. My fingers clutched the tiny stopper and plucked it from the vial. I dabbed the tiniest amount I could on my wrist and on my neck. With a snort of defiance despite already having done what was required of me, I tossed the bottle aside and the rest of it spilled onto the seat next to me. The flatfoot sneered at my tiny rebellion.

Sorry, Dad. But this is **disgusting.**

The doors opened. I quickly whipped my eyes away from the flatfoot. I stepped out of the tram, secretly grateful to have my feet back on solid – unmoving – ground. The flatfoot used the print-pad and opened a door that lead out into another hallway that looked identical to the one in Rhode Island. If I did not know that we had just travelled I would have inherently assumed it *was* the same hallway. After rounding a few corners he stopped in front of a large doorway, the meeting room, I already knew, since we had the exact same one in our division as well. Reality punched me in the gut.

Oh god. This is it. CAN I RUN? CAN I, CAN I??

My body tensed as a rubber band tightened around my lungs again. Without meaning to, I closed my eyes and allowed images of Reese to flood my mind. We were outside of the sealed passageways. His arms circled around me and his lips danced across my skin. All I wanted was to be closer to him. All I wanted was *him*.

I forced my eyes open again but I allowed the images to remain. I *did* feel calmer. I realized that even when Reese wasn't with me.. he was with me.

"You have two hours." The flatfoot spoke to me distastefully as if he wished he could bash my head in. The feeling was very mutual. He stepped forward and pressed his thumb to the pad. The door opened. I pulled my shoulders back. It was now or never. I had to do this.

Suddenly I forgot how my legs worked. Which muscles did I need to flex to move them forward? My feet clung to the floor as if they were glued. "Ruby?" It was Reese! He was here somehow! He was here and he was waiting for me and he was going to somehow save me from this nightmare and everything was going to be okay! My body snapped out of its paralyzed state and I rushed into the room. The door immediately slid shut behind me with a finalizing clink. I looked up, foolishly expecting to see the man of my dreams.

I was an idiot. No, idiot wasn't the right word for what I was. I was *insane*. Reese was not here. He could not rescue me. He was sneaky, no doubt, but it was one thing to go unnoticed while tiptoeing into old passageways and quite another to somehow infiltrate a whole different division and steal me away literally right under the nose of a flatfoot. If I hadn't wished so hard for Reese I would have noticed right away that the voice calling my name was different than his. This voice wasn't quite as deep or as low. It didn't tell stories while only saying my name, and it didn't bring back a rush of memories. I swung my eyes forward and I saw him. Not *him*. Not Reese, but someone else. I saw Connor.

Connor was physically quite tall, taller than Reese no doubt but there was no power coming from his height. Like all redheads his skin was pale but his face appeared even whiter than usual. Not that I had any idea what his "usual" looked like, he just seemed almost ghostly. There wasn't even a rosy color to his cheeks. He was skinny, almost gangly. Not much muscle to him at all. Maybe he would grow into that tallness someday, but maybe not. His hair was a bit wild; fairly short and spiky. I briefly wondered if he had ever seen a hairbrush but then I realized he probably styled it that way on purpose. Other young men I knew back in my division used to do that a few years ago. Maybe the "trend" hadn't died yet in Connecticut. With so few ways and opportunities for us to express our individuality I knew better than to comment on anyones chosen hairstyle. It was the only representation of autonomy some of us had.

Connor's "special outfit" was a pair of brown, slightly tight slacks and a collared light blue shirt tucked into his pants. He looked very "polished" as my mom would say, but the way his outfit clung to his body unfortunately made him seem that much more twiggy.

I shifted my eyes away from Connor because, to be honest, there was nothing about him that made me want to keep looking. Was I that put off by him, or was I that *put on* by Reese? Did my feelings for Reese blind me to even the possibility of finding anyone else attractive? Would I have thought Connor to be even remotely handsome if Reese didn't exist? These were pointless questions to ask myself because I knew I would never have the answers. Reese *did* exist. My feelings for him had existed for a long time and today I was given a glimpse of what being with him could feel like.

Just because I had turned away from Connor didn't mean he had turned away from me. I suddenly became inexplicably aware of his intrusive eyes roaming my body. The tiny hairs on the back of my neck pricked. I moved toward the brown couch against the side of the room and sat. I pressed my knees together like Mom taught me. I folded my hands neatly in my lap. I knew my position was polite but uninviting. Body language was important. Mom reminded me of that, too, but she had wanted me to be open and flirtatious. I just couldn't do that. It seemed like I could feel the exact moment when Connor stopped eyeing me. He cleared his throat. "May I sit?" I shifted my eyes but only slightly. I shrugged a shoulder. Connor cautiously sat down on the other end of the couch. I appreciated that. He was respecting my space. Good. "You're very beautiful." I did not blush. It was not Reese's voice saying that.

"Thank you." I replied curtly. I inwardly cringed. My tone was probably rude, but what was I supposed to say back? *So are you?* I knew this conversation was being monitored but there was no point in outright lying. Connor was not beautiful. Not to me. Probably not to many people at all.

"So um, I've been waiting a whole year to meet you."

Duh. We both went through the tests a year ago when we turned fifteen, so obviously you've been waiting a year. So have I. But I've been DREADING this for a year...

"Look, um. I'm young, you know? I'm only sixteen. I still have forty-four years left. I know you've been waiting a year and I'm sure you've been excited-"

WOW, really?!? Could I sound more egotistical if I tried?! Where is this even coming from? I'm the shy girl, the dreamer, the insecure one!

"-but we have two whole years of bi-weekly dates before our wedding. I'd like to take it slow, do you

73

understand what I mean?" This was strange. I suddenly found myself being polite as if I cared about his feelings at all. I *didn't* care. Connor's very existence represented everything I resented about Doctrine.

I had to be honest with myself. I wasn't being semi-polite in order to shield poor Connor's feelings, I was doing it because I knew the government was listening. I knew if I drew attention to myself or appeared to be uncooperative, they could watch me more closely which meant they would watch my whole family more closely. That would put us all in that much more danger. Even though I was my parents daughter, it was suddenly my responsibility to protect them now instead of them protecting me. For their safety, I couldn't outwardly reject Connor. I forced a fake smile to tug at the corners of my lips. I pressed my hands into the couch and shifted diagonally to face him. "I'm sorry," I forced myself to say. "I'm just nervous." That certainly wasn't a lie. Connor did not seem phased.

"Oh don't worry, I don't expect you to like me right away. No one really does." I raised an eyebrow. Was he *trying* to sound pitiful or was he stumbling with his words just like I was? "I'm shy, you know? It takes a while for people to get to know me." Fair enough. I could relate. "But I resolved to try and change that with you. I want you to know everything about me since you're going to be my wife."

I wanted to punch him in the face. I wanted to turn around and claw my way through the door with my bare hands if I had to. Who cared if my nails cracked down to the quick and who cared if my fingers bled? I would take the pain, the punishment, even being put to sleep long as I could get away from this freak. I didn't care what the cost would be for me to run.

But I cared about Mom, and I cared about Dad. I pressed my hands deeper into the couch and forced myself to stay.

Connor started talking, pretty much shoving past his statement that he was shy. At first I tried to listen as he told me about his parents, his interest in science and how he wanted to work in the labs studying genetics and viruses (yuck) but eventually his words all seemed to blend together and my mind wandered. Where was the little girl? Even if she was a liar she was still just a child. Did Reese go back to find her? Was she all right? Was she scared?

What if the girl wasn't lying? What if, somehow, her indication that she came from *up there* was true? Even if she wasn't lying, she was dirty, smelly, and skinny. Her rough appearance made her life seem like a struggle. Could I live without the immediate comforts The Complex provided? Part of me wanted to believe I could. I would take a life without bathing powder and steady meals it if meant being *free*, being with Reese, not having walls and ceilings always surrounding and limiting me. I would take a hard, unpredictable life if I could escape from listening to Connor talk about the time he got to dissect a fruit fly under a microscope. My mind wandered back to him after that statement because I felt sadness for the fly. Reese would not have done that. Reese would have refused. He would have wanted to save the fly even if he knew he couldn't, just like he tried to save the butterfly.

By the time the buzzer sounded that indicated this "date" was coming to an end I felt like I had been sitting on that couch for a lifetime. My muscles were stiff, and until I shifted to stand I hadn't consciously realized I had been tensing them. I reached down and ran my hand over the bottom of my dress so the thin green material would cover as much of my legs as possible. "Oh gosh, sorry, I've been talking all this time and I haven't given you a chance to tell me more about yourself! I'm such a jerk!" No arguments there.

"It's okay... next time." I knew next time meant in two week but I didn't want to think about or acknowledge that in the same way I hadn't wanted to think about or acknowledge tonight. Connor took a few steps toward me and my muscles tensed again. I couldn't help it. When he tried to slip an arm around my waist, my legs swung backwards. I tried to laugh very softly to cover my actions. "Sorry, um, I'm not ready for that yet."

Or ever. Not with you.

"My fault, I should have asked first. I shouldn't just expect to be able to do that because you're my wife – *going* to be my wife." If he hadn't corrected himself, I might have lost control. I might have ran, or my palm might have connected with his cheek and not in a pleasant way. I was NOT his wife yet. Not for two whole years. I closed my eyes briefly and Reese was there. He caressed my cheek and whispered in my ear that everything was going to be okay because he was home waiting for me. I took a small breath and opened my eyes. I held out my hand in an offer to shake. It was the best I could do for now. Connor awkwardly shook it and smiled. Even his smile wasn't attractive. It was overly toothy and way too eager.

"I'll see you in two weeks," I forced myself to say. I turned around just as the door opened. My flatfoot escort was standing right at the door as if he hadn't moved the entire time I was inside. He probably hadn't. I forced my chin up again in that same 'I am doing this

76

because I choose to, not because you are forcing me to' stubborn facade and marched out the door. This time, the flatfoot quickened his steps behind me as I headed for the exit to the tram.

The ride back to my division was thankfully projector-free, the only sound being the rumble of the tram. The flatfoot said nothing. My fingers clasped the metal rail as if it were a lifeline while the tram was moving and my mind was on anything but Connor. He was exactly as I feared; plain, uninteresting, no one I could ever see myself growing to love. Did I really feel nothing for him at all or had I pushed him away on purpose? I frowned with displeasure as that unwanted thought poked intrusively at my mind. It was a fruitless question because the more I unwillingly pondered it, the more I realized that it wasn't about hating Connor, it was simply a combination of my heart belonging to someone else and being opposed to what Connor represented that set him up to be doomed to mean nothing to me.

I shouldn't let myself get discouraged. My whole life I have known that I would be forced to marry at eighteen to a mate that our governments genetic matching system paired me with, but I also woke up this morning *knowing* all of us in The Complex were sealed from an unlivable outside world, *knowing* my feelings for Reese would forever go unrequited and *knowing* that my father was nothing more than a simple man who loved my mom and I and worked in the artificial gardens. I didn't know what my dad was involved in yet or what he was going to tell me, but I now *knew* that no supposed facts in life were as solid and unyielding as I was lead to believe.

The flatfoot was quick on his feet as we exited the tram. I paused for a moment and bent over as my stomach churned, but thankfully the moment of nausea passed and I hurried after him. He nodded curtly to me as we approached the door to my barracks and then turned and walked away. I was quite glad to see him go. A shiver ran through my body that I had unintentionally been holding in for quite a while. I felt dirty. I wanted this dress *off* of me. Connor had eyed it just like I feared he would. I wanted to douse myself in bathing powder and scrub my skin with my body brush until it turned red. I was tainted.

I couldn't go inside just yet. What if Reese was around the corner? What if he had spent the whole evening just as sickened as I was at the thought of Connor's eyes on me and his hands wanting to touch me?

STOP IT. You're holding on to a fantasy. Reese kissed you because you thought you were dying. He was proving to you that you weren't. He was helping you. Stop trying to turn it into more than that.

But, what if it *was* more than that? What if my panic attack was only an excuse and Reese had been waiting for a chance to show me how he felt?

Big things were happening. I was just forced to meet my mate. My dad was involved in something secret, maybe something bad. Either way, it was dangerous and scary. There was a little girl loose in The Complex that I wanted – needed – to know more about. Yet, my mind kept going back to one person only. Reese.

Am I absolutely insane?

I pressed my thumb to the pad and entered my barracks. I froze in my steps. Dad was on the couch, just like earlier today, only there were two flatfoots standing at his side while the division GP hovered over him. My whole body began to shake.

THEY KNOW! THEY KNOW MY DAD IS BREAKING DOCTRINE! THEY'RE GOING TO DRAG HIM TO THE TRANSITIONAL CONTAINERS!

GP Nolan walked over to me and smiled softly. "My, Ruby, you've grown up! Your father tells us you met your mate tonight. Congratulations! There's nothing for you to worry about here, we're just trying to trace down how your father is the first in the division to show symptoms of a new strain of nasopharyngitis."

Oh, no. Please no.

Dad sneezed again.

Chapter 4

R-0844, or GP Nolan as I knew him, spoke without a care in the world. If he had no ulterior motives, why were there flatfoots in our barracks? My whole body went numb. I slowly sank into our living room chair. My knees pressed together tightly and my fingers curled over each opposing hand. My teeth sank down into my tongue. The sting was a less than pleasant sensation, but if I were to relax my jaw I wasn't sure what my mouth would do. How could so many things go haywire in just one single day?

Where was Mom? I glanced toward the kitchen. There she was, standing by the sink, her face whiter than Connor's had been. Her hand was shaking so ferociously that she could barely lower the tea bag into her cup of warm water. If the flatfoots saw how frightened she was, they might get suspicious! Dad was not available to be her rock right now so I would have to do it. Ignoring the sting and possibly the blood that was filling my mouth, I stood. As slowly and casually as possible, I nodded politely toward the GP and then turned and walked to my mother. My hand moved over hers and finally, the tea bag was lowered. "It's okay," I whispered to her. "They'll be gone soon." I heard Dad speaking but his voice was low and I couldn't make out the words. I wanted more than anything to rush back to him, to stand between him and the flatfoots and demand they leave our barracks this instant before I tore off their heads and kicked them down the hallway like recreational balls. I ran after them with rage once before when I was only ten, what was stopping me from doing the same thing right now?

It wasn't just my age. At ten years old all I knew and cared about was that I loved Grandpa Logan and the government was unfairly putting him to sleep. Today I turned sixteen and simultaneously learned that the limited world around me that served as my prison might have an escape after all. I also learned with certainty that being genetically matched with a compatible mate did not stop the heart from wanting what the heart wants. The Complex, the government and Doctrine could not squelch my natural human desire and instinct to explore, discover, and find out the truth, whatever that may be. I couldn't demand that the flatfoots leave my dad alone because there was too much at stake. My father's secrets had to be protected. Without even knowing what they were, I knew that it was now partially my duty to help protect them.

Mom's eyes were wide and they blurred with tears of fear. I curled an arm around her back and tried to give her a gentle, reassuring hug. Her hand still trembled as she tried to pick up her cup of tea. I pulled out a kitchen chair. "Mom, sit." She sat. I had a feeling that if I told her to walk in a circle and make a monkey noise she probably would have obeyed me like a mindless robot. Compliance was how she reacted to fear. Her hand fell from the teacup to the table. She was a statue again, just like the day they took Grandpa Logan. I knew it was weak of me but I had to turn away. The memories were starting to cloak me like fire and they were burning my flesh. I wished I could be like Mom. If I couldn't run away physically, I wanted to run away in my head. I could simply close my eyes and go to another place where nothing scared me or limited me. I could fill the crevices in my mind with Reese again and I knew if I did that, I would be all right.

But I couldn't let myself escape. Not physically, and not into my own head. Dad needed me. I stood up straighter and taller as an invisible string tugged at my spinal chord. I walked back into the living room like I had nothing to prove and nothing to hide. I sat back down on the chair, pressed my knees together once more and leaned forward refusing to let intimidation and fear cause me to shrink away. Unless someone told me otherwise, I had every right to hear the conversation between GP Nolan and my father.

Protect Dad.

Remember Reese.

These convictions gave me strength. These two men gave me strength.

"Can you give me an approximate time in which the symptoms began? Any symptoms, including but not limited to stuffy nose, fever, headache, sneezing?" I shifted my eyes cautiously over to my father but he was sitting calmly as if this interrogation did not bother him in the least. He was a master at keeping his cool in terrifying situations. How long had he been involved in whatever he was involved in? How much time had he been given to perfect this facade? I had been given less than a day. Hours, only. I did not possess his skills, but I was trying my best.

Dad shrugged. "I think I only started sneezing this morning." I raised an eyebrow. Something was off about that. I recalled learning about nasopharyngitis in science class and how after being exposed to the virus it took one to three days for symptoms to present themselves, but hadn't he only run into the little girl earlier this morning? If his encounter with her had been earlier, she wouldn't have still been clutching his torn shirt, would she? How could he already be showing symptoms if he had contracted the virus from her?

"Have you traveled anywhere unusual over the last three days?" GP Nolan asked him.

I knew it.

One to three days. Dad nonchalantly shook his head.

"I've been working strictly in Garden 19 for the last two weeks. I've worked alongside 0-719, 1-004 and 0-832. Distributors arrived toward the end of my shift on Monday to transport some of the harvest. I don't recall their ID numbers but I'm sure if you pulled up the shipment schedules you could find out easily enough. I haven't participated in any social activities for at least a week so the only others who would have been exposed would be my wife, and my daughter." I inwardly cringed. Despite my dad being so calm and cooperative, did he *have* to mention my mother and I? Thank goodness she didn't hear that, she was in no emotional state to deal with even more fear. GP Nolan sighed and nodded toward one of the flatfoots.

"Put in a communication to Connecticut and have them quarantine C-2246," he nodded toward me, "Ruby's mate with whom she was meeting with tonight. His family, too. Anyone he's had contact with after he met with Ruby." How did GP Nolan know Connor's ID number, and why? Maybe Dad told him before I arrived back. At least, I hoped that was the explanation. "Just as a precaution, to prevent the virus from spreading inter-divisionally." Flatfoot One briskly walked to the door and exited.

Good riddance, Asshole.

I wanted to say that out loud so badly. My teeth sank back down into my already stinging tongue. I shifted my eyes back to GP Nolan. He was slipping plastic gloves over his fingers. I bit down even harder. "Hold out your finger please." My protective instincts were too strong to hold back any longer.

"Wait – please, please don't hurt him," I found myself pathetically begging even though my voice was barely louder than a whisper. GP Nolan turned to me with an almost amused expression etched on his boyish face before quickly shaking his head.

"Miss Ruby, I'm not going to hurt him. I just need a bit of his blood in order to test the amount of agglutinins." *Wow,* I was an idiot. All he was going to do was prick the tip of my dad's finger. Agglutinins were simply antibodies that the immune system creates to fight a virus. I understood why he was doing it; the amount of antibodies would tell him roughly how severe the cold is (measured by how hard his body was fighting it) and that would give him an approximate idea of how long it would take my dad to fight it off. I sank back down into my chair. I focused my gaze on the backs of my hands as the GP collected his sample. I didn't notice he had turned back toward me until I heard him speak. "I would like you and your mother to confine yourselves to your barracks for forty-eight hours, just as a precautionary measure. Have either of you displayed any symptoms?" I quickly shook my head back and forth. I felt the paper flower slipping out of my hair and before I could grab it, it fell from behind my ear. I didn't even hear it hit the ground.

"No, neither of us," I answered quickly. GP Nolan curtly nodded.

"Still, just as a precaution." He turned back toward my dad. "Robert, please remain confined for the time being. I'll be in touch once I receive your test results, and we'll have a better idea of your contagious-window and when you can return to work." The GP stuffed his plastic gloves and the small vial of blood into his shirt pocket. "I think we're done here." Flatfoot Two turned on his heel and briskly headed for the door. I hoped he could sense how much I hated him even though we both knew I couldn't say it. The GP glanced at me one last time and offered a small smile before exiting. I wanted to rush to my dad and hug him. I wanted to tell him how scared I was and how amazingly well he kept his cool, and then I wanted to be selfish and demand the answers he had promised but I knew my mom was still in the kitchen, still a statue, and terrified out of her mind. I stood. Dad looked up at me with calm eyes but there was something new in his gaze; appreciation. He spoke no words but I understood his wishes nonetheless. I knew I would have to wait for his explanation. I just hoped he knew that I couldn't wait long.

I headed back into our kitchen and sat down next to Mom. Her stillness was frightening. "Mom?" I said softly. She barely blinked. "Dad's all right. He's fine. It's just a cold. Remember earlier today when you didn't want me to worry? Now I don't have to and neither do you." Her hand finally relaxed and her fingernails stopped pressing into her palm. "Mom, do you want me to help you to your chambers?" She pushed her chair back and stood but she was still silent. I swallowed past a lump in my throat and tried to shove away the searing hatred I had toward the flatfoots. I wished they would all get put to sleep. It sickened me how they existed only to elicit terror. "...Mom?"

"Yes," she finally answered me. "I'd like to lay down now." I gently curled my arm around her waist and walked her to her chambers. I helped her sit on her bed. She slowly raised her eyes to gaze upon my face. "Oh, Ruby, how was your date? Tell me all about it!" I blinked with absolute surprise. She was a zombie only moments before and suddenly her tone was bright and curious. It was as if she had just snapped out of a trance she didn't seem to realize she had been in.

"Um, it was.." I should lie to her. I didn't want to lie because she was my mom, but she had been put through more than enough fear today already. "It was good, Mom. Connor is very nice. I think I'll really grow to like him." It was frustrating to me how I felt like my words were a slap in the face to Reese, even though he has never been, and never will be mine. The creases on Mom's brow-line immediately softened with relief.

"Wonderful! See, I knew this would work out! I know you were hesitant but I was sure if you gave him a chance, you would see how right this boy is for you. Do you have faith in the matching system now?" I sank my teeth into my sore tongue yet again just so the sting would jerk through my body as a reminder to keep lying no matter how wrong it felt.

"Yes," I said as calmly as I could. I even forced a smile to tug the corners of my lips upward. "I'm sorry I worried you before. Things will turn out all right."

"I'm very proud of you." Her pride was based on a complete and utter lie. "You've really grown up, Ruby. You're making good choices. You're being a good girl. That means you'll be a good wife and a good mother and because of those things, our kind can continue to survive. Do you understand?" I forced my chin to nod. I was sad for my mom that she considered this kind of existence a life. "You look tired." Finally, a statement that was entirely true.

"I am. It's been a long day."

"Well, I think we've all had a long day. Why don't you go get some sleep." I nodded once more.

"I'm going to go talk to Dad for a minute and then I'll send him in," I assured her. "I'm going to bed, I promise." I leaned down and gave her an obligatory daughterly kiss on her cheek. She smiled up at me gratefully. I fought not to look away. I hated deceiving her but it was the only way I could protect her. I turned and walked out into the hallway.

I approached the living room and sighed. I leaned against the wall and ran my hands over my face. Exhaustion *was* starting to take me over. My eyes were heavy and my body sluggish. Even if I *could* sleep with all of these unanswered questions swimming around in my mind, I knew my dreams would be disturbing and unsettling. I slowly approached my father.

Dad looked up at me with drooping eyes just as tired as my own. They were filled with tremendous sadness, and although I still had no answers, I felt such empathy for him. I sat down on the couch next to him and focused my eyes to focus on the backs of my hands.

"You're only sixteen," Dad finally broke the silence. "You're still so young." He sighed. I didn't bother to tell him that only a few minutes ago, Mom was just telling me how grown-up I seemed. Dad raised his hand and pointed toward the bathroom. I followed his gaze and I understood.

I rose first and slowly walked away from the living room. I stepped inside and backed up toward the grooming cabinet where excess bathing powder and a few other hygiene items were stored. Dad entered and softly closed the door behind him. He turned to me and sighed. "Ruby, I don't want you to end up like your mother." My eyes immediately narrowed. A rush of

88

defensiveness boiled through my system and pushed away my exhaustion.

"Mom loves me! She loves *you*! Why would you say that?" Dad held up one of his palms to halt my anger and then held one finger up to his lips. I sighed with frustration. It was hard for me to keep my voice low and quiet when he was saying things like that about Mom.

"Fear controls her life. I try my best to shield her from anything that could make her unhappy but in the moments that I can't, she retreats into herself. I worry one day she might become overwhelmed and I might lose her forever. I don't want you to be afraid like her." I loved my mom. I did. Because of that, I was ashamed that I wanted to admit that I didn't want to be like her, either.

"I can handle the truth," I tried to assure him, "no matter what it is. What I can't handle is *not* knowing." Dad rubbed his beard as if his mind was struggling with an important decision. I knew what it was. *To tell me or not to tell me.* "You *promised*," I reminded him. Dad's hand fell to his side. His shoulders rose with a deep inhale. He was preparing. He was gathering his thoughts. I could relate. When his shoulders sank again, he began.

"I belong to a secret organization. We don't believe the government is honest about certain things. Our basic agenda is to figure out what those things are." He cringed as if he expected to be punished for his words right then and there. After a moment his shoulders fell just a bit more into semi-relaxation. "We started exploring some of the old passageways. We drilled upwards into the hard soil and penetrated the Earth's surface." I gasped and covered my mouth with my hands.

YOU WHAT?! ARE YOU CRAZY? WHAT IF A CANNIBAL MONSTER ATE YOU? WHAT IF YOU SUCKED ALL OF OUR BREATHABLE AIR OUT THROUGH THE HOLE AND KILLED US ALL? WHY WOULD YOU DO SOMETHING LIKE THAT??

Both my mind and my body were begging to scream in his face, but miraculously I managed to hold back and my response was nothing more than an angry roll of my shoulders and a hanging jaw. I pressed my fists against my sides. Dad licked his lips and took a compulsive step closer to me.

"Ruby.. we could **breathe**."

Wait.... what?

"Once we broke through the surface, one of us volunteered to test it. He went up for twenty minutes, and he could breathe. The atmosphere is **not** completely decimated." I could not feel my legs. I could not feel my hands. Basically, I could not feel any part of my body.

"We knew the next step was to further explore the immediate surface, but not without precautions. We have no idea what's up there, we couldn't launch a mission like that until we were fully prepared.

"Extremely early this morning, we returned to the hole to temporarily seal it for our protection until we were prepared for a more extensive exploratory mission.

"Drilling upward caused a lot of dirt and debris to clutter the cement ground of the passageway. We noticed," he paused. "footprints in the scattered dirt. Small ones." He took a deep breath. "I told the others to focus on sealing the hole. I followed the footprints and then, I saw **her**. I saw a little girl."

She told the truth. She was a little girl *from the surface*. She was from **the surface of our planet** and she could breathe, walk, and talk just like we could. Didn't that mean...

"They were wrong!" I excitedly began to blurt. "They said we couldn't survive up there but we can! We can leave this place and we can see the sky! I know the oceans are gone and we're on the opposite side of the sun right now, but there are other sources of water, right? Water that I can see and feel? Water that can rush over my feet?" I couldn't contain my excitement. I kept my voice low but my body bounced as ideas and flashes rushed through my mind like fireworks.

WE

WERE

FREE!!!

Dad's hands practically slammed down on my shoulders like avalanches (or so I read) and the force knocked all of my weight back onto the ground. My ankles took the full impact and they ached a bit. His eyes were wild, darting from side to side as if he had lost his mind.

"NO!" He spat desperately through his teeth. I immediately quieted down. "Listen to me! We still have NO idea what's out there, *no idea* what roams that surface, and *no idea* why it's not as unlivable as the government has claimed all this time. *No one is free*, Ruby. Not until we learn the truth."

The Truth.

I thought that was what I was going to learn tonight. I thought that's what Dad was going to tell me. Now I knew his secrets, or at least some of them, but I *still* didn't understand. I still didn't know the truth, but I knew someone who did.

"We have to find the little girl again. She might have answers!" Dad shook his head quickly back and forth.

"No! We don't know what she IS, Ruby! She could be dangerous." I said that very thing to myself countless times today since meeting her, but hearing my father say it made me realize that somewhere inside of me, I had known since meeting her that she wasn't.

"I saw it in her eyes, Dad. She was terrified, but I know she understood me. She's not a monster. She's a person, just like us." He still shook his head.

"That doesn't mean she's not dangerous, either by intention or by existence." I leaned softly against our bathroom wall and folded my arms under my chest. The tip of my tongue ran over my lower lip.

"Just, let me get all of this sorted out in my head. You're part of a secret order. You did something dangerous, risky, because you wanted answers the government doesn't give us. You created a hole that went all the way up to the surface. Now we have a chance to find out *even more* about what's really out there and you're talking like you're too scared to explore! But if you were really that scared... you wouldn't be in the Order, Dad." Suddenly, his hesitation was clear. "This is about *me*, isn't it. You don't want *me* to be a part of this." Where was this insight coming from? I knew nothing about any of this until only hours ago and suddenly I was talking to my father like he was my equal instead of my parent, an equal that was trying to keep me from something I had every right to be a part of. But did I have that right? I only knew about any of this because I had been doing something I wasn't supposed to do. I let Reese take me into the old passageway and everything had snowballed from there. Maybe this was my punishment. I did something I wasn't supposed to do and it had opened Pandora's Box.

Even if that were true, it didn't change anything. I

did know and I couldn't go back to being the innocent naïve dreamer I was only hours ago this morning when I woke up. I couldn't erase today's events because they had already begun to change me.

"It's true. I don't want you involved," he admitted. "I want you to be safe and nothing about what the Order does is safe. You're only sixteen." I shook my head. I wasn't going to let him convince me to forget about all of this. I couldn't.

"I *saw* her, Dad. I spoke to her and I *know* she understood me. And Reese kissed me." I froze. Did I really just... no, no I couldn't have. I **did not** just open my mouth and say those four words out loud, even if they were only a whisper. I was the stupidest girl alive. My shock-face solidified my stupidity. My jaw hung wide open, my eyes unblinking and my body seemed to naturally pick up the statue-reaction from my mom. I understood the (ir)rationality of it better now. Whenever something awful happened, if I just stood still, very, very still, maybe no one would notice and the moment would somehow erase itself.

"...*What?!*" The word was barely distinguishable from a hiss as it was forced out between my dad's clenched teeth. My throat tightened as if it were swelling. I knew I would not be able to swallow. My eyes darted helplessly back and forth, not wanting to settle on his face at all. He took a step toward me but I was already against the wall, I had no where to escape to. "Ruby, *what?!*" I couldn't say it again. I just couldn't. Dad sighed. "Listen to me, they will *put you to sleep* if they find out." I closed my eyes. It was just for a moment. How ironic it was that all I wanted right now was for Reese to come rescue me from this.

"It happened right after we ran into the little girl.

I was having a panic attack and Reese was just trying to calm me down. That's all. He was just trying to help me." I cautiously opened my eyes again. The look on my father's face told me he wasn't any more convinced about the innocence of the situation than I was. I tried to clear my throat, it still felt swollen. "I didn't ask him to do that, it just... *happened*." I needed to stop whispering. Words that could mend this situation did not exist. Dad took a step back and rubbed at his beard again. His shook his head back and forth as if his brain refused to accept what I was trying to tell him.

"They're going to be watching us, Ruby. They're going to be watching and listening, do you understand? I don't think they know anything about either of us yet, but when they realize they can't trace the origins of my nasopharyngitis, they'll be suspicious. You can't see Reese anymore. If he comes for a visit I'll turn him away. You're not to meet with him under any circumstances. This is serious, this is about your life, his, mine, and your mother's. Look at me and tell me you understand." His words stung like a scalpel, cutting far deeper than a slap from my old schoolteacher Rita's ruler ever could. How could I not see Reese again? Besides Willow, he was my best friend. He was the one who had given me the strength to get through meeting Connor in one piece, even if he didn't know it. I knew the feelings I had for him were forbidden but they were there nonetheless and the idea of never seeing him again tore my heart in two. My eyes squeezed shut and my body trembled.

Ask me anything, but don't ask me to never see Reese.
I couldn't make that promise.

Dad's hands rested on my shoulders again. "I'm sorry, Ruby, but all of our lives may be at risk and we can't draw any extra attention to ourselves." Giant tears squeezed out from under my closed lids and slid down my cheeks. I gave up trying to stop them. I wanted to fight this. I wanted to tell Dad that I would rather die than never see Reese again because I wouldn't be truly alive without him anyway. But Dad was right, it wasn't just *my* life that was at risk. With Dad doing dangerous things and Mom being so afraid all the time without even knowing the dangers we were putting ourselves in, I was now part of a coverup/conspiracy/whatever you wanted to call it and I would have to do things that broke my heart into a million pieces to protect the people I loved. I lifted a hand to wipe at my cheeks. My father had created a hole to potential freedom, but I had never felt more trapped in my life.

"I understand," I found myself choking out as if the words were acid rolling over my tongue. "I won't see him again." Only then did my father's hands slip from my shoulders. I practically felt some of the tension roll off of him as he released a relieved sigh. It was nice that I could agree to something that comforted him, but what comforted him was already destroying me.

"Good, that's good," he muttered.

"But..what about the girl?" Dad tilted his head and sighed.

"There isn't anything we can do, at all, until we're cleared from confinement."

"But Dad, she's stuck in those passageways with no food or water. She's absolutely *terrified*, and if the Order mended the hole, she has no way out. We *have* to find her again."

"I'm sorry, but there isn't anything at all that we can do until we're cleared. We just have to sit tight." His eyes shifted to the right and then to the left as if he heard a noise, but I hadn't heard anything. Still, I stiffened. "We need to get to bed. We cannot discuss this again until our confinement is over. It's too risky." I silently concurred, but only because I was too exhausted, both physically and emotionally, to continue this conversation. It occurred to me in that moment that this was the longest talk I had had with my father in years.

"Dad...?" I whispered as I wiped another batch of sticky tears from my pale, freckled cheeks. I moved toward him and curled my arms around his broad shoulders, resting my head temporarily on his chest. For a moment – just one small, single moment, I was eight years old again. I had just beaten my dad in a game of cards (though now I realize he had probably let me win) and I was so proud of myself. I squealed and leapt at him without reservation. He caught me mid-fling and squeezed me against his broad chest. I snuggled warmly into his big arms and in that moment I knew that with a dad as big and strong, but gentle as him, nothing bad would or could ever happen to me.

I wished I had that kind of innocence and blind faith again. It wasn't that I didn't believe in his love or his desire to protect me, but I was old enough to know that there were things he could not protect me from. I first learned this at age ten when the flatfoots took Grandpa Logan away, but today had been filled with even more grim lessons. Dad was still here for me, but he was afraid. He was afraid *for* me which solidified the fact that I could no longer view him as my protector. What if the flatfoots came to take me away, but they didn't know about him? Would his love for me override his acceptance of the apparently inevitable power the flatfoots and government had and would he leap after me the way I had tried to leap after Grandpa Logan, or would he sit on his chair, still as a statue with his eyes downcast as they dragged me away screaming? Part of me suspected I was a horrible person for wondering that. Was I an inadequate daughter to doubt my dad in that way or was I simply being a realist?

Dad turned from me and carefully opened the bathroom door. After one sad glance at me over his shoulder, he walked out into the hall. I followed. "Goodnight Ruby," he said softly without turning around.

"Goodnight, Dad." I watched him enter the chambers he shared with my mother, but he came out again a moment later with a blanket and a pillow. I thought it was a bit silly for him to start sleeping apart from her tonight, if the cold he was carrying was passed to either one of us, we probably already had it by now. This action was probably more for peace of mind than for realistic precaution. I turned on the balls of my feet and trudged back to my own chambers. I closed the door. I leaned against it as trembles careened through my body like a seizure. More tears poured out of my eyes like the way Grandpa had described a waterfall. I brought my hands up to cover my nose and mouth, using my palms to muffle my sobs. When I woke up this morning I had been dreading meeting Connor. I couldn't have possibly known that things were going to get ten times more complicated than that.

I grasped the thin material of my special dress and tried to yank it over my shoulders but I had forgotten about the clasps. I reached behind myself and felt around with my fingers, pushing, pulling, trying to undo them until I heard something snap. I probably broke it but what did it matter, I would never wear this dress again. This was strictly a one-night garment. I yanked it over my head and threw it at the wall.

Stupid dress.

Part of me knew it was irrational to blame the dress for all of the crazy, unexpected, life-changing twists today had thrown at me, but I had to direct my confusion, anger and sadness somewhere. I pulled one of my regulation shirts and the matching slacks out of my closet and forcefully yanked them over my body. I was oddly glad to feel the thicker, harsher fabric against my skin because although I had spent most of my life wishing for change and freedom, at this moment it seemed strangely comforting to feel some kind of familiarity. I curled up on my bed and brought my knees up to my chest, wrapping my arms around them the way I often did when the government systematically lowered the temperature in The Complex a few degrees to simulate a surface "season" called "winter." I wasn't cold tonight but I still felt the urge to squeeze my body into the tiniest ball that I could manage. I laced my fingers together and closed my eyes. I expected sleep to provide a very swift escape for me but instead, the worms moving through the thick soil of my mind began to squirm with even more unwanted tenacity.

How did my father think that never seeing Reese again was a realistic possibility for me? We lived in the same division and even had a few of the same classes. Was I supposed to turn my back every time he spoke to me? Was I expected to ask my teachers never to pair me with him? How would I even explain that, in theory? Stepping away from the logistics of it all, *how* was I supposed to turn away from him?

Why was life such a bitter disappointment? I had daydreamed secretly for months about Reese, and I wished on every star I had ever imagined someday being able to see that he felt the same way about me that I felt about him. If there was even a chance that his kiss was anything more than a desperate way to distract me from my panic attack, my wish came true, but it did not bring me joy nor relief. If I hadn't spilled my secret to my father would I still be able to see Reese? Would we ever get the chance to face what happened between us, or was that chance now as assuringly gone as a candle flame once the wax was all burned away?

My body continued to shake with nearly silent sobs and I pressed my chin down into my knees. Was everything going to change now that we knew the surface was breathable? Maybe those who were sent on the missions didn't know, either. Maybe they were sent into space without having the chance to actually explore Earth. I obviously wasn't sure about any of the details of those who were sent on missions... no one was. The whole program was top secret except for the knowledge that it existed and the announcement every five years that another shuttle was being launched.

If I could wake up tomorrow and make different choices, would I? What if I had ignored Reese's message that he had given to Willow? There would be so many things I would be blissfully unaware of. I never would have done something forbidden. I never would have met the strange little girl that lived on the surface. I wouldn't know that my father was a part of a secret Order who didn't trust the government. Reese wouldn't have kissed me. I still would have been forced to meet Connor but maybe I would have been more interested in hearing him talk about himself if I didn't have all of these other alarming events tugging at my brain like small children all demanding my complete attention. I would still be laying here sad, but I would be in less inner turmoil.

My thoughts drifted back to my father. He was a

different man than the one I had known for the first sixteen years of my life. How had I not realized that we shared the same unsettled mind? I had always assumed that I got my curious nature directly from Grandpa Logan because he was the one who told me stories about the surface and encouraged me to be inquisitive, but what if my curiosity was more biological than environmentally influenced? Had Grandpa Logan known about my dad's suspicions about the government? How long had Dad been in the Order? How long had the Order actually existed? Who else was in the Order? Anyone that I knew? Probably, since Rhode Island was a very small division.

I tossed and turned and then paused to untangle the sheet from my legs. My eyelids were as heavy as stones but my brain was firing a mile a minute. Sleep verses thought, it was an epic battle but I suspected sleep would prevail in the end.

I could feel an oncoming dream trying to clear away the spiderweb of thoughts from spreading further into the corners of my brain. Images began to form behind the black of my closed lids, and although they weren't images I wanted at the moment, I was too far gone to try and stop them. Out rushed reality and in rushed dreamland to replace the void that reality had left behind.

Chapter 5

I woke up in the morning without the assistance of an alarm, but since I was confined to my barracks I had no particular reason to force myself to rise early. I closed my eyes again and rested my head back down on my pillow but sleep refused to return despite my body still feeling sluggish and heavy. Giving up on sleep but still unwilling to drag myself out of bed, I opened my eyes and stared longingly at the ceiling. When I was a child I used to gaze at my ceiling and pretend that I was looking up at the night sky. Did stars really twinkle? Was it true that the stars people saw didn't even exist by the time they could be seen because of how long it took their light to travel the distance to Earth? Science about our planet and about space was endlessly mysterious and fascinating to me.

Grandpa Logan had described the sky as light blue during the day and all sorts of changing colors during dawn and twilight. Night was supposedly a very deep blue, so deep that it was almost black and yet at the same time, the sky itself was clear. I would say "Grandpa, that doesn't make sense! Something can't have color and be clear at the same time!" He would chuckle, pat me on the head affectionately and tell me that there was no way I would be able to understand unless I saw the sky for myself someday. The closest thing I had was my ceiling and my imagination. I would try to picture where the stars might be. Maybe there was a big cluster of them over to the right, and just one star to the left. Maybe there was another planet between the stars but since it was so dark our eyes would never know it was there. Were the stars in different places each night? Since our planet moved so much slower on its axis than it used to, we measured time by counting the days (365 per year except for one extra day during leap year) but how slow were we actually drifting? Was time only a perception based on previous B-I science? Did it actually have any meaning at all anymore?

I sighed. Why did I have to turn nice, simple thoughts like imagining what stars look like into something existential and depressing? I supposed I knew too much now to daydream about happy things without knowing that there was no such thing as a good thing that did not coexist with a bad thing. Accepting the inevitability of bad things pulled my feet back down to the ground like magnified gravity.

I pushed my sheet back and slid my legs over the bed to stand. I stretched my arms over my head. My body still felt unusually heavy. I curled my toes against the floor and shook some of my messed up hair out of my face. I wished I could just sleep this whole day away, and then the next, and not wake up until confinement was over and I was sure my family and I were safe. But I knew that after yesterday, I would never be able to be sure of that.

The scent of banana bread tickled my nostrils. I quietly exited my chambers and peeked my head around the corner into the kitchen. Mom was standing in front of the juicer with a few oranges. YES, we had oranges! A bonus of Dad working in the artificial gardens is that we could sometimes get fruits that we did not grow in our particular division. Orange juice happened to be my favorite morning drink, but it was a rare treat. I slipped into a chair and Mom set a glass of juice in front of me with a warm, welcoming smile. Suddenly this felt like a morning no different than any other. In minutes I would have warm-from-the-oven banana bread to go with my juice and Mom would probably let me know what sort of harmless gossip she might hear today from the other woman in the sewing rooms – except, she couldn't go to the sewing rooms today because we were all under confinement. My momentarily unburdened smile faded. Well… at least I had a chance to feel normal for thirty seconds or so. How ironic that normality brought comfort to me when it usually felt like my prison.

Dad entered the kitchen a moment later. He said nothing to me, but walked over to Mom and leaned forward as if intending to give her a kiss on the cheek. Usually she would welcome it but today she held out her palm and pushed him away. "Not today Robert, not until your nasopharyngitis is completely cleared up. I don't want to risk it." He sighed softly but didn't argue with her. He sat down on the chair next to mine. I avoided looking at him and took another sip of my juice.

"So," Dad began rather loudly as he leaned forward in his chair. "Since we're on confinement, I thought we'd take the opportunity to spend some time together as a family. Remember the family days we used to have, Ruby?" I remembered. We had them every week when Grandpa Logan was still with us. We would gather in the living room and play cards or board games and engage in lighthearted conversation. The problem now was that no conversation was going to feel lighthearted and I didn't know if I had the strength to pretend otherwise.

"Yeah, but I'm tired Dad, I'm not sure if I'm up for a family day. I might just study or read in my chambers." Crap, I said the wrong thing. Mom was at my side in seconds.

"Do you not feel well? Do you have a fever? Stuffy

nose? Headache?" Her palm immediately pressed on my forehead as she hovered over me in an unintentionally invasive manner. I purposely refrained from pointing out that a minute ago, she had pushed Dad away from her because of his nasopharyngitis, but worrying that I may have caught it as well did not stop her from being near me. I quickly shook my head and squirmed away.

"Stop, I feel fine! Yesterday was just a long day and it took me a while to fall asleep last night. That's all, I promise." The crease on her brow let me know that she wasn't fully convinced, but she pressed her lips together and seemed to resist pestering me further. I was relieved but I tried not to let my face show it.

"Well, I think your father is right. We do need to spend some time together as a family. Especially," she paused for a moment. "Especially because you're only with us for two more years and then you will be a married woman and we will only get to see you on visitation days." I could see that she was upsetting herself. She dabbed at her eye with the sleeve of her shirt. I sighed softly as guilt enveloped my heart like a swaddling blanket. I caved because I didn't want to hurt her feelings or trigger her into another dissociative state.

"Okay, okay. Family day it is."

I ate my banana bread and sipped my fresh-squeezed orange juice but it didn't taste like it usually did. Well, that probably wasn't true, it was just that this was the first time I actually paused to think about what it tasted like. All fruits and vegetables were grown under artificial lights and pumped full of artificial supernutrients, but did they taste the same as they used to on Earth where they used to be able to grow under natural sunlight? I found myself wondering if orange juice from a "real" orange was stronger, sweeter, or did it have a different taste altogether? I halfheartedly finished my juice and raised an eyebrow as I wondered if I would ever get to taste a real orange, and for the first time in my life, I internally responded to my own thought with

maybe.

I followed my parents into the living room. Dad opened a cupboard and pulled out an old board game we used to enjoy called JOB SWITCH. It had been specially made after I was born. We each had our own game piece. A little girl figurine was supposed to represent me, a man figurine represented my father and a woman figurine represented my mother. We left the second male figurine in the box, it used to represent Grandpa Logan. There was a dial in the middle of the board and a pile of cards. First, you spun the dial. Whatever it landed on became your initial career. You moved your figurine to the circle that said the title of your career. After everyone was in a box, you picked a card. The card would either praise you on a job well done in which case you stay in your initial box, or it would force you to change careers. You had to move your figurine to the new career box, but that left your initial (or latest) career box empty. If it was already taken, you had to share the box but then there was no one to do your old job. You placed the card in a new pile. You kept going until there were no more career cards. Then you picked up the pile of discarded cards and read each career that no one has and you had to explain what would happen in The Complex if there was no one doing that job. The game was supposed to teach us about the different career options and how and why each career is vital within The Complex to the maintained survival of the human race, and also why we needed to continue to breed so there were enough people to do every job.

I could not have been less interested in playing this game. Where was the card for "Goes against Doctrine in secret and finds a little girl whose very existence might prove that the government has been lying to us?" Where was the card for "Life may be sustainable outside of The Complex after all?"

My mind refused to stop worrying about the little girl. I was terrified at the idea of her being discovered by a flatfoot or another government official. If that happened, they would put her to sleep for sure. I doubted they would even put out any type of alert or elicit a lockdown because they probably wouldn't want us to know anything at all. We might start asking questions that they did not want to answer.

Would Reese have gone back to find the girl and help her? He wouldn't have left her to fend for herself, right? But if he *had* gone back and helped her and they had been caught, he would be put to sleep immediately right along with her! Would the government tell us anything then or would they concoct a false story to explain his death? For that matter, what if my mom's fears about her own mother were actually substantiated? I squeezed my eyes shut as if that would somehow quiet the screaming questions bouncing around relentlessly within the grey matter between my ears. I couldn't bear the thought of anything happening to Reese. I was torn down the middle, half of me wanted Reese to help the girl because she was just a child, alone and afraid but the other half of me, the selfish half, wanted him to stay as far away from her as possible. Even if I couldn't ever see him again, I wanted him to live. I wanted to hang on to even the smallest thread of hope, so small that it was a dream again rather than a hope, that someday he could kiss me again. It might be the only wish that would get me through having to inevitably kiss Connor someday... and more.

I was a robot by the time the game continued. I got a job, then I was unemployed, then I shared work with my father, then I was unemployed again, and it went on and on like that until the cards were all gone. I glanced longingly at the door. I felt confined enough as it was being limited to a life within The Complex, but now I wasn't even allowed to leave my barracks. The living room was unbearably small, the walls obnoxiously close together. Every time I glanced at them I felt more and more anxious. Normally I would rid myself of my anxiety by taking a brisk walk, but I couldn't do that *because I couldn't leave my barracks.* We put the board game away and Dad produced a regular deck of cards. Blackjack commenced and our conversation was minimal. Mom was lighthearted, laughing here and there after making random corny jokes. Dad was his usual quiet self and I was the obedient daughter. It made me sad that I loved my parents so fiercely and yet not a single one of us felt we could be our true selves around each other. I didn't blame them for our distance. It was The Complex, government and Doctrine that made us this way which only made me resent these things even more, if that were at all possible. They had taken EVERYTHING from me; the potential for me to have an honest relationship with my family, the possibility that I could experience love with Reese, and the obvious one, my freedom. Now that I knew the imprisonment of hundreds of people in The Complex might be for nothing, sitting in this small room swapping cards for no reward other than the supposed thrill of beating my parents seemed like the most ridiculous waste of time I could imagine.

Just when I wasn't sure how much longer I could sit in this room without kicking down the walls, there was a knock on the door. I jumped to my feet faster than the speed of light and rushed to it eagerly, momentarily forgetting about the fact that I was under confinement. Dad was behind me in a flash. "Ruby, no! *Exposure*." I paused in mid-leap and landed unenthusiastically back on my heels with a frustrated huff. Dad stepped ahead of me and approached the door.

"Who is it?"

"It's R-1004. I have some papers from work I need you to sign, to authorize the grapefruit shipments to New Hampshire and Vermont." Dad reached behind his head and scratched at the back of his neck.

"Ah, well, I'm under a confinement order -" Did he just say *Order*? Had his tone changed when he said it? Had he used that word on purpose? "for nasopharyngitis. Can you slip them under the door?"

"Yeah, your guard let me know. Sorry to hear about that. The shipment sheets just need your signatures. I'll come back for them at eight AM promptly so you have time to look them over and check for errors." There was a *guard* at the end of the hall? Was he stationed there to make sure we didn't try to leave our barracks? *Was he technically holding us captive in our own barracks?* My stomach literally turned over on itself and a wave of nausea hit me like a punch. I tried to hold back a groan of pain as I doubled forward. One of my arms curled around my stomach while the other pressed against the doorframe. Just when I thought there couldn't be any more terrifying surprises in store for me...

"Sure, can do."

"See you back at work in a few days."

A manilla folder appeared under the door and Dad quickly reached for it. I turned my eyes on him suspiciously but he wasn't paying attention to me. He pressed the folder against his chest and cleared his throat. "I'd better tend to these now so I don't forget." Less than two days ago I wouldn't have thought anything of his eagerness to tend to work matters, but now, something about the quickness of his words and the protective way his fingers gripped the folder caused me to raise an eyebrow. He hurried back into the living room with me quickly in tow. "Sorry girls, count me out of the next few games." Mom stood and smoothed her hands down her pant legs.

"Actually, now is a good time for a break so I can get dinner started. I was thinking eggplant Parmesan?" I did not care, at all, what she made for dinner.

"Sure, Mom." Mom headed for the kitchen and Dad hurried off toward his chambers. I stood by myself in the living room and allowed my shoulders to heave with a few deep breaths. I *could* be the dutiful daughter, clean up the living room and put a few things away as my parents attended to business and dinner, or I could confirm my suspicions that the folder delivered to my dad contained more than just shipment papers from the gardens that needed his signature. I kept one ear attentive toward the kitchen until I heard a drawer, then a cupboard being opened. When I was satisfied that Mom was fully immersed in preparing dinner, I sprang toward her and Dad's chambers. If I knocked, it would give Dad a chance to hide or rearrange the papers and pretend like everything was normal, even if it wasn't. I couldn't take that risk. I curled my fingers around the handle and pressed it down. The door opened narrowly and I quickly squeezed myself in. The papers were spread out on the bed in a neat horizontal succession. Dad tore his eyes away from them upon my entry in obvious guilt and alarm. He then lunged for them. "STOP." I commanded forcefully. I paused as the echo of my own word blared in my mind like a foghorn. I had never spoken to either of my parents like that before. I was not proud of how disrespectful I sounded. I closed my eyes briefly and took a deep breath. "Dad, what are those?" I opened my eyes again. He had gathered the papers up in his hands in a disorganized and frenzied fashion. His face was tense and resentful. My heart twinged. I hated that I had just spoken to my father the way I did, and I hated how hurt he appeared to be because of it. "I'm – I'm sorry," I muttered softly. I knew that out of respect for my father I should have honored his privacy. I should have turned around and left, but I didn't. "Dad, what are those?" I asked again. He quickly shuffled them back into the folder without bothering to straighten them out. His eyes wildly darted back and forth as if someone else were listening.

"You know what they are," he replied a bit louder than he needed to, considering we were only standing a few feet apart. "Are you wanting to see them so you can acquaint yourself with some of the business aspects of the artificial gardens?" The tense creases on his face eased and his expression softened from a mixture of anger and hurt feelings to a quiet plea. Was he speaking in code? I shuffled over to his side and he set the folder back on the bed. He opened it and began placing the papers one by one on the blanket, systematically laying them out just as they were when I had rushed in. He leaned forward and my body naturally mirrored his.

"See this line?" He rested his index finger down on the first paper. "Thats the quantity of the order, and we have to check it against this line," he slid his finger down toward the bottom of that first page. "to make sure the quantity doesn't exceed the shipment divisions maximum allotted amount." I bit my lower lip and stared at the paper. It really *did* look like a regular shipping and receiving form. Was there some clue I was supposed to be catching on to that I was completely missing?

"And then here," Dad's finger jumped to the next page and rested on a random line that said nothing more than *'Vermont is prepared for incoming shipment.'* I raised my shoulders in a helpless, confused shrug. Dad lifted his finger and wiggled it. "Here's the agreed upon price or barter," he pointed to a new line with a few numbers and sentences. "You have to make sure a specified time and the name of the receiver is mentioned before signing off on it." He pointed to a few more places on each remaining page and explained what needed to be checked. "Do you want me to go over it one more time with you?" I shifted my still-confused eyes toward him and continued to chew on my lower lip. Dad's face softened again, but with just the slightest raise of his bushy red eyebrow he was letting me know this was important. There was obviously something I was missing.

"Yes please, just one more time." Dad patiently moved to the first page again and set his finger down. He started to go through the same verbal explanation but he tapped his finger three times on one particular word. *The.* A few sentences down he tapped his finger on another word. *Girl.*

And then it hit me, the entire stack of papers was coded! I wasn't entirely sure how to read the code as it didn't appear blatant such as every three lines or every fifth word on each of those lines, but there had to be a pattern of some sort or Dad wouldn't have been able to find each word so effortlessly. Then it hit me, the first letter of each word Dad was tapping on was a slightly different font than the rest of the word, extremely subtle but once I caught on, the code easily unfolded in front of me. I focused on each finger tap and I let the code stretch out in my mind word for word.

The
girl
is
safe
for
now
but
the
boy
is
in
danger.

For about two and a half seconds I was quite proud of myself for managing to understand the code, even if I did nothing but follow my father's tapping finger. Then the entirety of the message hit me like a boxing glove in the gut right after intestinal surgery.

But the boy is in danger.

BUT THE BOY IS IN DANGER.

Oh. My. God.

REESE.

The boxing glove that had just slammed into my stomach seemed to immediately grow claws in the shape of razor sharp knifes. It came at me again but this time the knives tore through my flesh and into the soft tissue of my organs, slicing upward toward my heart. I could feel my blood, loose from its veins, pouring freely and helplessly into the rest of my body like a waterfall. My chest tightened, my shoulders haunched over and my arms curled underneath my chest.

Did the flatfoots have Reese? Did they know he had been sneaking into the sealed passageways? Did they know about the little girl? No, the message said she was safe. She was safe but that didn't mean they didn't know about her! If they knew that she might be from *up there* and they knew Reese knew about her, he would be sent to the transitional containers for sure!

"I can't – breathe -" I choked out in barely a whisper. The walls in my parents chambers seemed to move in toward me, causing the space I had around me feel smaller and smaller by the second. The walls were closing in on me from the *inside*, constricting my chest so that when I tried to inhale my lungs were unable to expand and take in air. I closed my eyes as I felt my dad's hands move first to my shoulders and then to my back, systematically patting it.

"Slow, deep breaths," he advised. The concern in his tone caused guilt to swarm around me like the way my science teacher had once described bees. "Take it slow, Ruby." He was trying to help, I knew that, but I needed *Reese.* And then, there he was, behind the darkness of my closed lids. His deep blue eyes reflected something, *water,* and the water was moving and shifting like a live entity. He reached forward toward me and I raised my chin, wanting, *needing* to be closer to him.

"You can get past this," I knew consciously that the voice belonged to my dad but it was Reese's mouth that moved. When the words entered my ear canals, it was Reese's voice my brain chose to hear. I tried again to inhale, and this time, although it was a struggle and my lungs were resisting, I could feel some air managing to get past the constricted area. "Don't rush."

Thank you, Reese.

I tried again. It was still a struggle but a bit more air managed to get through this time, and even that little bit of air helped release some of the pressure. I waited a moment and took another breath, each one easier than the one before it until my breaths were steady and the walls that had been closing in on my lungs fizzled away. Only, with the pressure relieved, the clear image of Reese was fading away, too. Sadness replaced my panic. To see Reese, I had to be in distress. What was fair about that?

When Reese was only a silhouette faintly glowing in the darkness, I gave up and opened my eyes. Dad was still rubbing my back. "Ruby," his voice faded but the deep creases on his brow spoke volumes of the concern he had for what he just witnessed. I straightened my shoulders and stood tall on my feet.

"Sorry, Dad. I'm fine, it won't happen again." I wasn't completely positive that I could keep that promise. We stood in silence, my eyes ridden with guilt and desperation while his dimmed with concern. In that moment I truly understood the love my father had for me. I was his flesh and blood, created out of the love he and Mom shared. His life had been no different than mine was up until now; born in The Complex, told by government and Doctrine how to live, but the whole time I thought he was satisfied with being a nameless drone to The Complex, he was fighting for something more. His eyes told me that he was in this fight for *me.* He wanted to know the truth because he wanted my life to have meaning and freedom in ways his own never did.

I knew he truly loved Mom, which was lucky because neither of them were given a choice in their marriage but there was no conceivable way that every mated couple truly loved each other. I always suspected love was something that could not be forced upon the heart but until I had to face the reality of Connor and therefor was unable to deny to myself that I was in love with Reese, I never understood just how intricate and delicate our hearts truly were.

Dad's big arms wrapped around my smaller frame and he drew me to his chest in a protective and loving hug. His own slow and steady breathing caused my head to move up and down as his chest expanded and shrank with the flow of air to his lungs. All my life I had daydreamed and wished for a life different than the limited predictability of The Complex, but now that I had no idea what was going to happen from one moment to the next, I was afraid. I was afraid for my family, especially my delicate mother who knew nothing of the dangers yet. If things got very bad for Dad and I very fast, what would happen to her? I was afraid for Reese. What did the Order mean when they told my dad that Reese was in danger? What kind of danger? How much danger? Dad made me promise last night to never see Reese again but how could I keep a promise like that now? Reese may need me. I would give up my life for his in a heartbeat.

*Take **me**. Put **me** to sleep but don't hurt Reese. Please.*

Dad's arms loosened and I let myself fall out of the hug. He let go of me completely and rested his hands on my shoulders in a quiet but reassuring manner. There was love in his eyes in a way that I had never seen before. I understood why. Up until last night I never really knew my father. He had never let me in on his secret world for my own protection, but now we knew we shared the same secrets, the same suspicions and the same beliefs. We now knew each other in a way that was discouraged and even forbidden by Doctrine and that strengthened our bond and family devotion tenfold. Suddenly, a memory that seemed insignificant at the time crept up from the recesses of my mind and surfaced with a new meaning. I was nine years old and I was playing cards in the living room with Dad and Grandpa Logan. I was, as I often did, asking Grandpa questions about the surface and what it was like. I couldn't recall how the conversation had transitioned but I remembered Dad saying, "Every parent hopes that their children's lives are fuller and better than their own." I continued to pester Grandpa Logan and Dad grew quiet, just watching me as Grandpa's stories caused me to feel more and more enthralled.

Dad was in the Order for *me*.

Dad turned away from me and picked up the folder once more from the bed. He opened it, shuffled through the pages and pulled out the last one. He set it down. I walked to his side and leaned over as he set his finger on the paper.

Confirm shipment for 0900 hours. R-0832 scheduled to conduct the shipment.

I blinked and glanced at Dad warily. I was supposed to understand something again. I focused my attention back on the paper and re-read it. Wait, was there really a shipment? I supposed there had to be, I didn't get the impression that the Order would leave a paper trail for a false shipment and risk arousing suspicion. Dad tapped his finger on the ID number, R-0832. I re-read that again and it took a moment to remember whose ID it was. *Willow's mother!* Did that mean she was involved in the Order, too? When would the shocking secrets end? Did Willow know anything about the Order? I turned my confused and concerned eyes toward my father again, but he softly shook his head as if he knew what I was wondering. *No.* I supposed that made sense. After all, I knew nothing about any of this myself until just yesterday.

Dad stuffed the last paper back into the folder and set it neatly in the drawer of his night-table. "Maybe when confinement is over, you'll want to consider shadowing me at the job for a day, just to make sure you're truly interested in the career." Was Dad inviting me into the Order? I eagerly nodded. *Yes.* My hunger for knowledge was like a ravenous beast right now but the beast served something far more important than my dreams or my curiosity. All I cared about right now was finding my way to Reese again so I could help keep him safe.

"I have one important question about the job, before I commit to a shadow." Dad folded his arms under his chest and regarded me with patience. I was grateful.

"What is it?"

"Are you close with your co-workers? Do you all look out for each other and keep each other safe, **no matter what**?" I put special emphasis on those last three words. My eyes narrowed with intensity and I rested them on my fathers face, praying he would understand what I was asking. A soft sigh streamed out of his mouth and nose.

"Yes, Ruby. We look after each other. We work together and consider ourselves personally responsible for everyone's safety." I did not overlook the fact that he said *everyone*, not just his co-workers. That meant that he was accepting responsibility for Reese too, right?

Reese was not in the Order but he was in danger because of something the Order started. It was their responsibility to save him.

"Ruby, come help me set the table?" I shifted my eyes away from Dad. I hated being this helpless and I envied Mom right now. She was oblivious to the realities that we knew were crumbling down around us. She thought she was happy because she had me and Dad and she never allowed herself to desire anything more in life. Suddenly, lyrics from a very old song that existed B-I that Grandpa used to sing started interrupting my thoughts and taking over my mind.

"You can't always get what you want..but if you try sometimes, you might find you get what you need."

I had always wanted more. More choices, more knowledge, more freedom. When you're a kid and you dream of experiencing the scent of fresh air or the feeling of loose dirt against the soles of your feet, you don't think about all of the horrors it would take to achieve those dreams. I was in love with Reese. I could admit that to myself now and I knew it was true. It had been true long before I dared to face it. Now he was in some kind of trouble and I didn't even know how much, or if he was still alive or if I could save him. I made a promise to my dad last night that I now knew I couldn't keep. He knew it too, or he wouldn't have invited me into the Order, *if* that's what he actually did. I couldn't think of another explanation. I supposed he finally realized that at this point, the best way to protect me was to let me in. What about Mom, though? The best way to protect her was to keep her in the dark and away from her fears. Real love was about sacrifice. I understood that by the way my dad behaved. For me, he was sacrificing feeling secure about my safety because he loved me, and he knew that whether or not either one of us wanted this to be true, I was in love with Reese. For Mom, he was sacrificing an honest relationship with her because he knew she wouldn't be able to handle the fears that knowing about the Order would push upon her.

I would sacrifice for Reese. I walked into the kitchen and opened the cupboard. I reached for three plates. I helped Mom set the table and then I helped her finish preparing our dinner. We lived in these same barracks all of our lives and every evening when we all sat down to dinner, I knew without a doubt that until I was forcibly married, I would eat dinner with both of my parents at this same table night after night after night. Tonight I no longer had that assurance. I took special note of my mom's soft voice and loving smiles. I took a moment to notice and appreciate the way Dad would put a loving hand on the small of Mom's back or on her knee. Even the smallest of touches communicated his love and devotion for her strongly and purely. If he had to give up his life to improve or save hers I understood now that he would do it without question.

I made a silent promise to myself right here at our dinner table that I would do anything – *anything* – to save Reese. I would sacrifice everything I ever knew so that he could experience the freedom I have dreamed of my whole life, even if that meant I couldn't experience it with him. From now on every choice I made would be for him.

Chapter 6

The Complex had limited resources. As a result, items that were not necessities were kept to a minimum. Grandpa Logan used to tell stories about how, B-I, places called *stores* sold endless toys, people had closets the size of our barracks with clothes made from all sorts of different materials, and sometimes, people hoarded so many useless possessions that their homes were literally filled up to the brim with boxes, leaving them no space to actually live in. Apparently that last one wasn't normal though and people who had that many possessions were often on *reality tee-vee*. The concept of fictional broadcasting in general fascinated me. Broadcasting existed in The Complex of course, such as Commander SueLee's message on the train, but it seemed outlandishly frivolous to me that people used to utilize such an energy-sucking resource for nothing but pure entertainment. **Being an** *actor* sounded like such a fun job, though. Too bad fictional "storytelling" no longer existed as broadcasts.

The possessions I had were mostly things I made, or things made for me. Once a year we were allowed to take a photo of our choosing using "antiques" called Polaroid cameras. We were supposed to treasure those photos because sooner rather than later any and all Polaroid film would be used up and newer generations would not have the privilege. The government didn't bother to use its resources to create more Polaroid film for the same reason they did not bother to produce fictional broadcasting; it was simply not necessary for our continued survival.

Last year, rather than pose with my parents, I

chose to take a photo that consisted of myself and my two best friends, Willow and Reese. We posed outside of a classroom and another friend of ours, Sahara, snapped the photo for us. The image was proudly displayed on the wall above my bed. I had taped it next to the photo from the previous year which was taped next the picture from the year before that, and so-on.

Burdened with the frustration of claustrophobia, I stared longingly at my most recent photo and for the first time since it was taken I realized it was a lie. My best friends and I appeared as equals, threaded arm in arm with warm, inviting smiles plastered across our faces. I still recalled that day quite clearly and although I was smiling from cheek to cheek, it was not a warm, inviting happy grin but one of nervousness and impatience. I had wanted to stand next to Reese, but Willow had jumped into the middle of the photo and Reese and I were on either side of her. I felt helpless because I knew that if I asked her to switch places with me she would want to know why, and what was I supposed to say? The photo was taken months ago and I had not been ready to admit to myself, much less to Willow, that I wanted more from Reese than just his friendship. I was not happy in that moment, although I know I appeared otherwise. That caused me to stare at the photo-capture of my two friends and I with a new pair of eyes. What were both of them secretly thinking in that moment? Part of me wondered if Willow knew that I had feelings for Reese perhaps even before I realized it myself. As I let my memories roll backwards in time, countless instances suddenly surfaced where Willow inserted herself between the two of us or drew my attention away from Reese. It could all be coincidence, or she could have been subtly trying to discourage me. Or, just to throw a third possibility into the boiling pot, she could have simply been feeling jealous or left out by the unintentional extra attention I had been giving Reese and she was trying to stay as relevant and important to my life as Reese seemed to be. Mom once warned me that sometimes having two best friends could get dramatic during our teenage years.

But the boy is in danger.

Was Reese even alive? He *had* to be. I knew how ridiculous this sounded but I was certain I would know if he were gone. I would feel it. A treasured and important part of me would suddenly cease to exist.

I scrutinized the photo with even more intensity. Willow's almond shaped, doe-brown eyes were looking directly into the camera lens, *hamming it up*, as my mom would say, whatever that meant. Willow tended to get excited whenever her picture was taken and I didn't blame her; she was flawlessly beautiful. Personally, I was far too self-conscious and awkward to fully enjoy getting my photo taken. I was staring into the camera lens as well but my gaze lacked Willow's confidence. It appeared as though I was looking *through* the lens, staring at something else entirely or perhaps just lost in my own imagination, wallowing in disappointment that I was not standing next to Reese.

I hadn't noticed before that Reese had not been looking into the lens at all. His eyes were glancing just the tiniest bit to his right, perhaps caught in mid-shift as he was glancing over at Willow – or maybe over at *me.* His smile was a bit tighter than his usual grin and the tiny lines that stretched across the corners of his lips proved it. It wasn't his real smile which meant his thoughts had probably been elsewhere, too! What if he had been thinking the same thing I was in that very same moment? What if he was wishing that I was the one standing next to him instead of Willow?

I reached up and gently peeled the picture off of the wall. My throat tightened. My thumb caressed the glossy texture over Reese's cheek. Tunnel vision eliminated myself and Willow from the photo and my eyes remained on his face only.

I have to save you.

How could I save Reese when I couldn't even leave my barracks? While Reese was in danger, maybe hurt, maybe put to death, maybe hunted, I was sitting in my safe, cozy chambers with only a photo of him that would eventually fade, wishing I was by his side.

I tossed the picture across the room. The corner of the Polaroid hit the wall with a faint thwack and then fell to the floor. The picture was a lie. Our expressions were forced and our thoughts had been anything but genuine in the moment. Staring at a momentary capture of Reese's face was not going to save him. It was not *proactive*. Throughout the last two days I had made more than one promise to more than one person. I couldn't keep them all.

Sorry, Dad. I can't stay away from Reese. I love him. You wouldn't just leave Mom in danger. You would risk your life for her, so I have to do the same.

How was I supposed to save Reese, or even find him? A flatfoot was stationed in the hallway basically holding us prisoner. No, not basically, *literally*. Mom was content to convince herself it was for our own good as well as for the good of others so that we wouldn't spread the virus. Dad was the patriarch, the grown-up, the man with a secret he had to protect by acting as normal as possible when eyes were turned his way. His outer appearance of compliance truly was for the good of his

124

family and for others in The Complex. I understood why he was sitting tight, why he wasn't fighting tooth and nail to find out what kind of danger Reese was in and to save him. To risk saving Reese would be to risk the lives of the whole Order. I had no idea how many were in the Order. Was it just a select group of people that worked with Dad in the artificial gardens or was it all of the gardeners? Were there people in the Order from other occupations? How long had the Order existed? Did it reach outside of Rhode Island? Was the shipping invoice code something potential members in other divisions would be able to understand, too? That possibility actually gave me hope. If the Order was truly that large, maybe Reese had a chance. Maybe others were already working to save him. Only... the code hadn't said that. It had only communicated that he was in danger.

That was the last straw. One way or another I had to find my way out of these barracks and I had to find Reese.

I knew this was a foolish idea. I was putting Dad and perhaps the whole Order in danger but I knew that if Reese were killed and I had done nothing but sit in my bedroom staring at his picture and pining for him, I would hate myself too much to ever look in the mirror again.

The intensity of my resolve was unsettling. I felt as if a heavy blanket had draped itself over my body and plunged me into darkness, and then something heavy was pushing me down toward the ground. I closed my eyes and bent my body forward. I pressed my hands to my knees. Here it was again, the third time in less than two days that my lungs seemed to be caving in on themselves.

Reese.

Reese, I need you. No – **you** *need* **me.**
We need each other.

Reese's face came out of the darkness, again. I could make out the shadow of his jawline, the flow of his swept-back, thick hair and the way his cheekbones moved just slightly when his lips shifted from a smile to a frown. I reached for him but his hand was just a few inches too far away. I could see shapes – his fingers – wiggling, trying to stretch, trying to reach for my own. I did not care if it hurt, or if I fell because somehow I knew he would catch me. I leaned forward as far as I could on the balls of my feet, and then, I let myself go.

My fingers slid through his. I could feel them, solid flesh, warm to the touch and *real*. But how, when even despite this willful vision I knew it existed only in my imagination?

The compression across my lungs loosened. I could breathe again but in that same moment the comfort of Reese's hand in mine dissolved.

No! Come back!

I rocked forward on my feet again but this time gravity was stronger than my vision. I flailed my arms and almost fell flat on my face, in fact I would have if my palm hadn't slammed against the wall by pure chance.

I let the wall support me and I took a deep breath in, then slowly let carbon dioxide back out into the limited, artificial atmosphere. Another breath in. Another exhale. Once again, Reese got me through another panic attack. Once again, Reese saved me. Now it was my turn to save him. No more of this forgetting how to breathe nonsense. No more subconsciously almost shutting down my body because my mind did not know how to deal with the shocking reality behind the veil of lies.

I was in love. Painfully, irrevocably in love. But I was also still **me**. I was still the girl who was not content with the idea of being a wife and a mother while locked in The Complex with no other purpose than to breed so that humanity still existed on the day when we found a new home on a new planet.

Come on. Like that's ever going to happen.

And why should it, when it seemed that life was still sustainable on the surface? I wish I knew if the government realized we could live up there or not. If they did, why were they really keeping us down here?

NO. STOP IT.

These were all valid questions but they were for a later time. The only chance I had of getting myself through figuring out how to save Reese was going to be to take one step at a time, focus on one thing at a time. So...where was I supposed to start?

I would have to start with my parents. I knew Dad would never allow me to try and leave the barracks while under confinement. I was his daughter and it was his instinct to protect me. I couldn't ask for his help. He couldn't know my plan until it would be too late for him to stop me. But, how could I escape without putting my parents in danger? Even if I could somehow get past the flatfoot guarding our barracks, my parents would be under suspicion of aiding in my escape and the whole Order would be in danger which meant that if Reese was still alive – and he **had** to be – he would be put in even *more* danger. For a moment I considered that maybe the best thing I could do for Reese was to do nothing and let my dad and the Order *handle things*. I knew that's what Dad would tell me if he felt it was safe to speak freely. It wasn't that I didn't believe in or trust my father. I did trust him, even though I had just found out that he had all kinds of secrets and in a way, was a completely different man than I thought he was. I still knew he was a good man, and I knew he was my father. I still believed in him. But Reese was not his child. As far as I knew, unless one or both of his parents were in the Order too, no one had any reason to risk their lives to save his. No one except me because I loved him. Reese had no one to put him first but me.

There were very few perks of growing up in The Complex and (until last night's trip to Connecticut to meet Connor) being confined to only one small division throughout my whole life. I knew Rhode Island very well. I knew my way to each and every room and area and I knew the basics of how things worked. I knew we had large generators in each division that played the replacement role that trees and plants used to play on the surface; somehow maintaining our atmosphere by turning carbon dioxide into oxygen for us to breathe. I had no idea how they did this but I knew they existed and I knew where they were. I knew that ventilation was filtered into each and every barrack and the screen to ours was in our bathroom. I wondered, was the ventilation system as connected as our own hallways? It seemed ludicrous to assume that the generators had separate, non-connected passageways that not only brought air circulation to each and every barrack, but all of the community rooms and artificial gardens as well. They had to be interconnected, and if so, I could find my way around by climbing through them! Assuming I could fit through them. Truthfully I had no idea, at all, how wide they were because despite having spent my whole life in this barrack it never occurred to me to remove the screen and look. I knew Dad removed the screen and cleaned it every few months but it had never been of any interest to me. Maybe my idea was impossible but at least it was a place to start.

Assuming I could fit through the passageway, where would I go? All I had to go on was that one single coded message.

But the boy is in danger.

That... and my heart. Where would Reese go if he were in trouble? This wasn't the kind of thing we had ever discussed because up until less than two days ago there had never been a need to.

Reese had shared his secret with me when he sent that note with Willow. I now understood that had been was his way of letting me in, of asking for my help, of trusting that I could handle the truth, whatever that turned out to be. He had asked me to meet him at a place that meant something to the both of us, the place where he had found the butterfly. Suddenly I was sure that unless he was being held captive, that's where he would be. I couldn't explain it, even to myself, but I knew that if he was in trouble, and the Order made that pretty clear, he would be waiting on me to find him. In this broken, limited world where we seemed to believe that the more we love someone the more secrets we have to keep from them like Dad did with Mom, Reese and I were doing the opposite. We were counting on each other and letting each other in. I *knew* things without understanding how I knew them. I suddenly felt so sure that I was right despite having no rational explanation as to why. Love was my best guess. Maybe love wasn't just for fairy tales after all. Maybe it wasn't just a feeling either, but a connection that went beyond language or body movements. Love was not like the world we lived in. Love did not know deception, confusion or lies. Love was not complicated and it told our hearts only one basic message; *this person is the other half of my soul.* Maybe love, not just the love I had for Reese but love in general was the true key to unravelling the mysteries around us. Maybe trusting in each other is what would turn the darkness around us into light. Love was gifting me with a sense of strength and resolve that I never would have guessed I was capable of.

In "fairy tale" stories Grandpa Logan used to tell me, a damsel in distress always patiently, but sadly waited for her Prince to rescue her from a tower, a dungeon or a cottage embedded deep in a treacherous forest. The prince would battle her captors, take her hand and run off with her to the castle he ruled. She would become his princess and they would live happily ever after. Mom never approved when Grandpa Logan would tell me stories like that. I would watch the corners of her lips tug her mouth downward into a worried frown and as she tucked me into bed she would tell me that real love was far less flighty. She told me that I did not have to worry about finding love because the government would find it for me, like it had with her and Dad and I would never be in peril because our lives were safe and calm and always would be. Now, I understood that to Mom, fairy tales were probably scary because they made us daydream about adventure. She wanted to raise me to simply be content with the world around me because she knew that would keep me safe.

Sorry Mom, but I can't stay in a bubble and watch my prince fade away.

I was not going to let myself be a damsel in distress. Yesterday, Reese had shown me his secret and I had reacted badly. I had a panic attack and he had to save me by kissing me – *okay, fine,* so I was a cliché fairy tale damsel in distress in that moment and he was my prince in every sense of the word. But that was then and this was now. Now, Reese was the one in trouble and he needed *me* to save *him*. I would have to suck it up, accept all the chaos that was behind the thick layers of whitewashed Doctrine and dig deep within myself to find the strength and courage needed to do what had to be done.

I quietly slinked into the bathroom and softly closed the door. I would drive myself crazy for the rest of the evening wondering if the ventilation system was even a possibility if I didn't find out now. I crouched down on my knees behind the lav. The screen appeared simple enough to dislodge. I fiddled with the tiny slots until I heard something click. I pulled and off it came. The opening seemed small. My teeth sunk into my lower lip with worry. I subconsciously held my breath as I carefully stuck my head inside. The air vent was pitch black. I knew my way around my division quite easily but how was I supposed to navigate without sight? That wouldn't even matter though if it turned out that I couldn't fit my body through the vent in the first place. I tried not to allow my mind to go on a tangent while running through all of the worst-case scenarios. I could get lost. I could get stuck. I could DIE from either one of those possibilities.

NO. STOP. I MAY NOT EVEN FIT IN THE FIRST PLACE.

I eased myself further inside of the vent. I shivered at the slight sensation of the surrounding walls brushing against my shoulders, but I was in! That meant I could fit! But could I move? I stretched an arm in front of myself cautiously and then curled it backward. The sides of the vent ran across my arms but did not restrict them. It would be an extremely tight, horrifyingly claustrophobic fit, but it was feasible. I did not even want to consider doing this for so many reasons. Fear of getting stuck and of being in such a tiny enclosed space was only the beginning. Once I was in, I wasn't sure if I could ever go back. How long would it take my parents to realize I was gone (probably not until morning if I said goodnight first) and how long would it take the flatfoots to discover my absence? Would they hurt my parents? Would they torture them to try and get them to confess my whereabouts and my plan because they might assume my parents were in on it?

I had to stop this. I was psyching myself out and getting too far ahead of myself. I tried to focus on the best possible outcome instead of imagining the multitude of ways this plan could go wrong. The best possible result would be that I crawled to the place where Reese and I found the butterfly and he was there waiting for me. Maybe his danger wasn't immediate, maybe the Order was just worried that the flatfoots might find clues about the little girl that would lead back to Reese. Why hadn't they been more detailed in the message they sent to my father? Anyway, if Reese was waiting for me, then what? Now was the time to start considering the next step. Hopefully Reese would realize the level of danger he was in. Did he even know he was in danger? If he didn't, there was no way he would be waiting for me at 'our spot.' But then he would most likely just be in his barracks, so I could find him that way and warn him. I couldn't possibly plan any further than that because I simply didn't have enough information. I commanded my brain to stop looking ahead. I closed my eyes and focused on one thought only –

Find Reese and get him to safety.
I pushed my palms against the bottom of the air

vent and crawled back out. I carefully replaced the screen. I would leave tonight. No more doubting, no more fears.

I stood up and brushed off some dust that was clinging to my pants. I quietly walked into the living room. Mom was sitting on our couch paging through the weekly paper our division put out. It never actually said anything interesting. Without a word, I curled up next to her side, slid an arm through hers and rested my head on her shoulder. I didn't know if I would ever see her again. I didn't want to think in such dramatic terms but I had never faced uncertainty like this before and I didn't know how to process it very well. Just in case, I wanted the last bit of comfort I could get from my mom and I wanted her to feel my comfort as well.

Mom set the paper down and turned her head toward me with slightly raised brows. She lifted a hand and very gently ran her fingers through my fiery hair the way she used to when I was a child. "Ruby, are you all right?" she asked softly with concern. I briefly closed my eyes. I loved Reese and I knew I had to go through with my plan to save him. Only moments earlier I made myself a promise not to question my decision. It was hard not to because I loved my mother too and I didn't want to hurt her or put her in danger. Why was there no 'good' choice in all of this? Why was there no possible decision that would ensure the safety of everyone I loved? "Ruby?" I blinked and looked up at her with a badly performed smile.

"I'm okay. I just miss this. I miss being little." Mom kissed the top of my head.

"I miss you being little, too. You were such a precious little girl who is growing up to be a beautiful, intelligent woman. Connor is a lucky man." I paused.

133

Connor. I had barely even thought of him after leaving our mandatory 'date.' Should I be thinking about him? I knew I did not, and probably would not ever love him but with my future and even my life at risk because of what I was about to do, what would happen to him? I sighed softly. Strangely, it was Grandpa Logan's voice I heard in my head in the next moments.

Do what your heart tells you to do, Ruby. It's the only truth behind all of the lies and it's the only way to make things right.

My grandfather had been gone for six long years but his encouragement in my dreams and all the ways in which he believed in me still echoed in my mind and heart. His influence was still helping to shape the person I was growing up to be. I was lucky to have known him.

"I wish I didn't have to grow up," I said quietly, longingly. My mom's body was warm and comforting. I was tempted to forget about my mission and pretend like the world I knew was not crumbling down around me. But *it was*. I slowly sat up and shifted my eyes.

"We all grow up sweetie, but you're not being taken away from me just yet. We still have two more years together." It was both saddening and comforting to know that my mom actually viewed the parts of Doctrine that dictated the mating rules as negative. It meant she was not in complete denial. It meant that maybe there was some part of her that could someday understand why I had to do what I was about to do. I leaned against her side again and curled my arms around her waist to give her a hug. She returned the hug fiercely, as if this were the last time she would ever hug me. I knew she didn't realize just how accurate that could possibly be. I made a special point to treasure this memory in as much detail as I could take in because, just in case, I wanted to remember my mom exactly this way. I wanted to remember her soft-spoken voice, her love for me, and her albeit unintentional admittance that things weren't as comforting as they seemed here in The Complex even if she hid that knowledge behind a concrete wall of fear. If any of the worst-case scenarios happened for me, I wanted my loss to give her the strength she needed to defeat her fear. If something happened to me I wanted Dad to be able to tell her the truth so she could become his ally, join the Order and discover all the things that are hidden from us.

"I know." I replied with emptiness. I allowed myself another few moments with my mother. I shut out the world and I was grateful for her unconditional love. Then I raised my head, slid quietly away from her and forced my brain back into the adult role it had no choice but to take on.

I was distant with my parents for the rest of the evening. I wasn't trying to purposely avoid them but I had a hard time looking at them knowing that whatever way this played out, our lives were about to change. I took out a piece of paper and scribbled in the smallest, but clearest writing I could manage, *'Take care of Mom.'*

Mom retreated to her chambers and Dad was still couch-bound even though his sneezing and stuffed nose had receded. I tried to act as casually as I could as I entered the kitchen and filled my water bottle. I opened our refrigerator and took out a banana, and then grabbed a cookie from the cupboard. I turned to Dad, gave him a goodnight hug and retreated to my own chambers. I closed the door softly behind me. I wasn't hungry but I ate the cookie and the banana anyway just to fill my stomach because if this mission went badly and I wasn't able to return here, who knew when my next meal would be? Of course, if I got caught and put to sleep that wouldn't matter, but...

You can't think like that.

I pressed my lips together and waited. I concentrated on trying to shut my brain down which seemed like a nearly impossible task.

Get to Reese. Protect him. Make sure he's safe.

I couldn't let myself think past that. I couldn't start considering all of the possibilities or consequences or I would lose my nerve. It was getting late. Mom should be asleep by now. I wasn't sure about Dad. It was almost time. It was now or never. My heartbeat quickened. I tucked the note into my bra, grabbed my water bottle and very carefully tiptoed into the hall. I held my breath as I peeked my head around the corner into the living room. It was quite dark but I could make out my fathers silhouette. I could hear his breath, slow and steady with the tiniest hint of a snore. He was asleep.

It was TIME.

My heartbeat quickened even more. I bit my lower lip and curled my fingernails into my palms. I had to stay calm. No more of this panic attack crap. Frankly, I didn't have time for it. I had to face all of these fears and unknowns and I had to face them now. I drew my shoulders back. I took a deep breath in and then slowly let it out through my nose. That seemed to help. I was still nearly shaking with nerves, but I was handling it. I took another slow breath in, and another until I felt more confident. I turned and tiptoed to the bathroom. I slipped inside and closed the door as quietly as I could. I stood as still as a statue but I didn't hear anyone stirring. I opened the vanity mirror and pulled out a hair binder. My fingers smoothed over my thick red strands and pulled them backwards before wrapping the binder around them. I twisted the binder and pulled my hair through it again before pushing the binder against my scalp so my ponytail would remain tight and keep my hair out of my face. Then, I bent down behind the lav and felt the wall until my fingers grazed across the screen. I found the clasps and pulled on them until the screen popped off. Where could I put this so my parents might not notice if they were half awake and needed to come in here? I wanted to prolong them finding out I had gone for as long as possible. I slipped it behind the lav and prayed they wouldn't be observant until ... unless ... they had to be. I got down on my knees. My whole body shook and I had to take another few deep, calming breaths just to steady myself. I knew my way around. If the vents mirrored the hallways, I could do this. I picked up my small water bottle and tucked it between my breasts before pulling out the small piece of paper.

It's up to you, Dad.

I folded it up and placed it in the corner of the vent.

Goodbye, barracks.

I couldn't decide if it was better to hope that I would see these barracks again or if the best outcome would be if I never had to return, so I tried to shut down that part of my brain that wanted to turn confusion into fear. I scooted my arms forward, ducked my head and climbed into the vent. The impression of my knees against the – metal? Aluminum? I wasn't even sure what they were made out of - felt almost squishy. I paused. What if the vent couldn't hold my weight?

Slow down, don't get all panicky.

I had never seen the vents just freely, they were

obviously adjacent to the walls. I shook that thought away and very slowly began to move forward. The view in front of me was literally pitch black. I had no sight whatsoever so I would have to rely on touch and memory alone.

Reese. Just hold on, wherever you are. I'm coming.

My barracks were at the end of our particular residential hallway. There were nine more barracks on our right before the hallway split. I could only pray that the vent openings veering off toward each barrack were synonymous with the number of barracks, it was the only chance I had to navigate correctly. Moving was slower than I had anticipated. There wasn't enough room for me to be upright on my hands and knees so I had to bend and scoot at an awkward angle. After a few minutes, I had only passed two doors and the fear of being in such an enclosed, constricted space was trying its best to force me into panic-mode.

NO!

Panicking was not going to get me out of this space. Thrashing would not magically break down its walls and set me free. If I allowed a panic attack to take me over in here, I could die. That thought did not help in keeping me calm. I scooted my fingers forward along the right side of the vent and then I felt it; another passage. *Three doors.* The going was slow, but steady. I was fairly positive I knew exactly what was beside me. I closed my eyes and although the darkness was the same either way, with my eyelids lowered I could make out the faint image of Reese's silhouette. I focused on the way his well-defined jaw tightened when he was determined and the way his cheek bones twitched when he was antsy. I would see him again for real, and soon. That's why I was

138

risking my life. All of this was for him.

I opened my eyes and continued forward slowly in the confined darkness. *Four doors. Five doors. Six doors.* How long had I been crawling? It was probably only a few minutes but it felt like an eternity. Was it getting warmer? Was the air getting thinner? No, that was just fear trying to lie to me again. I kept going. *Seven. Eight.* I was almost to the end of the hallway! The flatfoot was somewhere near me, I was sure of it. Would he hear me crawling? I was being quiet. Once I felt the ninth door, I paused. I would have to take the following left, but would the vent stop in front of me and tee off like the actual hallway did? If not, how would I be positive I was making the correct turn? I would just have to trust my instincts. I winced as my knees started to ache a bit. I wanted to stretch out my body so I could limber up my muscles but the knowledge that I was in such a small space that I couldn't was trying again to escalate my fear into panic. I paused again, closed my eyes and allowed Reese to appear in front of me. The shape of his face gave me comfort. I continued. I dragged my fingertips along the left side of the wall this time until I felt a new opening. I bit my lower lip and very tentatively reached in front of me. It still seemed like the vent went forward.

Crap.

How was I supposed to know if this was the right opening? I pressed my knee against the bottom of the vent and crept forward just a bit more, reaching, and then I felt it! An aluminum wall! YES! Yes yes *YES*! I knew where I was! I carefully pushed myself backwards and felt around the opening again. It was one thing to crawl backwards and forwards in such a small space, but how was I supposed to make a 90 degree turn without basically contorting my body? This was not going to be easy. I briefly considered rolling over onto my side and or even onto my back and wiggling myself in but the fear of getting turtled – being on my back and potentially not having enough space to flip myself over to my hands and knees - was way too horrifying. I rotated my shoulders and started to bend forward. I pushed my knees down against the bottom of the vent and crawled forward some more, but my knee hit the side. I crawled forward again and angled my ribcage. This was NOT comfortable but it seemed like it was going to work. I scooted forward again and felt my knee scraping against the wall. So what? I pushed down on it harder until out of seemingly nowhere, something sharp jabbed right into my calf! My whole body jerked in response and my arms flailed, banging against the walls with a helpless echo. I bit down hard on my lower lip to keep from yelping. My instinct was to curl my leg upward and feel my calf to see what hurt me and how bad it was but when I tried, the walls were too narrow. My body started to tremble. I bit down harder on my lower lip. I could feel my eyes moistening with tears. Not being able to see what just ripped through my flesh was terrifying. Not being able to freely move my body was even worse. I was trying so hard to do this but it was starting to overwhelm me and I didn't know how much longer I could keep myself together, or what would happen to me when I no longer could.

Go back! Go back!

I hated my inner-voice in this moment. It was a coward. Besides, there was no way I would be able to turn around in this vent. I would have to crawl backwards the whole way. I *had* to keep going. I *had* to get out of here. I had to do both of these things now, and fast. I pushed down hard on my knee despite the fact that I could feel a trail of blood trickling from my punctured skin onto the floor of the vent. I tensed my muscles and forced my hips to squirm around the sharp angle until my whole body made the turn. YES! I wanted to crawl as fast as I could but I forced myself to pause and take a deep breath. I could do this. For Reese. I knew that nothing else on this planet, or any other, could get me through this but him.

There were no breakaway vents on this route, this was a hall that lead away from individual barracks and toward the common areas of Rhode Island. It was longer than the barracks hallway. It irrationally made me feel less sure of where I was. I continued to crawl forward until I was sure I had gone farther down this hallway than the barracks hallway. What room was first? No wait, this veered off and classrooms were on the right and labs were on the left. Finally, I felt the opening of a veered vent on the right. It might possibly lead toward classrooms, which would mean I wasn't far from the corner that Reese found the butterfly and the doorway that he had been sneaking through. Or – did the vents also line those forbidden passageways? They must, because they were at one time being put to use. So, was this vent adjacent to a veered off passageway or to the hallway?

I don't know! I don't know I don't know I don't know!

Tears started running down my cheeks and falling one by one onto the thin bottom of the vent. I sniffled and kept crawling. I needed **out**. The claustrophobia was starting to catch up with my determination to be discreet and to find Reese. I couldn't ignore it or cope with it much longer before it completely overwhelmed me.

I started curling and maneuvering my body

around the turn. I would have to risk it, wherever it lead, because either way it lead **out**. My ribs hurt as I jerked my body and rotated my hips but I ignored the dull pain. I pushed my elbows down and dragged my lower half into the turn and then immediately started moving forward again. My mind was starting to race. I tried to slow it down, I tried to take more deep breaths and get a rational idea in my mind of where I was and how long it should take me to find an exit but my thoughts were quickly becoming feral and refusing to let reason and rationality calm them. Tears were pouring out of my eyes faster and thicker. My fingers desperately groped the air in front of me, the walls on either side of me, and my leg, now dully throbbing, was being scraped against the wall with its open puncture.

Out. Out. PLEASE I need Out. Oh God, I'm gonna die in here.

I couldn't hold back anymore. I was panicking. I began to scurry. My arms and legs banged against the walls of the vent and although it was my intention to move faster I was probably moving slower. I started to sob and although I could hear my voice echoing, I was sure the sound would not fall on anyones ears. I scraped and scratched my fingers along the walls and just when I was about to give up, let my body slump, close my eyes and silently beg death to take me, I felt it; A SCREEN!

I didn't know where the screen was going to release me. At this point, I didn't care. I eagerly pushed on it and then suddenly I remembered something very important; the clasps to release it were on the outside!

oh god oh god I'M GONNA DIE oh god

I continued to sob and I gave in to my panic completely. My hands started pushing, then smacking, against the screen in helpless desperation. My digits

142

clawed at it, so deeply that I could feel the screen cutting into my fingertips but I didn't care, I couldn't stop myself if I tried. I clawed and clawed until I could feel a fingertip poking through. That only made my feverish desperation grow. I slid the first section of my finger through and then yanked it back. The tiny tear in the screen scraped against my skin. I did it again, and again until I could curl my finger all the way through the screen and pull. I pulled with all of my might and the screen tore just a tiny bit more. I slipped another finger in and pulled again. More tearing. Another. Even more tearing. Finally I forced my hand through it and then I moved forward so I could curl my whole upper arm through. My fingers were still grasping in desperation but I tried to direct them toward the clasps. Once I felt them, I was still panicking too much to rationally communicate to my fingers *how* to maneuver the clasps so I just grasped and tugged, hoping and begging for that familiar 'click' that would signify a release. Finally I somehow pulled it at the correct angle. I yanked my arm back inside and pushed on the screen. It flew off with minimal resistance and hit the ground below. I grasped the edges of the opening with my hands, yanked my body forward and literally propelled myself out of the opening.

I squirmed to the ground and immediately scurried away from the opening as if it were on fire. I tried to quiet my sobs but they were still shaking throughout my body and although part of my mind wanted nothing more than to flail my appendages any way they could go, just because I finally could again, instinct caused me to curl my knees to my chest and press my back against the corner of the hallway. I closed my eyes. I inhaled, and it was a difficult task. It was as if my body was shuddering so much that there was too much turbulence inside of me for my lungs to inflate properly. I squeezed my arms tighter around my knees and inhaled again. I concentrated on Reese once more, trying to forget about my claustrophobic ordeal and my extremely hasty exit that could have potentially blown my entire mission.

For a few minutes, two or maybe ten, I simply refused to accept my surroundings or my predicament. Nothing mattered – not Doctrine, not myself, not the mystery nor the danger around me. In my mind I was free. I was with Reese. My fingers threaded reassuringly through his as we stood barefoot on a beach near the ocean with the waves rushing over the tops of our feet. The wind caused my hair to flow backwards because it overpowered gravity and the sun shined down on my face like a gentle heater. What I wouldn't give just to have experienced the simplest things Earth had to offer before it was destroyed. What I wouldn't do to sit down in a field of grass and run my fingers through the blades. What did they feel like? Were they soft, or coarse? What about the soil that the grass grew out of? Could someone stick their hand into the loose dirt and roll their fingers through the tiny rocks or was the ground hard, the dirt clumped together? These burning curiosities brought sadness to me, but they also brought inner-calm back to my mind and slowly I managed to breathe easier.

When I felt ready I prepared myself to face my current predicament and I opened my eyes. No matter where I was, it had to be better than being stuck in those vents. I could only hope that I never, ever, had to do something like that again. It was probably ridiculously naïve of me to try and convince myself that the worst was over, but in order to press on, right now I had to try.

I opened my eyes. I pushed my fingertips against the ground and winced at the pain of the pressure on my fresh cuts, and scrambled to my feet. It was still dark but not pitch black like it had been in the vents. It was a HALLWAY! A normal hallway instead of a sealed off passage. I took a few cautious steps forward and let my eyes adjust. I knew where I was!

Thank you! Thank you thank you thank you!

Relief flooded through me like river rapids. I paused and allowed myself a few seconds of pure, absolute gratitude. I was only one corner away from the hallway I needed to be in. I forced myself to stand very still and listen. I heard nothing. My teeth returned to gnaw absentmindedly on my lower lip. The silence was both good and bad – on one hand, no one was chasing me, or running around looking for me nearby. If they were, I would have no place to escape to. But on the other hand, if Reese was waiting for me shouldn't I hear him shuffling? Maybe not, maybe he was standing very, very still as well. I wanted to run down the rest of the hallway but I forced myself to take it slow and step lightly on the ground. My heartbeat increased as I approached the corner. This was it – either Reese would be waiting for me, or all of this risk will have been for nothing and if so, I had no idea what to do next.

I rounded the corner. My eyes darted to the left and to the right, desperately hoping to rest on the relief of his form sitting, standing or crouching near the wall. But there was no one.

No. Oh no. No!

I literally fell to my knees and barely noticed the pain. I let out a single, anguished sob. Reese was not here. This was all for nothing. I would have to turn around and go back which meant I would have to relive the nightmare of those vents all over again

unless

he was hiding out in the passageway! If Reese was in trouble he might be hiding out, and if he was hiding out and waiting for me to find him he would probably be in the same place he was yesterday, not right here in the open where flatfoot could find him but in the passageway he just introduced me to, where he first found the girl! I crept further down the hallway and I could only hope and pray that whatever kind of trouble Reese was in, flatfoots had not re-sealed off, nor were guarding, the passageway door. If they were, I would be caught and put to sleep for sure but I couldn't go back without checking everywhere for him that I knew to check. I had chosen to risk my freedom and even my life for Reese and I had to see this through.

I grasped the rusty door handle, held my breath and pulled. The door groaned and creaked in protest as I tugged on it, but it opened at least enough for me to slip through. I quickly did. "Reese?" I called out in barely above a whisper. My voice was shaking. I took a few tentative steps forward. "...Reese?" I took another hesitant step. Suddenly my face came into contact with something fuzzy – and sticky – a horrifying combination of both. Before I could stop myself, my mouth opened wide and a loud, shrill shriek broke through the silence like a punch. I threw my hands up in defense of whatever combination of terrifying tactile things were attacking me. My fingers tangled in the same unfamiliar substance and then I felt something even worse, tiny, skittering legs crawling across my hand. I shrieked again and stumbled backward.

My arms flailed desperately in the air as my body weight rocked dangerously back on my heels but I couldn't regain enough momentum to balance myself again and down I went, landing hard on my tailbone. Pain shot all the way up my spine in fast, almost electric shocks. For a brief moment I could swear I saw blue lines zapping across my vision. I turned on my side and scrambled to my feet. Full-on panic was too great for me to rationalize and overcome and my feet scurried forward in a run. I was barely able to veer off to the left or right when I could tell there was a wall about to block my escape to – anywhere but here.

My heart pounded inside of my ears like a drumbeat and I barely noticed the quick in and out breaths I was working myself into. I didn't slow down until my legs began to ache and the muscles in my calves began to tighten and rebel. I was moving forward so swiftly that when I slowed my pace the upper half of my body veered forward and I nearly lost my balance again. I stumbled but managed to keep myself upright. The moment I stopped, I rested my back against the wall and pressed my hands to my thighs. I shut out everything else and just breathed. My heart eventually slowed and my breathing eventually started to come easier. I finally raised my head and forced the reality of the moment to become relevant to me again.

I had no idea where I was.

Reese was not where I thought he would be. I had been a lovesick fool to think that whatever danger he was in, he would just be waiting for me to rescue him like in a fairy tale in reverse.

Could I retrace my panicked steps and find my way back to where I entered these passageways? I doubted it and that filled me with cold fright. All of this was for nothing. My parents lives would be in serious danger the moment they realized I was missing. I could have potentially exposed the entire Order and who knew if Reese was even still alive?

All of this was my fault. If I had just followed my mundane life plan like every other teenager did, none of this would be happening. Whatever my dad was involved in and whoever was involved in it with him could have continued to operate in secret and therefor would remain safe. My selfish, overconfident, naïve determination could have just gotten everyone I loved put to sleep.

I was thirsty. I could still feel the small water bottle sloshing around in my bra, but I had no idea when, or if, I would ever find another water source so I was scared to drink it. I slumped down against the wall in utter defeat and closed my eyes. I should give up. I should remain missing and I should just let myself waste away right here in these forgotten, forbidden passageways. I deserved nothing less.

Chapter 7

Silence broke with the faint sound of water dripping. I quickly choked up my sobs of helpless defeat and curled my arms around myself. Where would water be dripping from? Pipes only went into barrack areas and gardens, I assumed. But what did I know?

The sound reminded me of my thirst but still I resisted drinking from my one small water bottle. The drips grew louder until they started to sound like taps. Maybe it wasn't water after all.. and louder still, I realized with the temptation to fall into blind panic again that the taps were footsteps.

FOOTSTEPS! SOMEONE IS COMING OH GOD ITS A FLATFOOT I'M GONNA BE SENT TO THE TRANSITIONAL CONTAINERS I'M GONNA BE PUT TO SLEEP

I scrambled to my feet and pressed my back against the wall. I was surrounded in darkness so maybe whomever it was wouldn't see me – irrational, desperate thought, but it helped me keep still. Whomever was approaching might not have any idea that another person was hiding in this hallway whereas if I ran, I would alert them to my presence for sure. The only thing I could do was remain motionless and hope against all hope that if the footsteps belonged to a flatfoot, he would not notice me. I held my breath and closed my eyes, irrationally convincing myself that not being able to see would in turn make the world unable to see me. The footsteps grew louder and my heart began to pound. I could barely tell the difference between the drumming of my heart and the menacing steps. They paused. I cringed and tensed every muscle in my body. I waited for the fingers of death to reach out and snatch my arm. I knew it, I was caught. I would be marched to the transitional containers. It was over.

Reese. I love you. Please find safety. I'm sorry I'm such a failure. I wanted to save you. I'm sorry.

"Ruby?" I held back a sob. Life was cruel. Love was cruel. I knew Reese so well that my mind just told me he spoke. I supposed it really *was* the end. I was hearing him so that I had something to hold on to in my last moments. "Ruby is that you?" There it was again, the soft concerned voice that brought precious memories of Reese to the surface of my mind. That was good. I would be thinking of him as I took my last breath.

Even though I had been bracing for it, fingers curling around my forearm still triggered my terror. My better judgement never had a chance to tell me not to scream. A shriek raced out of my throat. I instinctively yanked my arm away and my body rocked forward on the balls of my feet, preparing to spring into action. Some part of my brain tried to tell me that running would not only be useless against a flatfoot, but would probably ensure a more torturous punishment before being put to sleep but terror was overriding any rationality I was capable of, again. In the single moment before I took off, fingers wrapped around my upper arm this time and pulled me backward. I shrieked again but another hand covered my mouth and muffled my vocal trepidation. My eyes nearly bulged out of my head. Terror drove me to perform my next instinctive survival mechanism; my body went limp. My knees gave way and I crumpled toward the ground. The pressure on my upper arm increased. "Ruby, shh!" Even though these last moments of my life were showcasing me as a complete failure, I could still hear Reese's voice. The pressure on my arm loosened but whomever was holding me captive still did not let me go or remove their hand from my mouth. I simply gave up. "Ruby we have to get out of here."

Stop. I can't fight anymore. I'm so sorry Reese... you have to save yourself.

"I'm gonna take my hand away but you can't scream again."

Wait, what?

The hand slowly slid away from my mouth. I licked my lips but I refused to command my body to move. The flatfoot would have to carry me to my death. "Ruby, talk to me!" The tiniest sliver of rationality started poking at my mind with a stick. The voice was still Reese's. Was it possible that my captor was not a flatfoot? No, there was no point in hoping. If I turned my head and looked at him I would know with 100% certainty and I didn't want to give this government minion that kind of satisfaction. "Are you hurt? Can you even hear me?" Why did he care if I was hurt and why did he have to keep sounding like Reese? The poking grew more persistent. Something wasn't right. Something was off. I bit down hard on my lower lip and trembled.

".....Reese?" I tensed again and prepared for some type of physical retaliation, but it did not come. I could literally hear the relief spilling from his vocal chords as he replied.

"Yeah, it's me! Ruby, what happened? Why are you out here?" In an instant my eyes popped open again. I wriggled around to face him. It was *HIM*! It was Reese! It was wonderful Reese with his thick dark hair, his masculine, defined jaw and his strong arms that symbolized warmth and comfort even in the most dire situations, of which I was most definitely in right now. He let go of my arm instantly and curled his hands around my body instead, not to restrain me this time but to comfort me.

It's really you.

I was too overwhelmed with utter relief and gratitude to be able to vocalize the thoughts and feelings that were swimming around in my head. I curled myself up against Reese's chest and let my tears run. My shoulders shook with sobs and he held me tighter. "Talk to me, what happened? What are you doing here?" I couldn't form words. I realized that Reese not being a flatfoot meant my life wasn't over yet, but humiliation and defeat suddenly became sharks that unexpectedly invaded the sea of my feelings and they were hungrily chasing me down. I had wanted to be brave and gallant so I could save the person I loved but all I had managed to do was put myself and others in a very dangerous situation. Reese was comforting me, again, when I had wanted to be the person to comfort him. I didn't want to be a damsel in distress. I didn't want to be weak like this. Why was I so damned weak?

My sobs finally dissipated. My body continued to shake but I was silent as I trembled against Reese's warmth. His fingers soothingly rubbed my back and his silent strength flowed through me, into me, becoming a part of me. I released a long, exasperated sigh. "I wanted to save you," I choked out quietly. Reese didn't reply right away.

"What do you mean, save me?" I licked my dry lips. Did Reese not know he was in danger? But, if he didn't know, why was he wandering the passageways in the middle of the night?

"I know you're in danger," I whispered softly, carefully. My throat tightened. Reese sighed.

*So he **did** know.*

"How did you get out? There's a flatfoot stationed in your hallway." He knew! Did that mean he had checked up on me? Or had someone told him?

"I crawled through the air vent. It was dark and tight and horrible and then I had to claw out of a screen and then there was this fuzzy thing and then this crawly thing!" I began to shudder again. "I couldn't just stay put, Reese. I couldn't just sit in my chambers while something horrible might have been happening to you. I had to find you and rescue you." I closed my eyes again. I sounded like such a fool. Rescue Reese? I had done nothing of the sort. All I had managed to do was put myself and my family in a deadly situation. I found Reese – or, he found me – and now I had no idea what to do next. All I knew was that he had not needed saving and now I probably couldn't even save myself.

Reese gently pulled away from me and slid his hands from my back to my upper arms. He tried to move his eyes to my face but I looked away. "Ruby, listen." I was listening. I just couldn't look. "Do you think you could crawl back the way you came?" My jaw tightened as if I had been slapped in the face. He wanted me to go *back*?

"No." I replied adamantly. "It was horrifying, and besides that, I broke a screen when I"

completely lost my cool

"found a way out. When they find it they'll look at the cameras, right? They'll see and identify me and off to the transitional containers I'll go, not to mention my parents." I raised my hands and covered my face. That was going to happen whether I went back or not. How had I not rationalized this sooner? I knew that being discovered as missing would put my parents in danger but it wasn't just danger they would be in, it was certain death unless my dad could somehow escape with my mom beforehand. She would be forced to face her fears and her life would be changed forever as she plunged into the darkness and uncertainty that she was not raised to be prepared for, just like me. What had I done?

"You're right." I could hear the fear in Reese's voice. He was worried for me, and I still didn't know the extent of danger *he* was in. Did he? "You can't go back. Ruby…" Reese trailed off, but the way he said my name was a mixture of gentle pleading and sadness. *I* caused this. *I* made his already bad situation that much worse. I buried my face in my palms. "It's probably good you got out. I can't go back, either." I slowly let my hands fall below my eyes but I couldn't bring myself to look at him. "There's something I have to tell you and I'm – I'm not sure how." I closed my eyes again. I couldn't handle any more of this. This was all too much, too fast, and I was contributing to the destruction. "It's about your dad."

What about my dad?

I loved Reese with all of my heart but if he was going to say something horrible about my father I couldn't even hope to predict how I might react. I pressed my lips together and shook my head. "No. I don't want to hear it. Reese – I'm – I can't handle any more secrets right now! I already know about the Order and-"

"You know?" I paused. My lids blinked rapidly over my eyes. Did Reese know?

"Yeah,"

"Oh. Um, that's what I was going to tell you."

We sat in silence. The cement floor of the passageway started to feel cold against my bruised bottom and I began to notice the dull but persistent ache of putting too much pressure on my tailbone by sitting

154

after I had injured it earlier. My unhappy tailbone was only an ad-on to my discomfort from the throbbing cut on my leg, and the little stings of the cuts on my fingertips. I leaned against Reese's chest and closed my eyes again. This wasn't a vision I had to draw from my imagination, this was real. Reese was real. Whatever horrible thing came next, at least I wouldn't have to face it alone. "Are you on the run?" I finally asked him. My voice was barely above a whisper but it still broke the silent relief with the dread of reality even though it was the last thing I wanted to do. Reese didn't answer right away. I slowly raised my eyes to see if he even heard me. He dipped his chin and shifted his gaze. He avoided having to look at me. There was my answer.

"Yeah." He finally replied. "If they find me they'll put me to sleep." I didn't want any more details. It was too overwhelming to even attempt to wrap my head around the concept that in the short time between Reese bringing me to the little girl and now, a death sentence had been metaphorically stamped on his forehead. Now it was stamped on mine, too. I was so tired. I wanted to sleep. Maybe this was all a dream. I would wake up in my warm bed in the chambers I had slept in every single night for my entire life. I would feel disappointed about my inevitable future and sad that I would never be able to experience love with someone of my choosing, but I would be safe and so would Reese. I had been a fool, a naïve, selfish fool and now everyone I loved was doomed to pay a hefty price for my wanderlust.

"Tell me what happened." Reese and I were both silent again. I sniffled and scooted even further into his arms. I pressed my face into his chest. I never would have had the guts to do this even one day ago but the difference of one day had changed me in ways that could never be reversed. I was no longer self-conscious or afraid of Reese knowing how I felt about him. We probably only had hours to live and since my entire life up until this moment had been meaningless, I wanted my final moments to count. "Kiss me," I found myself asking before Reese answered my question. I sucked up my hesitation and raised my eyes to his face, hoping, searching, silently begging him not to turn me away. His kiss brought me back to life once, I knew it could do so again even if only in my heart. I wanted to feel the fire of being in love. I wanted it to burn me until there was nothing left.

Reese pressed his forehead lightly against mine. His skin was warm, his lips a few mere inches from my own. I gasped softly as the flow of my blood quickened in my veins. My lids fluttered over my eyes until I forced them to calm. I wanted to see him. I wanted our eyes to lock and I wanted him to let me see past them, into his soul. I wanted to feel something magical.

But Reese's lips did not crash down against my own. His eyes shifted away from my searching gaze and my hopes and heart began to sink. "Ruby,"

No. Don't tell me you don't love me. Even if you don't feel for me what I feel for you, LIE TO ME. PLEASE.

"you're my best friend." I tore my eyes away as my cheeks flushed with warmth and embarrassing redness. "Right now we need each other, but"

But what??

"I don't want to kiss you like this. I don't want to give up. I want to survive and if I kiss you right now, it would be like accepting that our lives are over."

Was Reese saying that he loved me or that he didn't love me? How ridiculous, selfish and frivolous was I being even thinking about love when the problems we were facing, and the danger that perhaps everyone in The Complex was in, was so much bigger in the grand scheme of things than an insignificant sixteen year old girl pining for her best friend?

I shifted in his arms and brought my leg closer to my body but I winced as the dull ache on my calf reminded me I hadn't tended to my injury. I lifted my head from Reese's chest and slid my arms down to my calf. I slowly lifted my blood-stained pant leg. Reese immediately leaned forward with narrowed eyes. "How bad is it?" I asked cautiously. I preferred not to look if I didn't have to. Reese's fingers pressed against the skin that surrounded my puncture wound and little electric stinging shocks quickly thundered up my thigh. I involuntarily twitched and gasped. Reese frowned and sat up.

"It's not good. It looks deep. It's still bleeding." I bit my lower lip. "Give me your water bottle." I frowned, it was all the water I had. My cheeks flushed again as I reached into my bra and pulled it out. Fortunately for my ill-timed and quite irrelevantly silly self-conscious moment, Reese didn't seem to pay any attention to where I had it tucked as he grabbed it and twisted the cap. "This will probably sting," he warned me. I closed my eyes and tensed my muscles in preparation. The moment a few drops of water hit my wound, more bursts of stinging pain shot up my leg. I twitched again and cried out. My slightly bleeding fingers curled against the ground, right now my leg was in much more pain than they were. Reese set the water bottle down and curled his fingers around my stained pant leg. He tugged on it, hard, and it tore. He kept tugging and tore it all the way around until the torn piece fully detached from my pants. "This will sting again," he warmed me.

NO!

I wanted to beg Reese to stop but there was still some measure of sensibility in me and I knew I had to let him clean my wound. In The Complex we rarely got injured because we were never allowed to do anything dangerous, but inevitable accidents did occasionally happen so we were taught basic first-aid from a very early age. Proper physical care was taken seriously because we were in a confined space and no one wanted any type of infection to spread, or any good breeding stock to die unnecessarily.

Breeding stock. That's all any of us were. That was our worth to The Complex.

Reese suddenly dug the torn material from my pant leg into my wound. My whole body jerked and I yelped again. His hand curled around my calf and held it forcibly down. "Almost done," his voice deceptively assured me but I could still feel every bit of the sandpaper material digging mercilessly against the flaming-hot injured nerves on the surface of the raw parts of my exposed flesh. Finally, the searing pain stopped but it left me with its cousin, a throbbing sting. Reese picked up the water bottle again, and this time when the cooling droplets ran over my wound, the burning sensation soothed. I shuddered. Reese grasped my pant leg again and tore another strip, leaving my leg that much more exposed. He curled the new piece around my calf and over my wound and tied it tight. I whimpered again as the pressure caused the electrifying sting to increase in intensity. "Sorry," he muttered again as he pressed his palm down on my wound over the tied tourniquet-bandage-of-sorts. I shuddered some more. I had experienced a few minor cuts and bruises growing up, but nothing like this! Had it hurt this bad from the moment it happened back in the air vent, or had my adrenaline and fear been so heightened that I was only noticing it now? "We're going to have to clean it and change the bandage a few times each day to avoid infection."

Every day.

Did we have any days left in our lives, at all? Reese raised his chin and for a brief moment our eyes met. His were fierce, determined, and although he usually had orbs that glimmered the way I always imagined the ocean to shine like, right now they were the shade of the hottest temperature fire could possibly get.

Yes, Ruby. We ARE going to have more days.

Reese's silent message was clear. I had no idea how we would manage to live because the only thing I had demonstrated in my ignorant attempt to save Reese was how incapable I was, but his determination fueled me nonetheless. I wanted to believe we had a chance, some way, somehow. "Are you hurt anywhere else?" The moment I raised my hand, the dull sting of my fingertips brought my attention back to the cuts I had received while trying to claw my way through the vent screen. I frowned and held my fingers forward for Reese to inspect. I tried not to shiver as his thumb grazed over my palm, but the small, sweet comforting gesture at least distracted me from the pain of my leg. "These aren't so bad... they'll heal." While that was a relief, he hadn't said the same thing about my leg. I chewed my lower lip with worry. He grabbed my water bottle again. I winced as he poured some droplets over the small cuts on my fingertips but the dull sting wasn't nearly as potent of a punch as my leg wound had been, and still was. He rubbed a bit of dried blood from my fingers. "Here, drink what's left," he suggested as he offered the small bottle back to me. I wanted to, but I shook my head.

"It's all I have." He wiggled it in front of me.

"Take it, Ruby. We'll get more." I had no idea how or where he thought we were going to find drinkable water in this dank abandoned passageway but I was too exhausted and thirsty to argue. I finally snatched it from him and brought the nozzle to my lips. I tossed my head back and closed my eyes as the slightly cool, refreshing liquid soothed my dry throat and calmed the dull thirsting ache that had been swelling up inside of me. I forced myself to stop when there were only a few sips left and I held it out to Reese.

"You need some, too." He started to shake his head but I narrowed my eyes and tried to mimic the same determination he had shown me. We were in this together. He relented and took the bottle. He threw his head back and gulped the last few sips. I glanced down at the cuts on my fingers, now blood free and barely visible. I didn't dare look down at my leg despite the fact that it was bandaged. It still throbbed. Reese moved to my side again and sat down with his back against the wall. He rested his elbows on his knees and lifted his chin as he stared blankly ahead at nothing. He was lost in thought and I wanted to know what was on his mind. I quietly curled up to his side again. I rested my head against his shoulder. "Tell me what happened." I requested once more. "How do you know about the Order and my dad? I need to know." If we had any hope of surviving, I needed to know everything he knew, and more.

Reese sighed. I waited. I understood his need to pause. The world as we knew it started spinning and dissolving the moment we snuck into the passageway, and it still hadn't stopped. "I went back to try and find the girl. I needed answers, you know? I went to the passageway where I first found her, but she was gone. I hadn't explored very far in the passageways before because I didn't want to risk getting caught or getting lost, but I couldn't just leave her trapped in there with no food or water." Of course he couldn't. He would never leave a child to die just to save his own skin. He was brave. He was selfless. He was everything I was not. "So I headed in the direction she ran off in. I started talking to her. I tried to tell her I wasn't going to hurt her and that I wanted to help her. I just wanted her to come out and to know I wasn't a threat.

"Then I heard footsteps. I didn't think they belonged to a little girl and," Reese paused. "I panicked. I thought it was a flatfoot. I ducked into the shadows and pressed myself against the wall. I held my breath and the footsteps got closer. Then I heard someone calling my name and I recognized the voice." My muscles tensed. *Who was it?!?* "It was Beau, you know, our biology teacher from last year." What would Beau, an older gentleman around fifty, be doing wandering around the passageways, looking for Reese? Unless – *unless he was in the Order!* I dipped my chin in a tiny nod to encourage him to continue. "I didn't move or respond, obviously, because how the hell did I know he wasn't looking for me on behalf of the flatfoots or something? But he kept trying to talk to me the way I had been trying to talk to the girl. He told me that he was part of something called The Order Of The Elements and they were trying to discover the scientific truth about the invasion and why we were all still confined in The Complex. Beau knew that a kid was lost in the passageway – I don't know how he knew, yet, but he swore to me he would tell me everything in time. He told me the Order had the girl and she was safe.

"They have a tap in the camera feeds. They had seen me sneaking into the passageways – the Order, that is, not the flatfoots – at least not yet – but their feed got interrupted when the flatfoots figured out someone else was tapping in. The Order knew it was only a matter of time before the flatfoots saw what the Order saw, so it was best that I went with him if I wanted to live. I didn't know if I should believe him but either way, I knew I couldn't go back to The Complex at that point so I stepped out of the shadows. If I was going to die I might as well take a chance first, right?" So, the Order was monitoring the security cameras somehow, too? How did that make them any better than the flatfoots?

NO!

I couldn't think that way! My dad was part of the Order and he would never be a flatfoot! He would never do to others what the flatfoots did! He would not haul off beloved family members to be put to sleep simply because they turned sixty.

"I didn't have much of a choice at that point but to trust Beau. I followed him down a few more twists and turns in the passageway and he led me to some sort of boiler room. He said it was the Rhode Island headquarters of the Order, but the Order had members all over The Complex." So it *was* Complex-wide! "Ruby," Reese paused again and lowered his head as if ashamed. I sniffled. My fingers reached forward seeking his and they ended up curling around his hand. I was patient. I waited. "I had to tell them you were with me yesterday. They hadn't seen you on the cameras yet. If they thought my life was in danger because of the cameras, that means yours was, too. The flatfoots would have eventually seen you on the feed." My breath caught in my throat. "The Order had already managed to get a message to your dad about me but by the time I told them about you, I-" he paused again and shook his head softly. "I'm sorry. I just, I had to be sure I felt like I could trust these people before I brought you into it. If it was a con and they were government moles trying to get me to tell them why I was sneaking into the passageways or to tell them what I knew about the girl, I wasn't going to hand them a reason to eliminate you, too. I'm sorry." I trembled. Why was this happening to us both? Neither one of us had the information we needed so we kept making choices that seemed to make things worse. It wasn't our fault. We were trying our best. It wasn't fair! This life wasn't fair.

I scooted forward and tucked my head under Reese's chin and against his chest. My fingers squeezed his hand. "Don't be sorry. I wouldn't have known if I could trust them either. How do we know even now?" I hoped and prayed that Reese had an answer to that question, not just any answer but a satisfactory one. I *hoped*, but I knew better at this point than to expect.

"We don't." I figured as much. "But we don't have much of a choice, either. They didn't want me leaving headquarters but with you being in danger, I had to find you and get you to safety so I snuck out. I knew there was a flatfoot stationed in your hall. When I told Beau that you'd been with me in the passageway and you'd seen the little girl too, he me about your family being under confinement because of your dad's virus." Reese ran his fingers through his thick hair to pull some of the longer strands away from his eyes with an exasperated sigh. "I didn't know how I was going to get to you. I thought of going to Willow again and maybe having her get a message to you by saying she was bringing you homework for the classes you were going to miss but then they might have searched her. I wanted – probably needed – her help, but I had to have a plan first, a way to get to you and a way to get you out. I was pacing and starting to lose my mind, I was just standing there trapped in the passageway while they could discover you breaking Doctrine any minute and come for you." He shook his head and closed his eyes. I squeezed his hand again.

"But they didn't. I'm right here," I tried to remind him in a soothing voice. He pressed his lips together and raised his chin again.

"And you ran right past me." I did..? "I would recognize your face anywhere, even as a blur. I thought maybe I was losing it but I ran after you anyway." I knew the rest.

And here we were.

"But, Ruby," I lifted my head again. There was more? How could there be more? "Once your parents realize that you're gone it's only going to be a matter of time before the government finds out, too. And that's only IF they haven't discovered you on the camera feed yet. Either way..." I squeezed my eyes shut.

NO. No no no no no no NO. Do NOT tell me my parents are going to die.

"I – I left a note for my dad," I admitted, though it didn't solve anything and it wasn't going to keep them out of danger. In fact, now that I said it out loud, I realized it was literally the dumbest thing that had ever come out of my mouth. "They're gonna get PUT TO SLEEP!" I started shaking again. What had I done? I hadn't saved Reese, in fact, he had already been en route to try and save *me*. I had literally accomplished nothing with my air vent antics except putting my parent's lives at serious risk.

"Hey, listen to me." *No.* I didn't want to. I couldn't look at Reese right now. "If you hadn't escaped like you did you might not have had a chance to stay alive." So he was admitting that my parents were doomed. How could I have done that to them? How could I live with myself knowing that it was my fault their lives were going to be taken?

"Why did you ask if I could go back?"

"I thought maybe you could get a message to your parents. But it's too risky."

"I can't." I was horrible. I loved my parents fiercely. The knowledge that my impulsive, life-changing decision had just put them on death's list was sickening to me, so much so that I was certain I never wanted to look at myself in the mirror again. And yet, the thought of crawling back through those air vents filled my veins with ice. "I could barely fit. My dad wouldn't be able to." Reese sighed. "Wait -" My selfishness seemed to know no bounds. I was terrified for my parents, but... "What about Gaia and Thao?" Reese lowered his head at my mention of his parents. This time, it was his hand that gave mine a squeeze.

"I don't know," he admitted. "I'm not even sure if they're alive."

Oh, Reese!

I **adored** Gaia and Thao. They had always been kind to me. Gaia often had a smile and a warm hug and Thao would always say things to me like, "My goodness Ruby, you truly are a gem! You get prettier every day!" What if Reese never saw them again? What if they were

165

*No. Don't even **think** it.*

"What do we do now?" I hated giving up like this, giving in, yielding any control over any possible choice and admitting to myself that I was in way over my head or capabilities, but I was so tired. My body stung in several places, I was cold, and the life I had wanted to escape from every moment since I was a toddler was already a life I missed. Irony was ironic that way, but there was no turning back. Ever. I realized that now. These dangerous choices were for keeps.

"We go back to the Order. We beg them to help your parents, if there's a way."

"And yours," I added, though the agreeing comment I expected hung silently in the ominous air like the way Beau once described storm clouds in class.

"Can you walk?" Honestly, I wasn't sure. Reese slowly slid his arms away from me and mine fell limply to my sides. He scrambled to his feet. He offered me his hand. I reached up, grabbed it, and allowed him to tug me up. The moment I stood, my blood rushed down to my leg and the pounding sting of my wound intensified. I gasped but I refused to be a wuss. I refused to be even more pathetic and helpless than I already felt.

"I can walk," I assured Reese. He slipped an arm around my waist anyway. I almost pushed him away but my pain battled my pride and quickly got the upper hand. I hobbled along, half-leaning on Reese for support and mustering up the very last bits of determination I had in me for the rest. The quicker we got to the Order the quicker I could demand that they save my parents. I just wanted to see them again. I wanted to tell my dad how sorry I was for letting him down. I wanted to rewind the clock so my mom never had to know about or face any of this. In fact, I wanted to rewind the clock so that I

166

never had to either, but I knew that was impossible. All I could do was learn to accept the new realities that surrounded me and take each moment as it came. It seemed like the only way to survive until – well – until there were no more moments. I would not let myself give up hope until I took my last breath.

Chapter 8

Reese and I rounded a corner as he led me back to the Order's hideout. The silence broke with a scuffle that did not come from our own four feet. Reese immediately curled his fingers around my forearm and yanked me into the shadows. We pressed our backs against the wall and my heart quickly began to race in my chest. My fingers curled in his as our hands locked. A mutual squeeze served as our own silent communication that if these were our last moments, we would face the consequences together. That didn't make me any less terrified but at least I was not alone. I was with the person I loved.

We didn't hear any more scuffles. Reese shifted his eyes in my direction. I widened my own. Had it been a random noise? Perhaps it had been air whooshing through a vent or water moving through a pipe. Although we had obviously both heard a noise, how could either of us be sure of what we heard? We were both on red alert, our ears keen to the slightest shifts in our environment and our minds ready to interpret the smallest clamor as a catalyst to our mortality. My body remained frozen until Reese loosened his grip on my hand. We cautiously stepped out of the shadows and continued to move down the passageway but we walked a bit slower, making sure that each time our feet came in contact with the cement floor we made as little noise as possible. We rounded another corner. Reese pointed toward a rusty door and dipped his chin. I understood. It was the Order's headquarters. I had to bite my lip to keep myself from crying out in utter relief. There were people in there – people that could help keep us safe. My brain wanted to remind me that being with the Order did not mean our lives were no longer in danger but I needed to believe, even if only temporarily, that these people would be our salvation. They Order keep us safe, they would rescue my parents, they would rescue Reese's parents, and we would all somehow manage to live happily ever after.

I wasn't quite sure how that would work out considering we were now fugitives and The Complex only had so many places to hide, but I needed something to believe in, something to look forward to, an ending, a resolution to calm my terror.

About fifteen feet from the door, Reese paused and gently touched my arm signaling me to do the same. I raised my brows with worry. He held a finger to his lips. He stepped forward without me and approached the door cautiously and quietly. He knocked three times, then paused, knocked three more times, paused again, then knocked twice. It didn't take a genius to figure out it was a coded knock. How had he remembered the pattern? I supposed when it was a matter of life and death our memories worked better than usual. I expected the door to open a crack and for a member of the Order to peer out, but nothing happened. I bit my lower lip. Why was no one answering the door? Was Reese's knock incorrect? We waited a bit longer. Slight but justified paranoia told me to look over my shoulder and then slink back toward the wall. Reese knocked again, repeating the same code. Still nothing. Maybe it was the wrong door. *Maybe it was the wrong code.* I leaned forward from the wall as Reese turned around, but then the door finally creaked. Reese took a step back. "Come in. Hurry." Reese turned around and gestured to me. I jumped forward on the balls of my feet. We both squeezed in the door and it was quickly shut behind us.

The room was pitch black and a familiar sense of panic rushed back to me.

    Dark space. *Confined* space! WHO WAS IN THIS ROOM WITH US?

    I whimpered softly. My hand reached forward, desperately seeking contact with Reese's. I felt the edge of his shirt and I scuttled to his side. I couldn't be alone right now, I would lose my mind.

I heard a footstep directly in front of us but all I could make out in the darkness was the hint of a silhouette. The footsteps moved away from me and around Reese. Then they were behind me. Then they were at my side. Someone was surrounding us, walking around us in a circle and it was deliberate! I whimpered again despite my better judgement. They were *trying* to terrify us.

    This is a trap. It's over. We're going to be interrogated and then put to sleep.

    Mom, Dad, I'm so sorry.

    "Who is the girl?" A low, raspy voice demanded. My throat tightened. My hand squeezed Reese's so hard that he was probably in pain.

    "That depends, who are you?" Reese challenged. All of my muscles tensed. Reese was brave but I feared it would only make things worse for him.

    "Evon, the Rhode Island Vice-Divisional Leader of the Order of the Elements." I did not relax. How did we know he was telling the truth? What if the Order had been discovered after Reese left to find me? What if the government stationed a flatfoot to pose as a member of the Order to capture anyone returning who did not know their headquarters had been compromised?

    "Prove it," Reese cheekily demanded as if mirroring my uncertainty. I trembled again.

    "We told you to remain stationary. We expressed

the importance of the Order, what we stand for and the lives we are trying to save. You disappeared of your own volition so we were forced to abandon our original headquarters and reconvene in a secondary safe location. I was ordered to remain behind in case you should return. Now answer me; *who is the girl?*" I wasn't sure if Reese was going to answer him or not.

"Ruby R-1046." I could hear Evon shifting his weight. My breath caught in my throat.

"How did you retrieve her?"

"I didn't. I couldn't figure out how. A flatfoot is guarding her barracks because she and her family are under confinement for the nasopharyngitis her father caught from the little girl. Ruby escaped her barracks by crawling through an air vent. It was blind luck that we found each other." Evon shifted his weight again. I shifted too in the uncomfortable moments of silence that followed.

"Why did she attempt such an escape?" It was my turn to perpetuate uncomfortable silence. Reese was afraid, just like I was. He didn't know if he could trust this man either. In that moment I realized that no matter how we answered, if Evon was a flatfoot we were already as good as dead. There was nothing left to do now but to be honest.

"It was the message," I finally responded before Reese tried to make up an excuse for me. "The message the Order sent to my father. It said Reese was in danger." More uncomfortable silence.

"You're Robert's girl. You're not mated with Reese. Why would you risk your life and the lives of your parents for him?" I let go of Reese's hand and slid my arm through his. I wasn't sure if I was protecting him, or seeking his protection.

"Reese is one of my best friends. I've known him since we were small children and I had to make sure he was all right." I was too ashamed to explain that Reese had been the one to find me and I had only added to the danger instead of saved him from it, but I suspected this man had already figured that out.

"Hold out your right wrist." I hesitated. My eyes shifted with uncertainty to the only person in The Complex that I could fully trust right now. Reese nodded his chin. Tentatively, I did as instructed. My hand shook a bit. Evon grabbed it and brought some type of contraption toward it. I could not see well enough in the dark to make out what it was, and instinctively I began to pull my hand back but his grip on my wrist tightened. Before I could struggle further, something on the device clicked and a blue shock wave hit my wrist. Instantly, my entire body jerked as a surge raced through my heart. I quivered and my eyes widened in terror. I managed to yank my wrist out of Evon's grasp and I drew it back toward my chest. It stung. "Just electricity," Evon said as if those words were supposed to calm me. "We've discovered that our ID chips have a higher purpose than simply our identification, occupation and mating status. They elicit an electronic pulse which is very likely a tracker. We will get around to removing your chip altogether, but a small shock disturbs the electronic output which scrambles the tracker." My eyes widened as I rubbed at my stung wrist.

"For how long?" I asked fearfully.

"Long enough until we can remove it permanently." Evon replied impatiently before quickly and intentionally circling the topic back around. "So you escaped to find Reese. But what of your parents? What do you think will happen to them when it's discovered that you are missing?" Irritation and sarcasm ruled his tone like an arrogant king. I closed my eyes and tried to ignore the burn of giant, messy tears welling up behind my eyelids. I bit my lower lip, hard. He had a right to point out how foolish I had been. He had a right to showcase that by not thinking things through fully, I might have gotten my parents killed.

"You're young and naïve. You can't imagine the extent of the government's lies. We suspected the subterfuge years ago. Gossip and questions travelled underground. As random members in each division started latching on to these questions, some of them began to suffer accidents. Others were taken to the transitional containers under false allegations. The government was trying to stop the truth from spreading. Over the years the Order developed. To protect our lives, absolute secrecy was of utmost importance. What began as a question of whether or not we could return to the surface to reclaim it for our species turned into paranoia and suspicion. It was obvious that these fairly raised questions were considered a threat to Doctrine.

"We've been able to discover some answers, but not many. Our interest is in preserving the lives of all of us down here in The Complex and finding a way to safely return to the surface so we can start over, rebuild humanity by working together, not by falling prey to a tyranny that took advantage of all of us in a vulnerable state A.I." My throat was tight and forcing air through my windpipe was a chore. My head spun like my body used to as a child, only I couldn't make it stop and the dizziness was no longer fun. It was just making me nauseous.

I thought I had an inquisitive mind. I was never content to settle with the life-plans laid out before me. I

174

wanted to experience Earth. I wanted to choose my own lover. I wanted to be able to decide for myself if I wanted children or not and I wanted to be able to pick a career out of a bigger pile than the mundane, brainless jobs in The Complex. I wanted to be able to use my mind. I wanted to question and explore and think and improve the lives of people around me but instead I had been told over and over again that my purpose was to procreate and my life had no other meaning. Grandpa Logan was right to encourage me. Dad was right to be a part of the Order.

What really happened to my grandmother? What if Mom was right and her death wasn't an accident after all? Had her 'accident' been the government's way of eliminating her? Poor Grandpa Logan. No wonder he encouraged me to reach further than the walls of this cemented cage. No wonder he wanted me to have a chance at a different kind of life. I opened my eyes. I wiped my whale-sized tears on the back of my forearm. "You say your interest is in preserving lives. Are you going to save my parents? What about Reese's?" I could hear him shifting his weight again.

No.

Hesitant silence right now was **not** acceptable.

"I'm not sure if we can try and save them without exposing the entire Order." I didn't care how dangerous or ill-fated my demand was, I was not going to stand here in the dark and listen to some speech about how sacrificing the few was for the good of the many. I heard that in school, a lot. During those lectures I thought that I hadn't paid much attention, but hearing various teacher's voices fresh in my mind right now proved otherwise. Those words **had** impacted me, just not in the way the teachers and the government hoped they would.

"My grandfather wanted me to believe that there was a life waiting for me somewhere out there that was better than this one. He never wanted me to let go of my imagination. He told me about his childhood on Earth in ways that made me want nothing more than to experience those things myself. My grandmother died in an accident, or so they say but my mother doesn't believe that. She believes my grandmother's death was engineered. She lives every moment of her life in fear of the government and what they might do. My father pretends to be closed off, quiet and accepting of the fact that his life was basically meaningless but I found out very recently that he is a part of this Order. He joined because he wanted me to have a chance at a better life, just like my grandfather wanted. He risks his life by being a part of this Order because it's what he believes in. He thinks he can make a difference. So you listen to me. If you mean what you said about valuing lives, you **will** find a way to save my parents."

My voice began to tremble with the last few sentences of a speech I had no idea I was capable of making. If I were anyone else and I heard those words coming out of me, I would probably have believed that they were coming from a strong, determined, capable girl and the irony was, I was the opposite of those things in every way. I was clueless, incompetent, incapable and a coward, but I loved my parents and if I couldn't save them myself, I refused to let pride or embarrassment stop me from making that demand.

This time, the awkward silence that followed felt different. I was still trembling, but rather than shaking with timid fear and feeling as small as a mouse, I was shuddering with self-surprise and determination.

Change didn't happen overnight, which was unfortunate because one day can change your entire life. My logical mind knew and understood that I could never return to my old life. I would not have to marry Connor after all; in fact, I doubted I would ever see him again. Did that mean I could spend my life with Reese? Maybe, that is, if we both lived through whatever was going to come next. We were fugitives now and that was terrifying because The Complex only had so many places to hide. Reese and I certainly couldn't spend our whole lives running and hiding. Either we would eventually be caught, or the constant stress and fear of being caught would age us and destroy us way before our time. Sending people to the transitional containers at sixty was far too soon and far too unfair, but if Reese and I had to live in constant fear we wouldn't even make it to thirty.

The darkness still made vision a challenge and although I couldn't see every detail of Reese's face clearly when I looked up at him with searching eyes, I sensed that our thoughts were the same. We still did not have freedom and we still did not get to choose our own path. We had to rely and depend on the Order's experience and knowledge to keep us alive. We had no other choice.

"If I take you to our secondary headquarters, you both need to swear an oath to me right here and right now." I raised an eyebrow with tentative suspicion and squeezed Reese's arm. He squeezed my hand back to remind me of the silent communication we had just shared. "You will not leave headquarters again unless we tell you to, and/or unless you are with an official escort. Your objective while we are stationary will be getting the little girl to talk. We need to know where she is from and what she knows about us. She doesn't trust us, she thinks we're holding her captive."

They essentially abducted an already terrified small child and then wondered why she wouldn't speak to them? Evon was an idiot.

"Up until now, every Rhode Island member of the Order has successfully lived a pretense of a compliant life so they've had barracks to return to and families to protect. That's all about to change. Right now, we have limited food and water and we have very little time to plan our next move."

Some small part of my mind wanted to resent the little girl. Presuming she really was from the surface, if she hadn't literally fallen into The Complex none of this would be happening. I would be in my barracks, snuggled under a warm blanket with my head cradled by a soft pillow. I would wake up in the morning to the smell of breakfast being cooked by my mother. I would head off to classes and I would enjoy spending time with Willow and Reese and my parents would go to work. Everyone I loved would be safe.

That's Mom talking.

I knew the life I just described was not the life I had ever wanted. I was never satisfied with the mundane future I knew I would be forced into. It would be easy to blame the child for turning our lives upside down and plunging us into a pit of fire, but I couldn't un-learn everything I now knew. Earth was habitable. We could live on the surface. We could breathe.

Was there water? What did people eat? What about the sun, was there any truth to our planet being slowed on its axis? Was there nothing but eternal darkness above our heads right now, or would we get to experience sunlight after all? I wanted to know everything and I wanted to know it as soon as possible. The Order would make that happen, right? They would find a way to save my parents and Reese's parents and then we would break through to the surface and we would start over. Everything would be different. Everything would be perfect. Reese and I could be together forever. I would get to experience everything Grandpa Logan described to me.

I couldn't hate the girl. When she stumbled into The Complex, she caused a ripple effect that could not be undone and I realized that I didn't want it to be. I wanted the life her appearance allowed us to glimpse, not the life I was going to be forced to live before she appeared.

What about her family? Did she have parents? Were they worried sick about her? Were they looking for her? What was the great big world above really like? We were so limited here in The Complex when it came to where we were allowed to go. There were so few places to hide and there was nowhere to truly get lost. Earth on the other hand – wow. I couldn't even wrap my mind around it. There was an entire planet above my head that people could get lost on, perhaps never to be found again.

After my parents were saved, I would help the girl find hers.

"I need you to both swear to these terms. If you don't, I'll leave you here to fend for yourselves." I pressed my lips together. Evon had not responded to my demand and I would not swear to anything until he did.

"My parents – and Reese's. Will you help them?" More silence.

"We will put forth every effort to retrieve your parents. But Ruby, you need to understand that we can't promise that we'll succeed. Their lives are very much in danger. All of our lives are. I *can* promise you that tonight, we'll convene and come up with a plan to try. Do you understand what I'm saying?"

No.

I wanted Evon to say that he would definitely save my parents. I wanted him to guarantee me that by tomorrow night I would be able to hug them again and whatever now-unpredictable life challenges lay ahead of us, we would all be able to face them together.

But I also knew Evon was right to be this honest with me. There was simply no way for him to guarantee a happily ever after. I closed my eyes briefly and took a deep breath. I allowed my shoulders to rise and then fall.

Remember, moment by moment.

"I understand," I forced myself to say. The words barely made it past my tightened vocal cords and the resentment I felt, albeit irrational and unfair, was not something I could mask in my tone. If Evon noticed it, he didn't react.

"And you?" Reese cleared his throat.

"I understand, too." Evon curtly nodded.

"Then follow me. Stay as silent as you can. Walk light on your feet. Do not run unless I run. Do not stop unless I stop. Understand?" I nodded and swallowed past a lump in my throat.

The man turned and walked toward the door. Reese and I followed him and he did not let go of my hand. I was more grateful than I could have ever expressed. I couldn't be strong on my own. I couldn't be brave on my own. Not yet, at least. I needed Reese. He needed me, too.

I unintentionally held my breath as we tiptoed down the passageway. In a way, our surroundings were completely silent and in another sense, the noise was deafening. I was a mouse, picking up every tiny shift, every trickle in the old pipes that lined the walls, every time one of our collective six feet touched upon and then left the ground. Every tiny noise almost made me twitch as it pecked at my fear that we were being followed. I tried to keep an even pace with Reese and Evon but every few seconds I had to glance over my shoulder just to be completely sure that greedy, claw-like government hands were not about to curl around my arm and steal me away. I started imagining said claws brushing across the skin on the back of my shoulder or grazing across my elbow and I would jerk. My eyes would dart toward Reese to make sure he had a good grip on my hand. More glances behind me assured me visually that no one was there but my mind and body simply refused to believe it. Panic was fighting with my desperation to try and stay calm. My throat tightened again. My feet became springboards and every time one of them left the ground, the muscles in my calves would tense as if ready to let loose any second into a full-blown run.

Finally after rounding yet another corner, Evon put out his hand and we slowed our walk before stopping altogether. He turned and glanced at us with a quick nod and stepped into another black shadow. We had no choice to but follow. Without the benefit of sight, Reese and I let the blackness cloak us and then stopped again to wait for further instruction. The consuming darkness only heightened my paranoia that we were being followed and I had to bite my inner cheek to fight the whimper that wanted to escape my mouth. My hand squeezed Reese's even tighter and I was fairly certain I was hurting him although he didn't try to pull away.

Evon knocked on the door three times, then

paused. He knocked three more times and paused again. After the last two knocks there was nothing any of us could do but wait. I rocked forward on the balls of my feet and held my breath.

What if they moved again while he waited for us what if they thought they weren't safe and decided to keep moving and not stay in one place what will we do how will we save our parents how will we even save ourselves?

The door opened. Evon's silhouette disappeared but I couldn't seem to muster up the bravery to follow him into even more darkness. Reese stepped ahead first and tugged my hand gently. Well – I supposed I could muster the bravery with him still by my side. My steps made it past the threshold. The door slammed behind us.

Before the total darkness had a chance to completely overwhelm the panicked side of me, lights started flickering on. My eyes immediately snapped to the right. The man holding the hand lamp looked familiar. I realized I had seen him working with my dad in the gardens! Another hand lamp flickered on, and another, and soon Reese and I were completely surrounded. How odd that being in a dank, unidentifiable room surrounded by mostly strangers all standing in a half-circle around us actually brought me comfort instead of fear.

Another man that I recognized from my dad's gardens stepped forward toward Reese and I. He narrowed his eyes at me as if trying to place my identity, but a moment later his brows relaxed and his lips parted Evon stepped forward and turned to face us.

"Reese disregarded our order to stay confined to headquarters because he feared Ruby, Robert's daughter was in danger. It seems that she too had seen the little girl." Evon paused and glanced accusing in Reese's direction. "Robert for some reason saw fit to explain our message to his daughter without impressing upon her the seriousness of the situation. She escaped her barracks through the air vents with the intention to find Reese, and oddly enough they apparently did manage to find each other."

We found each other because the place where we found the butterfly means something to us.

These men did not have to know that. That place was precious to me, and the reasons why were private. I wanted to keep it that way.

"Unfortunately, due to Robert's nasopharyngitis and the investigation surrounding it, his family is under confinement and their barracks under guard. When Ruby's disappearance comes to light, Robert and his wife will be at serious risk. Ruby and Reese have asked us to help them." I don't know what I expected to follow his speech, reluctant as it may sound. I suppose I didn't expect cheers and instant eagerness, but the silence that followed was like a knife piercing my skin and sinking past my ribcage toward my heart. Why were these people shifting their eyes and their weight, glancing at each other hoping someone would break the silence but unwilling for that person to be them? Some of these people knew my father! My father believed in this Order and risked his life, as well as mine and my mother's for its cause and these people were just standing around awkwardly staring at each other!

I let go of Reese's hand. I felt incomplete without the comfort of his touch and I had to fight to resist the urge to reach for him again. I took a deep breath and stepped forward. "When I was a little kid, my grandfather used to tell me stories about Earth. He made me want to see it and feel it. I started asking questions.

Why weren't we not allowed to leave The Complex? How could we be positive that we couldn't survive up there? I got slapped on the back of my hand with rulers as a result of my curiosity." I held out my hand to show off my scar. "Robert, my father, is one of you. He *believes* in your cause. He believes this Order can make a difference. He wants a better life for me than meaningless confinement. He risked his life and mine and my mother's because of your cause. So if you don't exhaust every effort you can think of to try and rescue my parents, everything my father believes about this Order is a lie." Silence followed my speech, but this time the people holding their hand lamps were not shifting or glancing at each other. They were all staring ahead – and I realized, they were staring at *me.*

One of the men walked forward. My fear urged me to shrink back but I planted my feet on the ground and raised my shoulders even higher. I would not budge. I would not stand down. I would not back off. My words were important. My parents were important. Every move I made had to consistently reflect that.

The man raised one of his hands and rested it on my shoulder. "Brave words, Ruby. You are your father's daughter. My name is Zane and I'm the Rhode Island Divisional Leader of the Order of the Elements. I give you my word that every effort will be made to try and save your parents, no matter what." Zane's promise was comforting and assuring. Evon raised his eyebrows. I resisted the tiniest of smug smiles. Zane's words were stronger, more determined and more honest than Evon's had been. I believed Zane actually cared for my parents and I believed he had an honest investment in their safety. My eyes blurred.

"Thank you," I choked out while trying to hold

my composure. "Thank you." I wiped at my eyes. Zane gave my shoulder a reassuring squeeze. "My parents mean everything to me."

"I know," Zane replied with the same gentle understanding and honesty. "and you mean everything to them."

Chapter 9

Reese and I were sparing as we ate some crackers. The Order had prepared fairly well, even in their secondary hideout, for the inevitable day when they were found out and could no longer return to their barracks and pretend to be obedient citizens of The Complex, but how long we would have to make their supplies last was, for the moment, unknown to me.

I was still thirsty but I only allowed myself a third of a bottle of water until morning. Water had to be even more carefully rationed than food; one could survive without food for weeks but without water, we would die within a few days. I recalled learning those basic survival facts in the classroom but I never imagined a day where I would have to put my minimal survival knowledge to use. The Complex was orderly. As long as everyone did their jobs faithfully and obeyed Doctrine, no one ever went hungry.

The members of the Order gathered on the other side of the room to discuss and decide on a plan of action to help mine and Reese's parents, and we were left to look after a completely terrified child. Every time I glanced over at the little girl huddled in the corner, my heart ached and went out to her. She was even filthier than when I first saw her. She was no longer clad in that strange, puffy suit. Instead, she was clad in our regulation uniform, albeit one far too large for her tiny frame.

Had someone in the Order forced the girl to disrobe? How horrible and humiliating for her. They could never even hope to earn her trust like that. Her long hair was probably sandy blonde, but it looked wild and almost painfully tangled as if it hadn't seen a brush in years. Her nails were nearly black with dirt. Her arms and legs were so skinny – almost twigs. Despite these things, she was a real person and she was alive. Now that I could see her tiny, frail body even more fully, I knew with certainty that she wasn't a mutation or a monster. She was just a person. If she really was from the surface, she was living proof that all of us in The Complex had been lied to.

In this little girl's mind, she was a prisoner and we were the enemy. We had literally captured her and we were forcing her to stay in this room. I wanted so badly to find a way to make her understand that we did not want to hurt her, we wanted to protect her. I wanted to explain that the Order only took her into their custody to keep her safe from the government, and that finding her before the flatfoots did had saved her from being put to sleep. But I couldn't imagine telling her those things would do anything to ease her mind, it would only frighten her more and who knows if she would believe me anyway? Why should she?

The selfish part of me was practically its own entity at this point and it was scratching at the insides of my skin in desperation to be set free. If I let that needy part of me take over, I wouldn't be able to stop asking her my burning questions and demanding immediate answers, one after the other after the other. Fortunately, the terrified version of me was working to keep the selfish part of me contained. Was I anywhere near ready for her to answer my questions, even if I could find a way to earn her trust? I suspected that the well of government lies ran deeper than I could comprehend. I was already on the verge of a complete emotional breakdown and who knew what might send me over the edge for good?

Reese and I had been given two hand lamps. They were turned on and they sat on the floor in front of us, but they were only strong enough to illuminate a few feet from where they sat. I readjusted my injured leg which was had settled into a dull throb and rested my head on Reese's shoulder. My lids were heavy and desperate for sleep but I couldn't sleep next to a terrified child. She appeared exactly like I felt; shaking, afraid, unsure of who to trust and unsure of what was true or even real anymore. My throat tightened. I wanted to speak to her, to offer her some kind of comfort but I couldn't even comfort myself.

"It's okay to eat," Reese tried to coax her with a gentle voice. He picked up a cracker and slowly extended his arm. Her eyes widened and she made no move to take it from him. She offered no response at all except the slightest narrowing of her eyes. I couldn't blame her for her mistrust. Reese did not lower his arm. "I'm sorry you're here," Reese continued to try to speak to her. "I can't imagine how confused you must be. If it makes you feel any better, Ruby and I barely know these people, either. They're not keeping you prisoner, you know. I realize it probably seems that way because they brought you here and they don't want you to leave, but they're trying to protect you." Her eyes narrowed even more and I gave Reese's arm a gentle squeeze to signal him to stop, or at least to not carry that topic any further. She couldn't handle things right now any better than I could. "I'll just leave this here, in case." Reese set the cracker down on the edge of the blanket that she was curled up on. There were no more blankets for Reese and I so we only had each other's body heat to keep ourselves warm. It gave me more of a reason to curl up against his side. I began to shiver and all of my limbs felt heavy. I was so tired. My whole life, I went to bed at around 10PM each night and rose around 6AM. I had the same bedtime day in and day out and the same rising time. Once in a while my mind would be racing too much to actually fall asleep at 10PM but after a while of laying in the pitch black with no stimulation, sleep always eventually found me. I had no idea what time it was, but hours had definitely passed since 10PM when I was supposed to have gone to sleep. In those few hours, I had changed my life forever, and the lives of those I loved.

Reese's fingers gently ran through my semi-tangled hair. The gesture only served to bring my attention to the dull sting of the cuts on my own fingertips. My lids, finally too heavy to keep steadily open, drooped once more. I jerked and forced them to widen again but an instant later they were drooping as if weights or anchors were dragging them down.

"Why don't you get some sleep. I'll look after you and the little girl," Reese offered and I immediately accepted. I was too tired to reason with myself that he must be just as tired as I was if not even more-so, or that if we failed to keep an eye on the girl, the Order might be unwilling to save our parents. Sleep was pulling at my weakened body and mind and I didn't bother to fight it. The instant I gave in, sleep overcame me.

As dreams often do, the one that currently captured my (un)consciousness seemed linear at the time I was experiencing it but the moment I woke up I realized that the things that happened made little sense to the logical mind.

In my dream, I was sitting on the couch in the living room of my barracks and Grandpa Logan was in his favorite chair. Somehow this didn't feel or seem odd despite the fact that he had been put to sleep six years ago. His dark pupils that were nestled in the middle of the green in his eyes – the same eyes I had. They were deep, bottomless, sad and defeated; two little black holes that lead to an unknown abyss. Something about their endlessness made me shudder with fear and I couldn't articulate why. The room was illuminated with a red glow which at the time seemed completely normal, although when I looked back on it after waking, it filled me with a foreboding, cold sense of dread.

"I'm sorry that I can't tell you everything," Grandpa said to me in a forlorn tone. I leaned forward, intrigued and wanting to waltz with the knowledge he had that was just beyond the reach of my fingertips despite the sinking feeling in the pit of my stomach that was trying to warn me I would be waltzing with something I was not yet prepared to face, and it would overpower and overwhelm me.

"Tell me what you can. I'll figure out the rest on my own," I coaxed him stubbornly despite the fact that I knew my words were too big for my britches. Grandpa rubbed his eyes with the backs of his hands only seconds before his whole body tensed. I bit my lower lip as concern began to flood my insides. "Grandpa, are you okay?" He didn't answer me right away but when he opened his eyes again, the whites had turned to a dark yellow. I didn't want to be rude but I had to look away. It was a sickening sign of decay. I was a horrible person to feel disgusted by my own grandfather.

"I'm tired, Ruby. You know I've been gone a long time." I *did* know. The scene of flatfoots dragging him away and me leaping after Grandpa demanding they give him back was never anything but fresh on the surface of my memory no matter how many years had passed. I knew Grandpa was dead, yet I didn't question his presence right now nor did I wonder how he could be here, talking to me. It seemed and felt reasonable. "You want answers that I don't have." He was right and wrong at the same time. I wanted answers, that was true, but I lacked the confidence to believe I could handle them. I also didn't believe Grandpa didn't have them.

"I'm in trouble, Grandpa. So are Mom and Dad." Wait, what kind of trouble were we all in, though? It was crystal clear knowledge and yet the 'why' kept evading me, like bubbles on the surface of water and the moment I tried to grasp them, they popped. "Didn't you know this would eventually happen? We have to save them!" Wait, weren't they in their bed? I suddenly realized they weren't, but then where were they? The red illumination that surrounded us intensified. Why was I back in our barracks, anyway? Wasn't I supposed to be somewhere else?

But, where?

"Ruby, you're old enough now to understand love. Love is sacrifice. That's what I tried to teach you through my stories. I wasn't just telling you about Earth B-I in order to make you wish you were there, I was telling you that if my father, your great-grandfather hadn't sacrificed himself so I could make it to the shore from our boat the day of the invasion, I wouldn't have survived and you wouldn't exist. Love has a ripple effect. When you sacrifice for someone you love, they will sacrifice for someone they love and that's how families survive and prevail in war. And Ruby, we *are* at war. We've been at war for a long time now and people just don't realize it. Sometimes, sacrifice is giving up your life for someone you love, and sometimes it's allowing someone else to give up their life because they love you.

Do you understand?" I understood nothing. What did love and sacrifice have to do with anything? How were we at war? War was a concept lost to us when we lost our planet. War existed in a time where many cultures lived across the span of many continents, and we went to war to fight for rights to the land or to gain freedom from one country lording over another. All that was left of humanity now, that we knew of or concerned ourselves with, was The Complex and those of us that lived in it. With one culture and one government, how could war exist?

Yet even as those skeptical thoughts raced through my mind I knew that I was wrong. There were vital facts that I was somehow missing, facts I knew, but I couldn't grasp them because they were swimming around in circles like panicked goldfish. They had nowhere to escape to, but they were still trying to get away.

Just like me.

My frustration intensified. I pressed my palms down against my knees. "Grandpa, who is giving up their life and why? Is this about you being taken? You didn't give up your life, it was **stolen** from you." It occurred to me in that moment that all of us in The Complex were not, in fact, united. One government ruled us but I hated them for their cruelty and their insistence that I was not an individual with rights and freedom. I had no freedom. I was not allowed to be an individual. I was being forced into a marriage that love had nothing to do with. I would then be forced to bear a child even though I did not yet know if I wanted to be a mother. I would die in The Complex the same way I was born into it, doomed and soon after, dismissed.

Again, something pecked at the back of my mind

193

that was trying to remind me these things were no longer true. But how could they not be?

The red intensified even more.

"So, who is sacrificing themselves, now?" I found myself asking despite the fact that I still wasn't quite sure what was happening around me or why. Grandpa leaned forward. The sound of marching footsteps began to echo in the distance.

"That's up to you." Up to me? How was it up to me? Was I supposed to sacrifice myself for something, and if so, to whom, and why?

The footsteps grew louder, so loud that I couldn't dismiss them as background noise anymore. The floor beneath my feet began to vibrate. I gripped the side of the couch with my fingers and suddenly, a stream of flatfoots burst through our door. Terror exploded inside of me. My lips parted and I shrieked while trying to scramble to my feet. They didn't even glance at me. They reached their elongated, green monster-fingers toward my grandfather and they yanked him out of his chair. "NO!" I screamed and scrambled forward but my feet slipped on the ground. I flailed to try and keep my balance. "DON'T TAKE HIM!" My demand affected nothing. They began to drag him toward the door. My shoes could not seem to grip the floor. I slipped and slid forward as much as I could and desperately tried to reach for him. "LEAVE HIM ALONE, YOU BASTARDS! TAKE ME INSTEAD!" This *couldn't* be happening, not again! They couldn't be taking him away **again**! Grandpa turned his head around over his shoulder as far as his neck would allow but his eyes immediately forced my body to freeze. They were now a deep, putrid yellow with red and blue veins weaving through them like enlarged DNA strands. Only then did it hit me that he was really dead. He had been dead for six years and he shouldn't have been in my living room at all.

The flatfoots, who wouldn't have allowed me to speak to them that way in the real world, ignored my insolence and slammed the door behind them. The very next instant, my body was set free from whatever bizarre force had kept me from coordination. I rushed to the door and tore it open but they were gone without a sight or sound. No Grandpa Logan. No flatfoots. I fell to my knees as utter defeat and infuriation washed over me like a blanket of suffocation. Hate boiled up inside of me like a tornado, twisting and turning as it started in my gut, then reached my heart with its icicles and finally entered my mind, making me wish horrible, torturous things on the devious monsters that comprised of our government and everyone involved with them.

Wake up

Something echoed in my mind.

Ruby, wake up.

"Ruby, wake up." The echo was clearer now and I recognized the voice. The red hot room around me turned to fuzz and began to dissolve. "Ruby?"

I groaned as my consciousness slowly and regrettably seeped back into the waking world. The dream around me completely faded and all I saw was black. Begrudgingly, I opened my eyes and shifted, grateful that I could still feel the warmth of Reese by my side. When I glanced at him he curled the corners of his lips upward and smiled at me softly before his doe-brown eyes shifted. I followed his gaze and watched the little girl. She was curled up in the fetal position, clutching her stick-like legs and twitching in her sleep. I wanted to wake her from whatever frightening nightmare she must be having but the tiny hairs that

195

stood up on the back of my neck alerted me to the presence of others.

I snapped my eyes upward and swept my gaze from side to side. Four members of the Order had surrounded us. I pushed my hand against the ground and sat up, shaking my head a bit to toss away the grogginess that was trying to tempt me into more sleep. The hand lamps on the ground illuminated the four faces in an orangey glow. Their serious and tense expressions silently let me know that going back to sleep at the moment probably wasn't an option. I decided against saving the little girl from her probable nightmare because for that poor frightened confused child, reality was probably even more terrifying than anything her dreams could conjure up.

"We've made a decision," Evon stated begrudgingly. He stepped forward. "Ruby, the flatfoot that is assigned to guard your barracks was informed yesterday evening while the coded papers were dropped off that someone would be returning to pick them up at 8AM. That's only a few hours from now." My eyes widened. How could that have only been last night? My father receiving those papers felt like a lifetime ago. "We'll be sending Fawke to pick them up; he's the same man that originally dropped them off. He'll enquire with the guard when the GP is scheduled to return to your barracks. Your parents will at least be safe up until that point. We will then intercept the GP before his scheduled visit." Evon paused and glanced behind him at the others before fixating his gaze back on me. "Ruby, you need to understand something before we go any further. There's no safe way to go about any of this. Beyond that, there's no way to cover this up. Even if we succeed in warning your parents in time and even if we manage to

196

coordinate getting them to a rendezvous point, our very best case scenario will be that, as far as The Complex will know, you and your parents simply disappeared, and obviously, there's no such thing as people in The Complex simply disappearing." My throat tightened and my eyes shifted helplessly toward Reese. Evon was getting at something and that something had formed into a metal ball that was pressing down on my stomach making it churn in painful protest. "This rescue operation, even if successful, will end the facade of all of us living an ignorant and obedient life under the rule of Doctrine. The government will know with certainty that somewhere in The Complex, traitors who know more than they want us to know are hiding in wait to expose the truth."

Traitors? Is that what the Order was? Is that what I was? Why did that word bring with it such a strong sense of deja-vous that didn't seem to easily connect back to a classroom lesson?

War. Grandpa Logan?

Bits and pieces of my dream flashed in short bursts just behind my eyes. I recalled talking with Grandpa. He told me that we were at war. I remember that I hadn't understood what he was talking about, but now I did. The word 'traitors' had been the trigger I needed.

All of this wasn't happening because of the girl, this was happening because of *me*. The Order could have made sure the little girl was never discovered by the government. They could have bided their time and found the truth when they were ready, without putting others in unnecessary danger. Evon was telling me, right here and right now, that I was the catalyst to a war. War meant countless lives lost, far more than just my parents.

I couldn't be a hero even if I wanted to. I could tell the Order to call off the rescue mission but I knew it wouldn't solve the problem. I created inevitable war the moment I crawled into the air vent and escaped while under confinement. I alone, and my naïve, ill-thought desperation to be with Reese again was about to change and endanger the lives of every single human being in The Complex.

Bile quickly boiled up inside of my stomach like a liquid hurricane. Acid and bits of undigested crackers raced up my esophagus, scalding it with a hot burn before pooling out of my mouth like a projectile river. I heard people around me jump backward before the chunky mixture splattered down onto the floor and began to cascade outward. The last of the vile concoction dribbled down my chin and I was so horrified by my emotions that I barely felt Reese gently wiping it off. "But - what if GP Nolan doesn't want to help us? What if he tells the flatfoots?" I managed to choke out as my lurching stomach, unconvinced of its new emptiness, still tried to expel contents that no longer existed.

"We have something he wants; something he *needs*. We're prepared to offer it to him in exchange for his cooperation.

"We will instruct him to inform the guards that he has identified your father's nasopharyngitis strain as a new mutation of a recently and previously identified virus in a nearby division. He will then request to re-examine your family without the government's direct presence, for their own safety." I doubted the guards would persist. When it came to viruses and the fear of catching them, people always listened to a GP's instructions. Well, almost always. I was the idiotic exception. "He will assure your parents that you are with the Order and you are safe. He'll instruct them to leave their barracks at the precise time they would normally leave for work. Instead, though, they will come directly here.

"He'll report to the flatfoot that your parents are cleared for work, but he'd like you to stay home one more day because you showed a possible symptom of potentially coming down with the virus. They won't expect to see you emerge from your barracks."

I bit my lower lip. This was *not* an iron-clad plan. What if my parents were still monitored even after GP Nolan cleared them? What if the flatfoot demanded to see me? This plan had only a small chance at success, not a guarantee. There were too many ifs, ands and buts. Even I could see that.

"But my mom, she doesn't know about any of this. The Order..."

"It will be your father's responsibility to enlist her immediate cooperation. Her life will depend on it."

"What if the GP can't be bribed? What if he tells the flatfoot, instead? What if the guards won't let him examine my parents alone? What if the guards try to follow them when they supposedly leave for work?" He sighed.

"Ruby, let me remind you again that this is risky and there are no guarantees. This plan is far from perfect, but it's the best plan of action we have." Evon confirmed my fears and it was the opposite of comforting. I wanted more answers. I wanted the Order to be prepared for the what-if's. I wanted them to have a solid, branched out plan of action for all of the variables that could go wrong. I wanted them to fix the mistakes I made, mistakes that had put my parents in immediate danger in the first place.

"What about Reese's parents... how will you warn them? And Sukie's family?"

Evon sighed. "For Gaia and Thao, there's only one of two possibilities. They are either not under suspicion of anything yet, or they have already been put to sleep. And I'll be frank with you, with Reese's crimes against Doctrine.." Evon did not need to finish that sentence. Reese's hand tightened over my own. My stomach lurched again but although my shoulders were thrown forward, I dry-heaved and nothing more spilled out of me. I slumped against Reese's side, weak and defeated. "After we deal with the GP, we'll pay their barracks a discreet visit and find out. We'll do our best to warn them and bring them here, but," Evon paused. I narrowed my eyes.

"But what?" Reese joined in the conversation with an impatient, frightened tone as he sat up a bit straighter.

"If they've already been taken, there won't be anything we can do." I couldn't look at Reese right now. I couldn't allow my eyes to shift in his direction because I didn't deserve to see his face. This was all my fault. If his family had been put to sleep, their lives would weigh on my shoulders. How would Reese ever look at me again? I had just found love, literally hours ago – and now it would be spoiled forever and always out of my reach. Reese's resentment of me would grow deeper and deeper every passing day until he couldn't even stand to be around me or acknowledge my existence.

Lives could be lost and I was sitting here mourning the fact that I could lose my one chance at love. I was a truly terrible, selfish person. I deserved every bit of resentment coming my way. I deserved to be punished for the lives that were going to be lost because of the things I had done.

"Do you have any more questions?" Evon asked me with a bit of sarcasm in his tone. I dug my fingernails into my knee.

"Just one. What are you offering GP Nolan that will convince him to go against Doctrine?" Evon paused before responding.

"An answer to a question that has plagued him for many years." When he didn't continue right away, I pressed my lips together with impatience. No one just casually asked another to go against Doctrine and deceive a flatfoot. We all knew what that kind of blatant insolence resulted in; being put to sleep. Convincing someone to risk their lives would take more than a simple bribe.

"What question?" Evon licked his lips.

"He's been wondering what happened to someone he was once close to. Someone that was carrying his child. Someone that wasn't his wife."

My blood ran cold. It was as if it literally froze in my veins and simply refused to circulate further. A shudder ran all the way down my spine and pooled into a deep pit of dread at the base of it. *What was he saying?*

"He fathered someone's child? *He had a secret lover...?*" The last five words passed through my lips as a whisper of realization. Despite my own very recent acceptance of falling in love against Doctrine, I had never really stopped to think about how many other people in The Complex might also have secret lovers. I couldn't possibly be the only person who fell in love with someone they weren't mated with. "What if the government already saw Reese and I sneaking into the passageway yesterday?" Evon stared at me with a furrowed brow, then a relaxed brow as if he couldn't decide whether to be disgusted by me or empathetic toward me.

"Then, it will be too late." I shouldn't have asked. I shouldn't have considered that. But, I had to, didn't I? I couldn't just expect everything to turn out okay, because it wasn't going to. Even if a miracle happened for Reese and I and all four of our parents were alive and brought to safety, we could never go back. My mom's world was about to crash down on her just like my own had, but at least I had chosen this for myself because my old life wasn't what I wanted. My mom was about to be forced into this fear and uncertainty against her will.

I rested my head back down on Reese's shoulder. I knew it was temporary. I knew that if things didn't go well with the Order's plan, there would be no more love between us and these two tiny days where my heart finally felt free to connect with his would be the only glimpse I ever had of happiness.

How ironic that I even considered the word 'happiness' in the midst of all of this fear and turmoil to be a part of my life. Everything had changed when Reese sneaked me into the passageway. Some of those changes were obvious; finding the little girl, realizing the government was keeping things from us, discovering my dad was a part of this Order and then putting my entire family's life at risk because I wanted to save Reese – but some changes were internal, too. I had resented the government from a very early age, and then even more-so when I had watched them drag my grandfather away but to have those hidden questions in the back of my mind confirmed – to know with certainty that our meaningless lives shut away in The Complex didn't have to be this way, it was like putting a stick of dynamite right on the balancing-middle of a teeter-totter. Both ends would be blasted to bits, the fire-cracker side of me that was filled with resolve and fury, and the tired, overwhelmed, regretful side of me that wished I could have been a different person from the day I was born. If I had never questioned Doctrine and The Complex, I might have lived out my lie of a life without knowing it was a lie like most others seemed to. Maybe living a lie was better than getting everyone you loved killed.

Evon turned around and walked away from me without another word. The others shifted their weight uncomfortably. I couldn't blame them for resenting me. I barely knew anything about the Order but I could tell they were smart, organized and careful. Now they were about to take incredible risks and ruin their secrecy because I had put my parents lives in danger. Even if they couldn't save them, the government will still know they were being defied. All of these people probably had families that were also going to be at risk.

Who was going to save them?

After the others awkwardly walked away I gently tugged on Reese's sleeve. He turned his head toward me and cast his eyes gently on my face. Why did he still look at me with such softness? He should hate me, too. I glanced away, but I had to voice my concerns. "Reese, why are they doing this for us? Why are they willing to risk their own families' lives for our parents?" Reese tilted his head ever so slightly in thought.

"Maybe your father has something they need or knows something vital, an item or a piece of knowledge that would be dangerous in the wrong hands. That would give him value, it would be worth it for them to risk a lot to try and save him." Maybe Reese was right. My father wasn't the leader but he was obviously an important member of the Order. "My parents though," Reese tightened his face. "I don't think the Order will be making it a priority to save them. If they've been taken, it's my fault." *His* fault?

"Reese, no!" I hissed. I ignored my throbbing leg as I scrambled to sit up straighter so I could look him in the eyes. "It's *my* fault, not yours! *I* did all of this when I escaped. People might die because of *me*." I closed my burning eyes and didn't even bother to try and wipe the salty tears that started pooling out from the bottoms of my lids. "Even if my parents, and yours get to safety, people are still going to die." Reese's arms curled around me and tugged me closer to him. My body tensed. I didn't want – no, I didn't *deserve* his comfort. I shouldn't be treated with kindness, I should be spat on.

"Listen to me. You did **not** cause this. The government has been lying to us for who knows how long. We can live on Earth's surface but they've been keeping us down here for who knows what reason! They put people to sleep who aren't sick all the time. We've been played for fools our whole lives and when you engineer a lie this big, the truth is bound to come out eventually. You and I are just," Reese paused and his fingers pressed into the small of my back. "in the middle of the explosion of truth. We're caught in the landslide of it and we just have to hold on and see where it takes us." I wanted to believe Reese. I didn't know if he honestly believed his own words or if he was only trying to convince himself that there was a valid reason not to hate me. Even if the comfort he gave to me, the comfort we gave to each other, was going to fall apart in a sea of darkness, I still needed it right now.

"What if it drowns us?" Reese rolled his

shoulders back.

"Then it does. At least no more generations will have to grow up like we did." Reese would sacrifice himself for the future lives of others. I knew his words were honest, I could hear it in his tone and feel it in his touch. He was selfless, brave, and he loved with his whole heart. He refused to let the possible consequences of his selflessness hold him back. Reese was everything that I was not. I didn't deserve him but I still wanted him. I wasn't as good as him, but I still needed him. If he wanted to love me I would let him for the time being because I knew one day he would see me for the weak, selfish person I truly was. If the world was going to crumble around us, I wanted to hold on to love for as long as I could. Right now, it was all I had left.

Chapter 10

Exhaustion was still weighing down both my body and mind but sleep refused to come back to me. There were no programmed lights in this dank, chilled room and no way to gauge when morning was upon us. Every second felt like it stretched on forever, and at the same time ticked by far too quickly. I imagined it was like being stuck in a wormhole. I wanted my parents rescued but I also dreaded the mission with such an intense ferocity that every time I thought about it, a sinking sensation whirled through the air and caused me to fear losing consciousness. I closed my eyes and practiced *stillness*; something we learned a few years ago in the classroom that had to do with keeping our minds isolated to only the present moment; thinking of nothing in the past and nothing in the future. I was never good at this practice because I could never seem to stop myself from asking questions, but right now, leaning up against Reese's warm body and feeling his chest rise and fall with his slow and steady breaths, I was briefly at peace. One of his hands rested on my forearm. The top of my head was safely tucked under his chin. I had imagined moments like these in forbidden secrecy for so long and despite the horrible choices I had quite recently made and the deadly unknown that stretched out ahead of us, finally being free to express my feelings for Reese felt just like I'd dreamed. I didn't have to use words and neither did he. Our connection reached beyond the barriers of human language and beyond the obligation of doctrine.

A rustling sound caused me to turn my head as my muscles stiffened. The little girl was stirring. I didn't want to move or leave the comfort of my *stillness* but I forced one of my hands to press against the ground so I could lift my upper body from Reese's. I bit my lower lip as I watched her scramble into a sitting position. Immediately, her tiny little legs folded and curled to her chest. Her twig-arms encircled her knees. She sniffled, then covered her nose and mouth with her hands as she sneezed.

If this child hadn't brought a virus into The Complex, would we all still be in the same predicament? What an idiotic question. Things were unravelling because we had been lied to, and eventually the fabric of any and all lies always unraveled. Her large blue eyes, seemingly too big for her head almost in a cartoon-like fashion, darted toward Reese and I with fear. My heart sank in my chest. She didn't know she was lucky. She didn't know that if the government found her before the Order did, they probably would have either tortured her, or put her to sleep. "Please let me go," she finally spoke in a raspy, frightened whisper as she shifted her eyes to me and rested her gaze on my features. For a fraction of a second, the fact that she spoke for the first time filled me with joy and hope but realizing she viewed us as her captors caused my heart to sink even more.

I knew it, I knew she understood my words! This proves it, she's not feral! She's not a monster.

"I don't want to die." The little girl could definitely speak, but her words crept under my skin and lit a fire under the heavy ball of guilt rolling around in my stomach. I bit my lower lip and reached for Reese's hand. How was I supposed to explain to her that she was safe here, or, at least as safe as the rest of us?

"I'm sorry," I whispered and closed my eyes for a moment. Reese squeezed my hand and I forced my eyes open again. He was trusting - maybe even expecting - m

208

to somehow sooth her. My throat tightened. "It's not what you think." Her expression of terror did not change. "We're not going to hurt you. We're trying to protect you." Her large eyes narrowed. She thought I was lying to her. "This place, it's called The Complex. I was born down here just over sixteen years ago and I've lived here my whole life. I was told things – lead to believe things – that aren't true, and I know that because you're real and you're here with us right now." I took a deep breath and kept my voice low. "I've never been allowed to go above ground. All of us down here, we've been told that after the invasion, Earth was decimated – um, ruined. The government told us that the air above wasn't even breathable and the only way anyone or anything could have survived on the surface was by adapting and mutating into savage monsters." The last word I spoke caused the girl to tighten her arms even more around her legs. She was afraid of the word *monster.*

"You're lying!" The child suddenly spat at me with an accusing tone. "*You're* the monsters!" I sat back with shock and glanced toward Reese helplessly. I understood that the girl didn't realize we were trying to keep her safe but the intensity of her words made me feel like there was more behind them than just her present perception of captivity.

"What do you mean?" I asked fearfully because I wasn't sure I was prepared to hear the answer. The depths of the government's lies and manipulations seemed to have no end. "Why do you think we're monsters?" The child narrowed her eyes even more. It wasn't just anger that was pulling her skin tightly across her cheekbones or forcing air to enter and exit her lungs only through her nose. She was filled with hate. I

209

recognized it because I was all too familiar with it myself.

"You killed my daddy." I immediately shrank back as if her words were a fist that was flying toward my face. I didn't fully understand her words but I knew they meant something important, something serious, something that would cause me to question my assumption of who the bad guys really were.

"W-what do you mean," I asked hesitantly, cautiously. "Are you really from," I paused and swallowed past a constricting lump in my throat. "*up there*?" I paused again. "Are there others? Do you have family? Do other people really live on the surface?" I knew I was pushing her too far, too fast but words were spilling out of my mouth quicker than I could control them. The girl fixated her hateful gaze back on my face. Her small fingers curled into her palm. My heart sank even deeper into my chest cavity. I wanted to reach out and embrace this little girl because we were the same; both of us lost in the undertow of a giant wave receding to reveal a shore we didn't even know existed. I wanted to tell her that everything was going to be okay. I yearned to protect her. My previous distrust of her identity and motives melted away like candle wax and all I wanted was to be someone that she could trust, someone that would never lie to her; someone that would make sure no harm ever came her way.

I had no actual siblings. It was rare that anyone in The Complex did because most mated couples were only allowed one child in order to minimize cross-breeding in future generations. The only exception was if the genes of a mated couple were especially elite, but I had no idea what that even meant. Still, looking at this frightened child, I felt protective of her the way that I imagined an older sister might. Her lower lip began to tremble. I wanted to embrace her now more than ever, but I knew that would frighten her even more. It wasn't right. A small child should not have to cling to her own frail body for comfort.

Why had the little girl accused the Order of killing her father? Where was her father from? Had he been a citizen down here – or, was he from *up there?* I drew in a deep breath. I couldn't jump to conclusions. Even if the little girl had been *up there*, that didn't mean that there were others. Maybe she was a secret child, like the girl who asked Koi to save her from the government's wrath because she had become pregnant by being with a lover she was not matched with by Doctrine? That could also explain why she had no ID chip in her wrist.

Maybe the little girl's family were rebels like the Order, but maybe her family didn't know about the Order and attempted to explore the surface on their own. There were so many possibilities, but all of them still meant the little girl wasn't safe from the government. She didn't feel safe with us, either. What was I supposed to do?

"How old are you, sweet heart?" I asked cautiously as I scooted up against Reese again. Her accusing glare still did not falter. She pressed her lips together, probably fearing she had already said too much to these strange, untrustworthy people that were holding her captive and then trying to tell her that they were trying to keep her safe. We must seem awfully cruel to her, as if we were messing with her mind. No wonder she remained terrified.

The girl was so small and her limbs seemed so delicate, to the point of appearing malnourished. I could not guess her age on my own. By her body only I would not think her to be more than six, but her eyes, her facial expressions, they all made her appear older.

"What do you eat?" I kept gently trying. If she was indeed from the surface, was she really a – a cannibal? Did she eat other people to survive? Even if she did, it didn't seem like she got to eat very often.

The child finally ripped her hateful blue eyes away from my face. I felt immediate relief. The intensity of her anger had begun to feel like a pile of bricks were slowly being stacked on top of my shoulders.

"What about your mom?" Reese tried asking her softly. "Is she still alive?" The girl's face, which had started to relax, immediately tightened up with tense, defensive hatred again and this time she zeroed in on Reese. "How do you live? Where do you live? Do you have a home? Do you really not know what this place is?" She continued to glare at him the same way she had spat her angry eyes upon me only minutes before.

I held up my palm toward Reese to signal him to stop. The little girl wasn't ready. She didn't trust us. She wasn't going to talk unless we could somehow convince her that we were not a threat.

The child didn't respond to Reese, but finally, the defensive fear in her eyes began to wane and the tightness of her cheeks relaxed a bit. I knew that didn't mean she had suddenly decided to trust us. Fear was exhausting and all-consuming, her mind was probably trying to protect her.

I can't let this girl turn out like my mom. I can't let her disappear inside of herself.

This unique child may not trust the Order, but if had any chance at all at getting through to her, it was now, when her fear was exhausting her mind. "I know we seem scary to you, but we're scared too. Reese and I, we're hiding here because there are bad people that want to hurt us. We don't want them to hurt you, either. We want to get you home, okay? We want to help, but we can't unless you tell us where home is.

"I know you don't want to right now, and that's okay. I'm not going to make you tell me anything, okay? But I want to prove to you that you can trust me. I'm going to work at it, okay? I'm going to take care of you and you have my word, my PROMISE, that no matter what, I'll get you home."

My eyes blurred as I spoke and I wasn't even sure where my words came from. I had spent the past few days lost in a sea of fear, wallowing in my naïve idiocy and incredible skill of messing everything up. But every word I spoke to this frightened child was spoken from honesty, from a determined place in my heart that I hadn't even been aware of prior. I was compelled to protect her, to help her, to sooth her fear by being someone she could depend and rely on. Her well-being from moment to moment suddenly mattered more to me than the fact that she potentially had answers to questions that had plagued me, and others, throughout our whole lives.

The girl curled her arms around her tiny body and shivered. "I'm cold," she whispered. "I need my suit." I was afraid to ask her if the Order had forced her to change out of that strange, puffy covering I first saw her in, and I was afraid to ask them why. With a soft sigh, I reached for the woven blanket underneath me.

"I'm sorry, I don't know where your suit is," I told her honestly. I leaned forward and gently wrapped the blanket around the girl's shoulders. At first she jerked away from me, but her eyes finally softened. She remained still as I let go of the blanket after it draped over her, but then her small hands reached out and tugged it tighter across her petite frame.

I folded my legs under the rest of my body in what Grandpa Logan used to call *Indian Style*. Without the blanket for myself, the cement under my bum felt cool but the little girl had stopped visibly shivering and that made giving up my blanket well worth my own minor discomfort. I lowered my eyes and let my hands fall into my lap. I wanted to reach for this tiny human and take her into my arms.

The little girl shifted her gaze over to me once more. The vulnerable child underneath the angry exterior shined through like a blinding light. Her lower lip trembled and her eyes blurred. As I watched the thick layer of fear and suspicion melt off of her as loneliness took over as her dominant emotion, I saw myself in her more than I cared to admit. I regarded her as well but I resisted the urge to reach for her in case found the gesture threatening. I rested my head on Reese's shoulder. He sighed and curled an arm around my torso. I understood what was going through his mind just by his gentle need to keep me close. He was scared, too. He needed me in the same way that I needed him. In the middle of the tornado that was tearing through our once stationary lives, I had something to be grateful for. I had love.

"I want my mom," The girl whimpered with a trembling tongue. The tears that had begun to blur in her eyes started to fall down her cheeks in large drops. She made no move to wipe them off and as I watched her, she was me all over again.

My chin trembled. "I know," I whispered softly. " want my mom, too." The girl raised her eyes toward my face and for the first time, allowed me to see into them, past them, through them. She *finally* believed me. She finally understood that I wasn't going to hurt her. Relief flowed through my body like a river and I felt Reese's arm around me tighten. He saw the shift in her, too. He knew she was starting to trust us.

The shuffling sound of shoes against the cement caused me to raise my head instantly. My body, still resting against Reese's, tensed and prepared itself to lurch forward if necessary to protect the child. Three men, led by Zane, stepped into the reach of the light from our hand-lamps. I relaxed a bit but I kept my eyes on them steadily, unafraid to let them know I was wary but willing to listen. "It's time," Evon spoke as he took another step forward. "I wanted to remind you that we can't make any promises, and from here on out, the probability that we will be heading into a war is," he paused. "an inevitability." He had already mentioned all of these things.

"We know the air above us is breathable," Reese spoke up, to my surprise. "If the mission is successful, why don't we just go up there before the government can hunt us down?" Zane shifted his gaze. I furrowed my brow. Reese's question was not only entirely valid, but it seemed like a viable way to continue to stay alive. It seemed ludicrous to even consider staying down here in the Complex and playing hide-and-seek until we were all caught and put to sleep if survival above was possible.

"We don't know enough about what's up there to risk it yet." His answer was flimsy. I wasn't buying into it. I slowly inched a bit closer to the girl. Reese climbed to his feet to face Zane.

"You said the air was breathable *up there*, which means survival is possible. But you're telling me that you aren't willing to lead us to safety *up there* just because you're afraid?" Zane shifted his weight, but Evon took another step toward Reese and arched his back in a menacing haunch. My protective instincts rushed through my blood. I dragged my aching leg under me and rose to my feet.

"I'm afraid too," I admitted. "I've been scared out of my mind for the last two days. Every single thing I believed about why our lives are the way they are has been a *lie*. I watched the flatfoots drag my grandfather, a healthy, sound of mind sixty year old man, out of our barracks when I was only ten. I knew I was never going to see him again. I never got the chance to know my grandmother because she died in an accident, or so we were told but it might not have been an accident. I've never even seen the sky! And why? Why are they LYING to us?" Reese's hand curled around my shoulder but his touch offered minimal comfort to the repeated question I couldn't stop asking despite knowing that right now I had no way of finding an answer to. I lowered my head and tried to stop my body from trembling. A deep breath in filled my lungs. I drew my shoulders back. "If you succeed in saving the lives of my parents, the least we can do is try to maintain those lives by leaving this prison." There, I said it out. I called The Complex what it truly was; a **prison**. I learned about prisons in the classroom. Before The Complex and its much simpler method of dealing with people who broke Doctrine by putting them to sleep, countries would punish "law breakers" by confining them in small spaces for years at a time. A more accurate description for what has been happening to us our whole lives didn't exist. We were in a prison. We were prisoners who had committed no crime, and I wanted to be free.

Zane continued to shift his weight from foot to foot. There was something he wasn't telling us. I moved closer to the girl once more and a quick glance behind my shoulder told me that the calm that had slowly come over her with Reese and I was completely eradicated. Her eyes bulged, her body shivered and her breathing was short and labored. "After my parents are rescued," I refused to say *if.* I refused to let the Order think that they had a choice in the matter, or that they didn't have to lay down their lives for my parents. They might be keeping even more secrets, maybe bad secrets, but I trusted that my father wasn't. I trusted that as far as his involvement in the Order, his heart was in the right place. "I want to know that we will do everything we can for the right to LIVE. I want to know why you hesitate to bring us *up there* to safety.

"If you **don't** rescue my parents, I will assume you left them to die and if that happens... you will pay. Do you understand me?"

I had no idea who this person was that was speaking with my mouth. I had never even imagined confronting someone like this before, much less an adult; my elder. I was the fearful one. I was the one with questions and dreams, but also frustrations and the desire to protect others even when I no knowledge with which to do so. I was the one who clung to Reese ever since we were reunited and I had hated myself for my stupidity and my weakness. Yet here I was, fixating my bright green gaze on the men before me with challenging eyes, spitting forceful words from between my lips, and even making threats that I felt within every ber of my being I would hold in truth. I wasn't me anymore. All of my failures over the last few days didn't matter. The danger I had put others in because of my naïve desire to be a hero, the selfishness in which I based my choices off of – all of that was gone, in the past, unchangeable and useless to dwell on. Right now, I didn't trust most of the members of the Order. Right now, a scared little girl separated from her family and wanting to find her mother needed me. The desire to protect an innocent person was different than my past desire to find Reese. That desire was rooted in selfishness even if hadn't wanted to admit it at the time. This was rooted in selflessness. This child deserved to be reunited with her mother. Every single person stuck in The Complex being fed a lie deserved freedom. We deserved to breathe real, fresh air. We deserved to look up at the night sky and see the stars for the first time. We deserved to have all of the questions we were too afraid to ask, answered. If I had to make demands, if I had to stop relying on others, if I had to find my own way no matter how many times I stumbled, I would do so. I wanted Reese by my side, always, but I had to stop leaning on him. I had to grow up. I had to be brave. I had to stop daydreaming about being a hero and learn how to actually be one.

"I understand you, Ruby. We will either be back with your parents, or," Zane paused. He actually paused because he realized I was going to accept nothing less. My demands and my determination actually had an impact. With only a small nod of acknowledgment to replace words, he turned his back on me and walked back off into the darkness. Evon's gaze lingered and his eyes screamed with resentment. He blamed me for setting frightening, life-changing events in motion that he was not ready to face. I refrained from reminding him that he was in the Order on a voluntary basis, one would assume, and that uncovering the truth was what the Order was supposed to be all about. Instead I simply remained silent and met his gaze. Finally he turned and followed his leader. Zane was the braver one by far, but would Evon continue to follow him into the unknown when it was clear he wasn't ready?

None of us were ready, but that didn't matter. Changes happened with or without our permission.

Did I trust the Order to rescue my parents? Fear wanted to quickly rush in and take over my pride when I realized I wasn't sure, but I knew that I did not have the means, ability, or knowledge at this time to assist them. My rash choice to try and "rescue" Reese had only served to put others in danger so I couldn't take matters into my own hands again. Even if I didn't trust these strangers, I trusted my dad. I closed my eyes and forced myself to trust that he got the note I left him in our bathroom before I crawled into the vent. I knew that I had to trust him to know what to do. I had to trust him to keep himself and my mom alive. Right now, the best thing to do was stay put, wait, and gather as much knowledge as I could about the outside world. I had to keep working to gain the little girl's trust because she came from *somewhere*, she had answers that we might need in order to preserve our lives. But I knew I couldn't force those answers out of her, she had give them willingly. She had to trust me – trust us – or we would never be able to get her back home, wherever home was. She had to help us so we could help her.

Chapter 11

The silence was only broken by the shifting of bodies; my own, Reese's and occasionally the little girl's. I felt her eyes on me even when I wasn't gazing in her direction. They were heat lamps illuminating only so much space around them, warm by nature but exposing at the same time. I was positive by now that she wasn't lying to us. She was from the surface.

Did this child question her life the way I questioned my own? Was there a government on the surface, too? Did they know anything about The Complex? I wondered how different her life was from my own. Was it busy, meaningful and stimulating? How did she survive the sub-zero temperatures of the surface? What was her home like? Did she have family? No wonder she afraid to talk to us. She was just a young girl and she literally fell into an underground world she didn't even know existed, filled with people who chased her, kidnapped her, and told her that others would want to kill her. She didn't have the protection of her family or familiar companions. She started this journey of peril all alone. I could see why she would be terrified and wary to trust, but she wasn't alone anymore. She had me.

As humans, we accept the world as it is presented to us. Okay – maybe *I* didn't, but could I even take credit for my questioning ways? I understood now more than ever that maybe Grandpa Logan deliberately conditioned me to challenge my surroundings and my questions were simply flowers growing from the seeds he planted.

Or maybe they were weeds.

The faint sound of vibrational breathing quickly caused me to turn my head. I relaxed a tiny bit as I saw the back of Reese's head gently resting against the wall. Part of me wondered how he could sleep at a time like this when our entire world was crashing down around us, but I'd had my nap despite the chaos and now it was his turn. Our bodies needed sleep to function, that was a scientific fact and no amount of chaos or life-changing events could alter. I rested my head gently against the wall as well but despite the exhaustion that was still weighing down every cell in my body, I knew sleep would not come back to me. Not until I knew that my parents were safe – or dead.

The sound of shuffling feet caused my muscles to tense. I raised my brows as a familiar woman sat down quietly next to me and rested her elbows on her knees. My curiosity was immediately piqued. I waited for her to speak but her gaze was fixed forward into the darkness. Her breathing was slow and steady. Was she angry at me? Worried for her own family? Did she blame me for the unknown that now stretched out before us, and the danger? I knew that letting her sit in silence would have been the respectful thing to do. Yet, seeing her in person in this situation broke my heart and caused a whole new worry for me; it forced the reality of just how many people whose lives were at risk to punch me in the face.

"I'm sorry," I whispered in a voice so ashamed that I wasn't sure that my words would travel to the woman's ear canals. But they did, because a moment after the words left my lips her head slowly turned toward me. Her brows were not furrowed and her lips were not tight. Her hands clasped together, finger pressing against finger and her chin lowered in sadness. Sorrow seemed to be the only emotion she had room for

"It's not your fault, Ruby." Willow's mother whispered back to me. She shifted her gaze once more toward the darkness. "When you and Willow were very young, her father taught you girls to play a game called *Cats Cradle*. Do you remember?" I did. "You would thread your fingers through a long string that was tied together. One of you would reach toward the other's fingers and slide more strings over your fingers, and you would both have to be careful and concentrate or the string would get tangled and you would lose the game." She sighed softly. "Life down here is like that. We all have to be vigilant or things get tangled. You may not have fully thought through your decision to escape while under confinement, but everything that's about to happen isn't because of that. No matter what happens from here on out… you can't blame yourself. Do you understand?" My throat tightened and my eyes stung. No, I didn't understand.

Sukie was right to call me out on my bad choice, but she was wrong to minimize it and to say that it wasn't the cause of so many lives now in danger. Maybe we did live in a world of strings that got tangled if even one of us wasn't careful, but I was that *one*. I hadn't been careful.

I wanted so badly to know if Willow was in danger. Well that was a dumb thing to wonder. *Everyone* was in danger. Reese and I were now "missing" and if the government hadn't discovered that yet, I was sure they would soon find out that Willow was close to both Reese and I. Just because of that, she was in danger even if the government knew nothing of the Order, and that was a big *if* at this point. There was nothing I could do to fix it, there was no way for me to save her. I could feel her mother's sorrow as if it had elemental form; a thick vapor that surrounded her that caused the temperature to rise around us and the air to feel heavier in our lungs. That was answer enough, wasn't it?

"Her father knows about the Order," Sukie said to me as if anticipating my worries, my shame and my fear. "He knows what to do in an emergency." She had obviously intended her words to be reassuring, but her tone revealed that she couldn't even assure herself.

How was it that I hadn't even thought of Willow in all of this chaos? She had always been a loyal friend to me. She never judged me, always listened when I needed to talk and had a kind word for everyone no matter what because that's the kind of person she was; genuine and sweet down to the core of her soul. She had briefly entered my mind when I saw her mother's ID number and realized she was in the Order, but then I was focused on Reese, and on my parents, and on the little girl. I had failed Willow as a friend when she needed me the most. I had put her in danger just as much as I had put my parents in danger. I wanted to pry more but I couldn't add to Sukie's distress. I would have to bite my tongue, sit back with Reese as he had his temporary escape into slumber and wait, because every time I opened my mouth or decided on an action, life in The Complex for everyone, just like the strings in a game of Cat's Cradle, got more and more tangled.

My body became a mimic of Reese's sans the actual sleep. I glanced at the child as she curled up in the fetal position again. I narrowing my eyes at the occasional twitch of her wrist or crinkle of her nose. I was thankful that she had finally dozed off as well, I was sure her exhaustion mirrored my own but allowing herself to sleep in our presence at least communicated some level of trust, even if it was minimal and based on shaky ground.

The hand lamps flickered like candle flames. My lips tightened in slight apprehension because I knew the flickering meant they weren't going to last much longer and when they went out, we would be plummeted back into the helplessness of total darkness once more.

Don't think like that! Willow's mom is here with us and she'll make sure no harm comes our way.

Oddly, reassuring myself in that way actually helped calm my nerves. The hand lamps flickered again and it was almost comforting. I used to enjoy reading at bedtime when I was younger and if I really concentrated, I could almost convince myself I was safely tucked into my own bed once more with a school book and far off daydreams about the world above that I truly believed would never come to pass.

The flickering increased in frequency and eventually the light dimmed and then disappeared altogether. I sighed and closed my eyes. There was no point in keeping them open when there was nothing to see. Instead, I concentrated on my hearing. To my right, the slow steady breaths of Reese's deep, overdue slumber gave me comfort. To my left, the slightly more erratic breaths of Willow's mother told me that although she was trying to get some rest, there was no such thing as peaceful sleep for her, not while her family was in danger and their safety was unknown. It was a comfort to have that connection; to know that I was not alone in my fear. I understood what must be going through her mind. She was thinking, if she hadn't made the choice to join the Order, would her family be in danger right now? No wonder she didn't solely blame me – she was too busy blaming himself. That was downward spiral I was all too familiar with.

I realized in that moment that although feelings of guilt were valid and understandable, indulging in them did nothing to solve our problems regardless of how they were created. Feelings were just interpretations; they were not absolute. The truth about our very existence and why we were here had been shrouded in mystery underneath a blanket of deception for so long that we didn't even realize it was hidden in the first place. Without knowing what those truths were, I couldn't rely on my feelings and fears to decipher the lies that surrounded us. I would have to acknowledge and accept my feelings without allowing them to overwhelm my rationality.

Rather than the slow creaking of the doors to our hidden quarters slowly alerting us to someone entering or exiting, a loud bang slammed into my ear canal like a bomb as the door was thrust open. It wasn't just the sound that took my auditory sense by surprise, it was a slap of doom that echoed throughout my entire nervous system and chased away any drowsiness left in me like a predator locked onto its prey. Without consciously communicating with my brain, my limbs flailed into overdrive and I scampered to my feet like a bolt of lightning. My eyes darted in uncontrolled desperation to my right, then to my left and I quickly realized that both Reese and Sukie had the same reaction. Sukie instinctively took a few steps forward and then one to the side, standing protectively in front of me. The silhouette of Reese did the same with the little girl. My heart swelled, Willow's mother had a reason to want to feed me to the wolves rather than protect me, but I also understood that as a mother, her instincts were probably outweighing any resentment she might be harboring under her sorrow. And Reese, would he have chosen to protect me or the girl if Sukie hadn't stepped in? Why was I even thinking of such things in a moment like this? My blatant selfishness always seemed to rear its ugly head in moments of panic when I had no time to tap into my moral compass before instantly reacting.

I could still see virtually nothing in the darkness, but the sound of two systematic feet clicking, clicking, clicking in their approach told me someone knew we were here.

OH GOD IT'S A FLATFOOT! WHERE ARE MOM AND DAD THEY'RE DEAD AREN'T THEY WE'RE ALL GONNA GET PUT TO SLEEP

"I'm sorry," a deep voice begun, and then hesitated. My entire body went numb. I could no longer feel the floor underneath my feet. My calves dangerously wobbled and then buckled. I fell hard onto my knees, and although I registered on some level the pain that was shooting up my legs from my kneecaps, I was immune to it, experiencing it as something barely noticeable from a distant place. My consciousness was somehow detached from my body as my eyes, unblinking, stared into the darkness where my final doom rested probably only a few feet in front of me. I heard another click, and a moment later, a hand lamp illuminated the darkness. I was tempted to rip my eyes away because I wasn't ready to see who was standing in front of us; friend or foe. If it was a flatfoot, if we had been found and were about to be put to s- **murdered**, I wanted to look this bastard in the eye and send waves of negative energy into him with such potent ferocity that it filled him with icicles of terror. I wanted my hatred to be so mighty that it would make him tremble like an abandoned infant long after the memory of my existence was nothing but a faint, single ripple on the ocean of humanity.

The distinct but indescribable ether between utter relief and a brand new wave of fear was a strange and mystifying place to be. Before me stood not a flatfoot, but Zane, the leader of the Rhode Island branch of the Order. The forlorn look in his eyes did not appear to be good news. Already reduced to my knees, my still-numb legs sank down even more until my backside rested on my heels. "I'm sorry," he began again. "but I'm afraid I have bad news."

A single sob tore its way painfully out of my lungs. My upper body fell forward and cocooned itself around my folded legs.

Mom, Dad, I'm so sorry, I'm sorry I'm sorry oh god what am I going to do without you how could I have done this to you?

Some part of my mind registered arms curling around my back but I couldn't bring myself to respond. In order to acknowledge the gesture, I would have to force all of my consciousness to be present within my body, and not only did I not want to do that but I doubted I was capable of it in the first place. I didn't *want* to be capable. It felt like whatever it was that made me *me*; my spirit, my soul, or maybe nothing more than electric neurons firing in my physical brain, was peeling away from my body like the skin of an orange.

"Reese... I'm sorry. Flatfoots took your parents into custody under suspicion of treason." The arms around me tightened. For the briefest moment, I was able to register that the news wasn't about *my* parents. The selfish monster that comprised at least half of my personality actually allowed a moment of relief to flood my distant system. My consciousness was re-connected to my bloodstream. A moment later though, a deep wave of sorrow washed over me like a blanket of suffocation.

Reese's parents... no. No, this can't be happening!

I rose on my knees and curled my arms around Reese, allowing him to tug his trembling body against mind in desperate, needful despair. He had meant to comfort me, but in an instant the roles we needed to play in each other's lives reversed. He tucked his head and buried it against my shoulder as his sobs undulated throughout his physical form. I held on to him with even more ferocity than he was holding on to me. If his parents were taken into custody, all of the disaster I had known we were on the verge of exploding into was now officially underway. The flatfoots knew about Reese sneaking into the sealed off passageways which meant they almost certainly knew I had been doing it, too. They took Reese's parents to punish him. It wasn't fair. His parents weren't a part of the Order. They had no warning and no way to protect themselves. Reese himself hadn't known anything about the Order, he had just been sneaking into the passageways to be a teenage rebel. His actions were innocent, but now his parents were prisoners.

Well – we were *all* prisoners. We just hadn't fully realized it until now.

I felt a tap on my back. I opened my eyes just enough to turn my head and watch as the little girl sniffed back her own tears and gently curled her tiny twig-arms around Reese as best as she could in his greatest moment of despair. I was touched, unblinking at her incredibly brave act of kindness and empathy. I slowly uncurled one of my arms from Reese's trembling torso and gently drew her closer, inviting her into our comforting embrace. She was lost in an underground

229

colony that until very recently I had believed to be the only civilization of human beings left on the planet. Even if she knew nothing about us or why we were being kept down here, she had answers, or at least the potential to help us find the answers, to our desperate questions. We needed her for our survival, and she needed us for hers.

I turned my bloodshot gaze back to Zane. "And... my parents? Were you able to intercept the GP?" He took a step forward and gently pried my arm away from the little girl. He slid his fingers through mine and gave them a soft squeeze. "Things didn't go exactly as planned, but your parents are not in government custody." My heart tightened in my chest like a rubber band. "We couldn't get to the GP but when the government came for your parents, they weren't in their barracks."

They weren't there.

How could that be? Where would they have gone – and why?

Suddenly, utter gratitude for my stupid, simple life-saving action hit me like a sledgehammer and I unintentionally let my other arm slip away from Reese. It was my note, it had to have been! My brief, vague, inexplicable request scribbled on a tiny, torn piece of paper that I left behind when I crawled through the vent had to have saved their lives. As insane and inappropriate as it was, my lips parted, my head tilted back and my vocal chords released just a few high-pitched laughs of pure, complete delight. I had done everything wrong; I left my barracks on a whim with no realistic plan and no survival skills, crawled through a vent with the blind hopeless notion of magically finding Reese and 'saving' him, but the only thing I had actually accomplished was nearly getting my parents killed. The must have found the note and my dad must've gotten my mom out just in time. How had they gotten past the flatfoot guarding our barracks? Had my dad figured out why I left? Did he know I had left to try and find Reese? Who found the note, my dad or my mom? What had my dad told my mom and how did he get her to escape with him? She must be so afraid, so angry, so confused...

No. Stop.

I couldn't fret about my mother right now. Even if she was terrified, she was *alive.* I knew my dad loved her very much and I knew in my heart that he would do everything he possibly could to keep her safe.

"So – so they got out in time..." I muttered out loud. "Does my dad know where this location is? Will he know to come here?" Zane shifted his weight.

"He knows roughly where it is, but getting here will be difficult for him." Something in his tone caused my relief to dwindle.

"...Why?" He sighed. I glanced at Reese again as the child continued to cling to him. His eyes were completely glazed over with giant teardrops that streamed down his cheeks like a waterfall. He was silent. He was grieving. He was in his own world surrounded by sadness he might never overcome, and he wasn't hearing anything.

"The government's system is," Zane paused again and ran his tongue over his lower lip. "fragile. I know it's difficult to view it that way because we're conditioned from infancy to see the government as the be-all and end-all to our civilization, but when you're ruling with lies, it's like living inside of a giant house made of glass. If someone finds the bravery to throw a single rock, the whole house shatters. Do you understand what I'm saying?" No, I didn't, not really. Or maybe I did. I already knew that life as I had always known it was over; it would never be the same but was he trying to say that the lives of everyone in The Complex were now in danger? "The government has lots of secrets, Ruby." He pointed toward the girl. She widened her eyes in fear before tucking her head against Reese's arm. "She is proof of that. Now, there's a pattern. They have Reese, and you, sneaking into the passageways on camera. They have the test results of your father's nasopharyngitis, which is a strain no more harmful than any other that we have recorded, yet a strain that cannot be traced back to anyone or anything within The Complex." He paused again. I leaned forward and narrowed my eyes in a silent demand that he continue. "Because of the combination of your father's untraceable strain of nasopharyngitis and the discovery of you sneaking into the passageways, when they came for your parents an hour ago, they had plans to take them into custody on suspicion of treason, just like they took Reese's parents. But, yours were gone."

"Do you know how they escaped? There was a flatfoot guarding our barracks.. that's why I had to leave through the vents."

"The guard was found unconscious, with a head injury and a spilled cup of tea next to him."

Mom!

Mom had to have brought that filthy monster a cup of tea probably laced with belladonna, one of her favorite herbs with sedative qualities, but how on earth had my dad convinced her to do that? I closed my eyes briefly as an estimated description of the scene unfolded inside of my head. Mom, with her hair combed to perfection and an apron wrapped around her waist over her uniform, must have walked out of the barracks cautiously with the tea – which didn't even seem possible knowing how frightened she was of flatfoots. She must have struck up some type of conversation with *the thing*, causing him to let down his guard. It was the only explanation that made any sense, even if it didn't seem likely. She loved my father with all of her heart, though. As terrified as she was of everything, if he asked her to do something, maybe her love for him gave her the strength to overcome her fear. I glanced over at Reese, still lost in his overwhelming grief, and suddenly I believed in the possibility of my mother finding her strength. After all, there's nothing I wouldn't do for Reese

"But, where are they?" I asked in desperation. "Why will it be difficult for them to get here?" Zane shifted his weight again. The fingernails on his right hand absentmindedly scratched the knuckles on his left.

"We barely made it in time, ourselves." I wrinkled my nose. What did that even mean? Had they almost been seen?

"We were lucky this time. We overheard a few flatfoots and government officials talking outside of the hallway that lead to your barracks, hence how we know about your parents' escape and the flatfoot assigned to guard you all having been incapacitated. They're planning to lock down the entire complex. Then, they'll search and interrogate every single citizen, one by one."

Oh my god.

"Do they know about the Order?" I asked immediately, but my panicked thoughts refused to allow Zane time to respond before more words streamed out of my mouth. "What about all of your families, the families of everyone else in the Order that's already here? What will happen to them?" I already knew; they would be taken into custody, just like Reese's parents. Mothers, children, everyone found with a missing family member would be either tortured, or put to sleep. Zane was right. We were living in a glass house and the glass was shattering around us. The shards were coming down like rain and piercing the skin of countless innocent people. "When are they doing this? When are they locking down The Complex?" Anger boiled up inside of me again as it took on a life of its own, turning my blood into ice and causing carbon dioxide to be expelled from my lungs in short, intense bursts that should have been fire. I darted my eyes back to Zane, rationally knowing that there was nothing more he could do to help anyone, especially my parents, but my anger had flesh-hungry fangs that needed to sink into *someone.* "So what do we do??" I raised my voice in desperation. "We have to help them! We have to do SOMETHING!"

"No," Zane answered as if prepared for and even expecting to be lashed out at. His demeanor was calm and his expression firm which only caused my animalistic fury to grow.

"DO YOU HAVE FAMILY?" I shouted at him as my fingers curled into my palms. "DO YOU EVEN CARE WHAT HAPPENS TO THEM?" A quick glance at Reese was the only thing that had the potential to sooth the wild beast that wanted to take me over completely, but as I watched the girl cling to him even tighter and biting her lip toward me in fear, I took a deep breath and held it in forcing the tornado to shrink. It wasn't gone – by far – but I managed to hold it at bay at least enough for me to hear my own thoughts.

Zane strode forward intent on quickly closing the gap between us. I instinctively leaned away from him, but before I could do anything else his large hands clamped down on my shoulders. "Listen – of course I care!" He hissed through his teeth. The anger that had flowed through me and threatened to take me over shifted and was now threatening to possess him instead. "I have a family! I have a TEN YEAR OLD DAUGHTER. But rushing off without a plan is not going to save her. We wait. We wait for the government to initiate the lock-down. We wait to see if your parents make it back to us. We wait until we can come up with a plan." He paused again and finally loosened his grip on my shoulders. I shook my shoulders to try and lessen the pain. I didn't dare allow myself to ask the follow-up question that was swimming through my mind like a menacing shark. *Then what?*

Zane was running on desperation, just like I had been. I understood his rage, his panic and the utter helplessness that was eating away at his insides. He was handling it better than I had, at least. I had run off with no realistic plan or method and I hadn't helped anyone in the process.

Or, maybe I had, inadvertently. Zane said that when they came for my parents this morning, they were already planning on taking us all into custody because they knew that I had snuck into the passageways, and they knew my dad's strain of nasopharyngitis had not come from inside The Complex. We would have had no way of knowing any of that if I had stayed. The Order had done the best they could in getting a message to us, but they had no prior knowledge of just how much danger we were in and therefore could not have warned us about our grim fate. If I had stayed, my parents and myself would all have been taken as prisoners.

Realizing that I had potentially saved myself and my family with my ignorant, desperate, ill-thought out plan washed over me like an internal massage, instantly loosening my muscles from their tensed, tightened grip around my skeletal system and freeing more space for my lungs to expand with each breath I took. I turned toward Reese again, bypassing the reminder that he was still lost in a black hole of grief as I threw my arms around him and rested my head onto his shoulder. I loosened one hand and gently rested it on the little girl's back to remind her that she was still under our protection. I turned my head back toward Zane. "Then, go come up with a plan." I said to him quietly, but firmly defiantly. "We can't just leave everyone to die." We locked eyes as if challenging each other. I could tell he didn't appreciate my attitude, and probably not even my presence. His resentment of me was understandable; I was temporarily safe while his own daughter was potentially being tortured or put to sleep, right at this moment. If she didn't survive, he would resent me even more and that wouldn't exactly help him feel motivated to want to save my parents. His own family would be his first priority.

The moment these facts hit my consciousness, I tore my eyes away because I realized Zane could no longer be fully trusted. Reese, myself, the little girl, Reese's parents and my own were not his priority. I didn't blame him, his own family was now in danger and that would consume every thought he had and tailor every plan he made because he loved his family like I loved mine. What it meant, though, was that the three of us were truly on our own.

Zane's gaze softened with empathy but he couldn't seem to find more words of comfort when he probably couldn't even comfort himself. I understood. "Suki, come with me." Willow's mom pressed her palms to the floor and rose. She leaned down and gently rested her palm on top of my head for just a brief moment before turning to follow Zane, leaving the three of us to cling to each other in utter darkness once again. Reese finally shifted. I brought my hands up to his face, gently resting my fingers on the slight prickles that were growing out of his cheeks. I pressed my forehead against his and breathed slowly, softly. How deep in grief had he been? Had he heard a word Zane said to us, or had he just been too sad to process and to care?

"Baby.." I'd never said that word in reference to Reese before. I'd never even considered it. Loving him had been a very secret daydream but I was not the same person I was just a few days ago. We were fugitives now with a very probable death sentence hanging over our heads. Maybe we could pull off a miracle, save The Complex and re-emerge on the surface to live happily ever after but the realist in me knew that we were sitting in the middle of a man-made lake of government deceit in a thin layer of ice, and it was cracking all around us. We knew we were being lied to but we didn't know why. There was still so much to discover. Would we be able to find answers or would we be put to sleep within a day? Not knowing the answers to even those questions caused all of the fears built around my forced inhibitions to melt away like butter. My eyes fixed on Reese's and refused to look away from his pupils until I knew he was looking back into mine instead of past them. "Baby.." I whispered to him again. "Your parents may be still be alive. We're fugitives... they might be keeping your parents alive for leverage." I hated my words. I hated how disgusting they tasted while they rolled past my tongue and out into the world, but I couldn't deny their truth. I'd known for six years, since the moment I lost my emotional innocence watching the flatfoots drag Grandpa Logan away, that there was no limit to what the government was capable of or how far they would go to devalue the life of an individual.

Reese didn't reply to me. I could tell he was *with me*, his pupils dilated in fear and need, but no speech followed my attempt to verbally sooth him. I closed the gap between our mouths and pressed my lips to his. A moment later I felt his tensed body loosen and he leaned forward, returning my kiss with passion and almost overwhelming need. Electric shocks spread through my body like wildfire and I let my head fall back. In the middle of all of this chaos, I had something to cling to. I had someone who needed me as I needed him.

My lips parted just a bit and the tip of Reese's tongue slipped through them and gently caressed my own. My body went limp and his arms quickly curled around my back and steadied me from tumbling. Then, a tiny voice interrupted my moment of pure bliss which I might not have been able to stop on my own.

"Ew." Immediately, Reese tore his mouth away from my own and we both tossed our heads to the side a a hot, searing redness spread across my cheeks. In the darkness we could only see the silhouette of the little girl, but I chuckled with slight embarrassment.

"Sorry," I muttered as Reese laughed a bit.

"Are you two in love?"

Wow.

I was not expecting that question. At all. I stared at the girl's silhouette and shifted on my knees, pressing one hand against the floor as the blood that heated my cheeks warmed even more to a fiery crimson. Uneasy silence followed her exclamation and all I heard was

Reese shifting his weight like I had done only a moment earlier.

The blazing, screeching wail of some sort of alarm suddenly tore through the darkness like a knife. It was so loud and bracing that my whole body tensed and jerked. As I involuntarily rose on my knees, my body wobbled and almost toppled over. It didn't help that an equally startled and frightened child leapt at me and I had to catch her, but a painful, impulsive flexing of my thigh muscles kept me somewhat upright and I was able to steady us both. As quickly as the volatile screech began, it suddenly stopped only to be followed by a series of urgent-sounding, loud beeps. Other noises began to threaten us from – well – all around, I couldn't tell where the noises were coming from but they sounded like doors slamming shut in empty rooms that echoed. I felt Reese's arms embracing me while my own clung protectively to the girl. The three of us, an odd, makeshift family unit, could do nothing but cling to each other in the darkness and pray that whatever these noises were, they would soon stop and that the end wouldn't bring about our discovery and destruction.

The beeping finally did stop after what felt like forever, but was probably only thirty seconds or so. The return of eerie silence did nothing to ease my fear. No hurried footsteps approached us to check if we were all right although I did hear faint rustling noises of others moving about in the very large secret room. Tiny hand-lamps were clicked on, but they were far too distant from us to be of any use to our eyes; just dots of light. We all clung to each other even tighter and the frightened little girl in my arms whimpered ever so softly as her head pressed into my chest.

"Attention. This is Commander SueLee."

OH GOD OH GOD OH GOD

This was it. We were all going to die. We were going to get captured, we were going to be tortured, and THEN we were going to be put to sleep. **Killed. Murdered.**

"Until further notice, nothing and no one will be traveling between divisions. Everything has been locked down. Anyone attempting to access connecting tunnels between the divisions, current and past, will be immediately escorted to the transitional containers to be put to sleep.

"There are several fugitives at large. They are very dangerous. The Complex will not be returned to its normal activity until every last one of them is apprehended. Every Doctrine-abiding citizen is to report to your division's meeting hall at once to be briefed and questioned about these fugitives. Anyone not accounted for at these assemblies WILL be considered in league with the fugitives, located, and taken to the transitional containers.

"These deranged criminals have taken it upon themselves to defy their purpose and put every member of The Complex in terrible danger from the perils of the world above. While these turncoats remain at large, you are not safe. Your children are not safe. We demand you cooperation in exchange for your continued protection."

Another shrill series of beeps announced the end of Commander SueLee's threats. My eyes, although unable to see, darted around in irrational desperation. The broadcast had come from nowhere – from everywhere – seemingly all around us as if this entire room had been fitted with speakers. I had only heard Commander SueLee do a Complex-wide announcement one other time during my existence, and it had been to warn any woman who tried to carry an un-approved pregnancy to term that her and her fetus would be brought to the transitional containers. Couples were often only allowed to have one child; more than that could supposedly lead to too much inbreeding a few generations down the line. I knew I was an only child and I as well as my family were safe, so I didn't think on it further.

I was now one of the "fugitives" in question. So were my parents. The government was trying to manipulate the entire population into thinking we were up to something horrible. I had always felt like the black sheep among this civilization because of my dissatisfaction with the virtually meaningless life I was told to lead, but most people in The Complex quietly accepted their fate. Some accepted their lives out of ignorance and others, like my mom, accepted their lives out of fear. If the government threatened their "safety" by telling them to look for "fugitives" I had no doubt they would turn us in without a second thought. Now I understood why Zane told us it would be difficult for my parents to get back to us. With The Complex on lockdown, they would be trapped wherever they are, and hunted.

I tried to run my fingers gently through the little girl's long, impossibly tangled hair but they got stuck almost immediately and I didn't want to hurt her. She shook so violently that I was afraid she would make herself sick.

"We're trapped here aren't we?" She whispered, but loudly enough for me to hear without a problem. Reese gently kissed the side of my head.

"We'll find a way out," he tried to assure her but

his words were empty. Maybe she wouldn't be able to tell, but I could. "We'll get through this."

I remained silent because I couldn't bear to tell this little girl that I didn't think we would make it. Why hadn't anyone else from the Order come over to us? I had realized already that we would not be their priority, but something felt cold in the pit of my stomach. This block of ice swelled inside of me and forced me to silently acknowledge that not only were Reese and I basically on our own, but that protecting this girl wouldn't be the Order's top priority, either.

The three of us may be frightened and helpless in the dark; hunted, mistakenly viewed as the enemy and possibly catalysts to whatever torture the government was going to inflict on several innocent citizens, but it wouldn't be dark in this room forever. Soon, we would have to stand, and we would have to fight.

"I'm Silver." I froze. I wasn't even looking in Reese's direction but I could sense that he froze as well. A wave of warmth flowed through me even in the dank hopelessness that we were drowning in. *Her name.* She finally trusted us enough to tell us her name. I turned toward her.

"It's lovely to meet you, Silver." She slipped her rain-thin arms around my waist. I held my breath for just a moment.

"I'm sorry you were captured." My eyes widened

"Sweetie, we're not captured. Not yet. We won't let them capture us, okay? Reese and I, we're going to protect you no matter what."

"But you already were. That's why you're down here, isn't it?" Reese's gentle footsteps moved closer to us.

"Well, in a way, but we didn't know that. We're

going to make it to the surface, where you live." I knew those words to be true by now, that the girl, Silver, was from the surface, and yet saying them out loud still felt unreal. She tightened her grip on me even more.

"Even if we go back up there, I don't know how to find my mommy."

"We'll find her," I tried to assure her even though I knew I could potentially be making a promise I might not be able to keep. But how could I let her down?

"But we never stay in the same place. We have to run from the hunters."

The hunters? What was Silver talking about?

No.

I couldn't hear any more of this. The surface meant freedom. The surface meant safety. Silver was making it sound as if it was just as terrifying to be up there as it was to be down here. I had to erase her words from my mind. I asked her questions when she wasn't ready to answer them but now that she was, it was I who wasn't ready. I needed to believe that there was even the slightest, furthest possibility of escaping this prison into a limitless world of the unknown where we could choose our own destinies and live in peace. I had to believe in the pot of gold at the end of the rainbow to get through this – not just all of this, but even the next five minutes. If Silver had things to tell me about the surface that would spoil the last thread of light I was clinging to in the darkness, I wasn't ready to know.

Don't forget to check out
Dark World : Logan's Journal

A **completely free to read online** ongoing prequel first person diary style series that follows Ruby's grandfather's experiences after the invasion of 2022 when the overnment first corralled the survivors into The Complex.

<u>www.kellfrillman.wordpress.com</u>

Dark World : The Lockdown

Sometimes change happens gradually, so gradually in fact that we fail to notice its subtleties until we face an event that we find ourselves reacting to differently than we thought we would. Other times, change hits us like a sledgehammer and creates a mirage effect so we still identify with who we were before while at the same time trying to accept and get to know the person we are now.

When I look back on the days right before the A-I Revolution, everything seems to blur together and the only clarity I have in my memories is daydreaming about my teenage adoration for Reese and then opening my eyes to view the beautiful, perfect black sky for the first time in my life. The events in-between those absolutes were short, yet packed with so much blurred intensity that attempting to retrieve any specific memory as a casual reminisce is equivalent to trying to find something tangible to hold on to while being tossed around like a rag-doll inside the funnel of a tornado.

As I sit here and watch Finnian play in the yard wide-eyed and filled with the wonder of innocence, I try to imagine how I will someday tell him the tale of my own childhood. I try even harder to imagine how I will explain to him that the comfort he has now will not last forever. I don't want to think about these things because it makes me feel like a failure despite knowing there is nothing I can do to prevent the future. However, it does give my mind some ease to know that I don't have to destroy his innocence just yet. He may have hard times ahead of him but his childhood will not be based on lies. When he is old enough to start asking questions I will answer them with honesty.

I raise my right hand and run my left index finger softly over a faded scar that runs from my right ring finger to about halfway toward my wrist; a forever reminder of how my questions were answered during my own childhood. I was raised in an underground complex beneath the soil, surrounded always by walls and ceilings, limitations that not only inhibited my body, but my mind and spirit as well. My parents were raised the same way. We were told by our government that after the otherworldlies pillaged our oceans in 2022, our planet was no longer sustainable and we were left with nothing but a giant fall-out shelter to consider our home until the theoretical day long after our bones were dust when our legacy discovered a new planet that would give humanity the chance to flourish once again.

Trying to clear away the cobwebs that tangle my memories together is both a desire and a fear. I try to live in the present as much as possible because looking back on the past is like choosing to stay on a merry-go-round long after you've become dizzy and nauseous; fruitless and unavailing. Still, when I see Finnian gently pluck a moonflower from the ground, his wide eyes transfixed on its delicate intricacies, I can't help but think of Silver. If I close my eyes and wait patiently, the cobwebs clear as if melting away on the ends of a lightly swept broom and there she is in my mind, as perfect as the first day I met her.

One day in the very, very far-off past, humanity used to believe the earth was flat. When they found definitive proof that our planet was in fact round, I wonder how they reacted. When I was sixteen years old and Reese first lured me into the off-limits passageways, that was already enough to make my heart race with the thrill and anxiety that doing something forbidden naturally brought, but then there she was – a frightened little girl unlike any other little girl I had ever seen before with no ID chip implanted in her wrist, no idea what our complex was after having literally fallen into it, and wearing puffy, body-covering clothing that I had never seen before. She told us stories about her nomad family traveling around on the earth's surface, constantly running from soldiers who were always trying to kill them and they didn't even know why.

Silver was my catalyst, her presence alone spiraling me down a path of danger and discovery. She was also my beloved child, in spirit rather than physical form but I loved her fiercely and as we plummeted head-first into what would later come to be known as the A-I revolution, I found myself valuing her life far more than my own. Caring for her forced me to develop years worth of maturity and wisdom nearly overnight. Loving her as much as I did – as much as I *do* - not only saved her life and mine, it might have been the very thing that saved us all. Love is a very motivational thing because its one of the few emotions that has the strength to overcome fear.

Although genetically impossible because they shared no blood link, I swear by my soul that Finnian has Silver's eyes, her soft smile, and even her gentle, quiet laugh. I see Silver in the way he bounces when he's filled with excitement and I feel her spirit when he holds my hand. Finnian's trust in me clears away the cobwebs even more and I find myself sitting back in my wooden porch chair as I allow my lids to lazily fall over my retinas. I embrace even the early moments when Silver was fearful of me because working to earn her trust was a treasure that brought me strength.

Trust is delicate, a thin layer of glass serving as a floor that stretches from point A to point B forcing you make each step as gentle as you possibly can as you make your way across. Sometimes we *do* make it to point B, but other times the glass shatters. Sometimes we fall.

Finnian bounces over to me, his chubby legs making his jog look more like a series of hops. He presses his small hands on my legs and heaves himself up into my lap. I can't resist curling my arms around him and covering his puffy cheeks with kisses. It means so much to me that although he has the curious spirit of an explorer just like I did, he knows that when his explorations are done for the day he had a warm lap to climb into and arms that will protect him. His independence would grow as he did, and when he yearned to explore out of my sight-range, I would panic. But I would force myself not to call out for him every few minutes because even more than I wanted to keep him close, I wanted him to see and explore the world around him. It was not a perfect world, but it was without four walls and a ceiling. It was a world where those of us on the surface were no longer hunted by the government. We were *free*.

"Grasshopper won't move," Finnian tells me with his lower lip puckering out in a sad and frustrated pout. raise my eyebrows as he points to a patch of grass illuminated by a hand-lamp. I saw it; an insect on its side, its tiny legs un-twitching. Finnian is too young to understand the concept of death and I am too protective to want to explain it to him just yet. I adjust him on my lap and soften my expression.

"It's just sleeping honey," I tell him gently.

"For how long?" Clever kid. Always asking questions. I smile softly and think of how proud Granda Rogan would be of him. My father would be, too.

"Probably for a long time. He's somewhere in dreamland." That wasn't a lie, exactly. Maybe death really *was* like a dream.

I pause in my satisfaction and question my approach as a dull chill makes its way across the surface of my skin. Maybe I shouldn't be correlating sleep with death. After all, the government used to sugarcoat cold-blooded murder by saying that they were only *putting people to sleep.* This wasn't the same thing though, was it?

I look up at the sky, my eyes transfixed on the waning moon. I would never be able to stare at the moon and stars and not feel awe-struck. Still, shadows linger in my mind. I am free now but the invisible chains I had been shackled with from birth sometimes try to trick me into thinking they are still here. Strange, unexpected noises cause me to glance over my shoulder. Wandering too far from home triggers my anxiety and irrational fears that I am going to be *caught* and *punished.*

I rock back and forth with Finnian still in my arms, humming a soft tune near his ear. Maybe someday all of the ghosts from my past would leave my mind and heart forever, but I doubt it. As much as I hate to admit it, the complex is a part of me and always will be.

Even though she was older when I first met her, I used to hold Silver like this when she missed her mom. I found strength in reminding myself that she needed me but the truth was that I needed her just as much. Silver was a barrier between me and insanity. At the beginning of the A-I Revolution, stuck in a room without light and surrounded by people we weren't sure if we could trust, clinging to each other gave us both the resolve to fight for the freedom we deserved.

The cobwebs were clear, and with my eyes closed and Finnian's warm body snuggling against my own, my mind drifts backward in time to the days we spent hidden away in that dark room with nothing but fear and helplessness to keep us company. There was nothing we could do but wait. We waited to see if my parents were alive, and we waited for an opportunity to escape the complex before the government found us and put us to sleep. Every breath might be our last, every word could be the final one spoken. "Don't let me die," Silver once whispered to me after several moments of defeating silence. A single tear escapes my eye. I don't know if I will ever be able to forgive myself. I probably never should.

ell Frillman resides in the heart of Pioneer Square in eattle and enjoys coffee houses, movies, and appletinis. 'hen she's not writing, sleeping, eating or doing other ecessary human activities, she works hard at her day job 'ith an animal rescue that saves lives one dog and cat at a me. Although she tolerates the human race and enjoys the iller coaster rides her fictional characters take her on, 'ie first and foremost attributes the successful completion f each novel to the patience and support of her beloved ets.

Made in the USA
San Bernardino, CA
07 August 2016